BE NOT AFRAID

This Large Print Book carries the
Seal of Approval of N.A.V.H.

THE BAYOU SECRETS ROMANCE, BOOK 2

BE NOT AFRAID

DEBORAH LYNNE

THORNDIKE PRESS
A part of Gale, Cengage Learning

 GALE
CENGAGE Learning·

Farmington Hills, Mich • San Francisco • New York • Waterville, Maine
Meriden, Conn • Mason, Ohio • Chicago

GALE
CENGAGE Learning

LIBRARY OF CONGRESS CATALOGING-IN-PUBLICATION DATA

Lynne, Deborah, 1953–
    Be not afraid / by Deborah Lynne. — Large print edition.
        pages cm. — (Thorndike Press large print clean reads) (The Bayou secrets romance ; #2)
    ISBN 978-1-4104-8091-0 (hardcover) — ISBN 1-4104-8091-7 (hardcover)
    1. Large type books. I. Title.
PS3612.Y5517B4 2015
813'.6—dc23   2015014540

Published in 2015 by arrangement with Barbour Publishing, Inc.

Printed in Mexico
1 2 3 4 5 6 7 19 18 17 16 15

I dedicate this book to
the Lord
and my family in Christ.

God has given me the gift of enjoying
what I do . . . writing and sharing stories
with others who love to read. My dream
growing up was to be an actress.
Momma and Daddy always believed I
would be the new Doris Day. God had
other plans, giving me a husband and a
family who encourages my writing. So
my childhood dream came true. Now,
by writing novels, I am acting . . . only I
get to play all the roles. How wonderful
is that? Plus I get to share my love for
the Lord, woven in to all of my stories.

ACKNOWLEDGMENTS

First and foremost, I want to thank my Lord for giving me the passion for writing. He burned this passion in my heart many years ago and has since been refining me and helping me to grow and write so that He is exalted in my stories. He's blessed me and continues to do so, and I give Him the praise and the glory. We all know He never gives us more than we can handle, nor will He ever give us something to do and not give us the way in which to do it. Thank You, Lord.

Over the years He's blessed me with critique partners: first with Elaine Grant, Sylvia Rochester, and Sharon Elliott . . . and now Emy White and Marie Barber. They have all been a blessing, trudging with me through my efforts and helping me finetune my stories. I thank each for their help.

God also put one very special lady in my

path a few years ago that helped relight the flame for writing. When I was about to give up, Mrs. Lucille Montgomery, who at the time owned The Christian Book Store in Baton Rouge, Louisiana, came to me and asked to read one of my manuscripts. She was visiting our church at the time and had heard from ladies there of my writing. When I gave her a manuscript, *Be Not Afraid,* she loved it. As a bookstore owner, she felt confident she could promote my book with no problem, and she did just that with the first two novels that were released: *Grace, a Gift of Love* and then *All in God's Time.* Thanks to her encouragement, this is my third novel being released. I hope, like her, you enjoy the read.

In loving memory of my dear friend,
who went on to be with the Lord on
December 23, 2009.

Let not your heart be troubled,
neither let it be afraid.

JOHN 14:27 KJV

CHAPTER 1

A scream pierced the darkness outside the office. Samantha Cain's head popped up as she glared out the big window. She froze. Her heart pounded as an icy chill slid slowly down her back.

"What was that?" she whispered to herself as she slowly rose to her feet.

Fearfully, her eyes searched the night through a large picture window in a futile attempt to find the source of the scream. A black void filled her view as the moon hid behind a large cloud.

Standing still, Sam listened for another scream. Almost perfect silence flooded the room. Neither the hum of an occasional tugboat chugging down the Mississippi River nor the steady rhythm of a train crossing over the bridge on elevated tracks was heard. Only country music played softly in the background, barely audible over the pounding of her heart.

Was it a scream, or was it her imagination? It could have been a squeal from tires. Kids raced along the River Road all the time. A cat could have called out in the night. Possibilities flashed through her mind.

It could have been anything. Why am I reacting this way? I've worked nights too long to start jumping at every sound. . . .

Fear comes from the devil. Peace comes from God. That wasn't a straight quote from the prophet Isaiah, but Sam got the message her mind had sent her. She took a deep, cleansing breath to calm her nerves and slowly released it.

A moment later, the scream replayed in her mind.

She shivered. That was what unsettled her nerves. It wasn't tires squealing or a cat screeching. It sounded like a human scream . . . a woman's scream.

With unsteady hands, Sam reached for the knob on the radio and turned it off. Straining, she listened again. Nothing. Silence.

Her fingertips iced over, and goose bumps lined her arms. The bitter taste of fear settled unnaturally in her mouth.

"This is silly," she scolded herself. Sucking in a gush of air, then quickly blowing it out again, hard and fast this time, she tried to shake off the feeling of alarm.

Fear not. I am with you. Words of peace crossed her mind as her heartbeat settled to a steady thump.

Maybe I just imagined the scream. To further convince herself of her strong imagination, she unlocked the double locks on the wooden door to her office. Standing in the entryway to the glassed-in lobby area, she saw first her own reflection: a woman barely over five feet tall, with long brown hair cascading down over her shoulders. Her bangs almost covered her green eyes as she leaned toward the glass door and cupped her hands around her eyes. She peered through the glass door leading outside. With the fluorescent lighting on inside, she could see only vague, indistinguishable shadows through the glass.

Pushing the front door open, she stepped out into the night air and listened again.

Still nothing.

Sam's eyes adjusted to the darkness. The one streetlight, near the gate's entrance to Liquid Bulk Transport, exposed an empty highway.

The clouds shifted slowly, unveiling the moon one slice at a time. Patches of grass-covered ground became apparent beyond the road where the levee rose to contain the flow of the mighty Mississippi. Tracing the moonlit summit of the levee in both directions, Sam saw nothing out of the ordinary.

Confident now she'd imagined the scream, she relaxed, unclenching her fists. A slight breeze stirred strands of her hair, blowing them softly across her face as she turned back toward the building. Grabbing the door handle, she was about to pull it open when she heard a rustling.

She stopped and turned in her tracks. What was that? Was it the wind? Was it something . . . or someone?

She perked her head, twisting toward the highway as she strained to listen. Then she heard it again . . . a scuffling. A couple of dogs, maybe? She wasn't sure what, or possibly who, but she knew she heard something. Sam jerked her body around in the direction of the levee. Staring hard, she tried again to find the source. Her eyes squinted, slowly tracing along the levee for something — *anything* — making that sound.

The noise stopped again. With her left ear cocked toward the levee, Sam stilled, straining to hear the sound again. Nothing.

If only it were distinct, she could find it. Identify it. Maybe then she could prove to herself it was nothing to worry about. Possibly even discover it was two dogs fighting over a bone. And, who knows, maybe a cat tried to interfere.

There it was again!

Something was out there, but what? A thrashing sound came from the direction of the levee, but she didn't dare move closer. It was louder this time. More grunting or groaning noises.

What was it? Was it those dogs she so hoped for? She didn't hear any growling. Sam stared, squinting, focusing her eyes intently toward the sound.

Finally, she saw it. Over there, on top of the levee, an eerie light cast from the moon shone upon two silhouettes, a large form locked in a struggle with a small figure of a woman. The shapes appeared for a second or two, then vanished on the other side of the levee. A woman was being attacked. Sam's heart pounded as she swiftly turned on her heel.

Running back into the building through the glass door and past the wooden door leading back into her office, she punched 911 on the telephone. As it started to ring, she glanced out the window and back at the door to the office. Oh no! She forgot to shut and lock the door behind her. Her stomach knotted as panic choked her. Her chest tightened.

There isn't time for fear, she told herself just as she heard, "This is 911 emergency. What is your emergency?"

In a rush, she said, "This is Samantha Cain at Liquid Bulk Transport on River Road. I heard a scream and saw two people fighting on the levee. By the sizes and shapes of the shadows, it looked like a man attacking a woman. Can you get help here quick?"

"Stay calm, ma'am. I'll dispatch help right away. All cars in the vicinity . . ."

Sam listened while the operator broadcast the situation and location to deputies on duty. *What if help doesn't get here in time?* she wondered. *How can I stand here holding a phone while someone is being attacked? Can I let her be a victim, too?*

"I've been trained," she reminded herself aloud, thinking of all the self-defense and emergency courses she'd taken over the past year. She slammed the phone down on the countertop. "I can't just sit here. No way. I've got to try and help her." *Greater is He that is in you, than he that is in the world.*

With that scripture in mind, Sam grabbed her purse and pulled out a small black container of mace. *Help me, Lord,* she prayed. *I can't stand by and let him hurt her. I*

16

need to slow the man down, distract him or something, until help arrives. Please help me make smart moves. . . .

Now she knew exactly what she was going to do, and she knew she wasn't alone.

Racing out the door, across the graveled parking lot of the trucking company toward the levee, she didn't give herself time to worry about the consequences. She hastened toward the fight, holding the mace tightly in her grasp, ready to spray the attacker when she reached him. If nothing else, it should buy time.

As Sam rushed closer, she noticed that the woman's hands were hanging limply at her side. It appeared all of the fight had gone out of her. Sam prayed she wasn't too late.

Hold on, her thoughts whispered. Aloud, she screamed, "Leave her alone! Let her go!" Sam closed some distance between them as she started across the highway toward the levee.

The man's head snapped up, and he peered in her direction. Even from this far away, Sam saw his eyes. They blazed with a sick, detached, almost possessed look. His hands stayed locked around the woman's neck, appearing to squeeze even tighter, if that were possible. Sam knew she had to be crazy to continue toward this crazed man, but she couldn't stop now. She had to do all she could do. It took all the courage she could muster to keep moving forward and not run back to safety.

As she started up the levee, less than fifty feet away, Sam shouted again, "I said, leave her alone!"

The attacker's eyes widened as he slowly turned toward Sam, twisting the limp body still in his grasp in the same direction. The woman wasn't fighting back anymore; nor was she standing on her feet. He was holding her airborne, by her neck.

Sam's steps slowed slightly as her grip tightened on the mace.

Suddenly the attacker released his hold, and the victim crumpled to the ground like a fallen leaf. His gaze locked on Sam, and he took one step toward her.

Sam's heart skipped a beat. *I'm next. He's going to come after me now. Am I strong enough to hold him off till help gets here?* Her heart began to pound even harder.

Then she heard that still, small voice in her head: *I can do all things through Christ which strengthens me.*

There was no turning back. She gripped the can tighter and her fingertip felt for the button, ready to spray him, to stun him . . . to bring him to his knees.

CHAPTER 2

Slowly, he moved toward her. One step, and then another, his crazed gaze locked on Samantha all the while.

A lump caught in her throat. Sam tried to swallow it, to push it down so she could breathe freely. Instead, she held her breath and squeezed harder on the can in her hand.

Suddenly, a shriek of sirens filled the air. For a moment, the crazed man hesitated, looking past Sam, as if estimating the time left before help arrived.

She wanted to turn and look behind her, too. She wanted to see what he saw . . . to know help was almost there. But she couldn't. She didn't dare take her eyes off the enemy.

Flashing lights filled the semidarkness. They appeared in all the dark shadows. They were close . . . had to be.

Then, in an instant, the sick smile on his face wiped clean. His brow flicked up as he eyed her with a dare. She knew what he wanted to say. She felt it in her gut. *"Until next time,"* she heard him say, only not aloud. Then he turned and fled.

Even after he was gone, she couldn't move for a second or two. When the high shrill of the sirens sounded like they were on top of her, she managed to look toward the highway. There they were — sheriff cars and an ambulance all pulling to a stop at the bottom of the levee.

She rushed to the victim's side. The first thing she noticed was the woman's face. Eyes closed. Skin tinged blue and swollen. Blood oozing from her nose and at the edge of her mouth, with lips slightly parted. Was she dead? Had Sam gotten there too late? She prayed not. At a closer look, she detected a slight rise and fall of the chest . . . very slight. There was still hope.

Sam leaned down and touched the woman gently. "Stay with me. Open your eyes. Help is here." She stroked the side of the woman's face as she heard doors slamming and feet running. "You're going to be all right. Just hang on. Can you hear me? Help is here."

As she tried to rouse the woman to consciousness, Sam was vaguely aware of a sudden commotion around her. In a heartbeat, the help arrived and surrounded them, but something was terribly wrong. Instead of looking for the attacker, the officers' guns were drawn and pointed directly at Sam. Was this some kind of sick joke?

"Put your hands up and step away!"

"But I'm the one who called for help. I'm Samantha Cain. The guy who did this is getting away," she cried.

"I said, get up and back away. Hands on your head." The guns pointed in her direction emphasized his words.

Sam's heart raced. It was bad enough she could have gotten herself killed by a crazy man, but now — ?

"Get up slowly; put your hands up where I can see them, then place them on your head. Now!" the voice barked.

Dropping the can of mace to the ground, she started to rise, lifting her arms up in surrender. For what, she did not know. "This is ridiculous," she muttered, placing her hands on top of her head, fingers clasped together.

"Step back." He waved his gun in one quick jerky motion. When she moved away, the one who seemed to be in charge, keeping one eye on Sam, leaned over the woman's body. A second later he motioned for the paramedics to approach. "She's still alive."

Not if you don't hurry, Sam thought.

After the paramedics moved in to stabilize the victim, the officer turned his attention to Sam, motioning her to move further away from the victim. It was all she could do to contain her annoyance of the men in blue . . . well, technically, green, since it was the sheriff's office that came to the rescue.

"I'm telling you, I didn't do anything wrong," she tried to explain. "I'm the one who called for help."

The officer didn't listen, nor did he seem to care. He led Sam further away from the woman on the ground. "Keep your hands up over your head. Stop. Spread your legs." He patted her down. Keeping his gun trained on her, he said to the others, "I'll take care of this one. You three spread out. Canvass the area. See if someone else is hanging around like she claims."

It's about time.

With the barrel of his gun steadily pointing at her, he used his radio and called in to headquarters. Sam was terrified. Angry, but terrified. How could they hold her here like a common criminal? All she had done was try to help . . . try to do the right thing.

"You can turn back around now. What did you say your name was?"

"Samantha Cain." Sam started to put her

hands down.

"Slowly," he said.

"I told you I was only trying to help. My purse is over there." She pointed in the direction of the yellow building across the street. "At my office. I'm a dispatcher at that trucking company right there." The building sat in the midst of one very large parking lot. The lot was filled with many tanker trailers and several bobtailed tractors. And who knows, maybe by now even that sick man who hurt this woman.

"My license is over there if you need proof of who I am. I'm the one who called 911 for help."

"If you're telling the truth, you have nothing to fear."

"Only that the attacker is getting away," she mumbled slightly under her breath, "or hiding over at my workplace."

At that moment, she heard her name confirmed as the emergency caller over the two-way radio. Then the officer peered around one more time, as if scouting for trouble hidden in the darkness.

"All right, Ms. Cain. You appear to be the one who called it in. You should have stayed in your office. You could have been hurt, too." He slipped his gun back in the holster and pulled out his pad and pen. "All right.

Start from the beginning and tell me what happened."

She breathed a sigh of relief. *Finally.* "I heard a scream. I saw the woman being attacked. I called for help. Then I came and tried to distract her attacker until you got here."

"Again, that was a foolish thing to do. You could have been killed. What if we had been delayed in getting here? Do you think you were big enough to take down this man you saw?" He shook his head, as if disgusted, and didn't wait for a reply. "What did the man who attacked the woman look like?"

As he mentioned the victim, Sam cast a glance at the paramedics. "Is she going to be all right?" Sam asked.

"They'll do all they can for her. Please. Give me a description of the man."

"It was dark." She shifted her feet. "I couldn't see him clearly. He was wearing a hat, kind of like a ski cap. It covered his hair and ears and even part of his face. He was tall compared to the woman. His huge hands wrapped around her throat." The whole time Sam talked, her hands were moving as if trying to do the talking for her, making her description clearer for the deputy.

"And the look in his eyes. . . ." She shook

25

slightly as that image replayed clearly in her mind and goose bumps raced down her back.

"You said you couldn't see him clearly, yet you saw his eyes?" The tone of the officer's voice confirmed he didn't believe her.

"Yes. By the moonlight? The streetlight?" Throwing her hands up in the air and waving them around, she shrugged. "I don't know, but yes. I saw his eyes." Sam closed her eyes and tried to see his face in her mind but couldn't. All she saw were those dark eyes glaring at her and the look that said, *"I'll be back."*

Her eyes popped open, and she glanced all around her. "Have y'all found him yet?" Where did he go? Where was he hiding? She stole a glance across the street at her office. Could he have slipped over there? Would he be waiting for her? She trembled.

"What else do you remember?" the officer asked.

"They were dark . . . His eyes, I mean. And the look in them" — she shuddered as she spoke — "it was sick." Her hands tried again to emphasize what she was saying. "I believe he told me what he wanted me to know. Not in words, but in his eyes, he let me know he would be back. At least that's what I think he was trying to get across to me without opening his mouth. 'Cause he never said a word."

The officer scribbled a few more notes on his pad as he continued to question her. "Think back to before the scream. Did you hear anything then? Or see anything unusual?"

Rubbing the temples on either side of her head, she tried to think. "No. Not that I can recall." She shook her head.

Her thoughts strayed back to the attacker. The threat in his eyes was real. She was sure of it. Who was she kidding? She could have been killed. That man was ready to come after her.

He still might. *No,* she told herself. *That was the heat of the moment. He wouldn't be crazy enough to come back after me. But look at what he did. . . .*

Suddenly, overwhelmed by the reality of what had taken place tonight, her head started to spin and her knees turned to liquid rubber. All strength eased away from her. For a moment, Sam thought she was going to faint. She wrapped her arms around herself, holding on tightly, trying to stop the shaking inside of her, trying to stay upright.

"Are you okay? Hey, Joe," he called to one of the paramedics as he moved quickly to catch her. "When you get a chance, come check this one out. All the color just left her face." To her he said, "Sit down for a minute." He helped ease her to the ground.

The pounding of her heart lessened as she slowly breathed in several deep, calming breaths. *I'm safe now, and the woman is alive. I did the right thing. Thank You, Lord,* she reassured herself as she looked up at the officer.

Swallowing hard, Sam nodded. "I'm okay." She gathered up her strength and confidence. "Sorry. I guess it just hit me what happened and the fact I could have been killed. I'll be all right. Thanks."

She waved off the paramedic as the officer stepped away to converse with one of his fellow deputies. "I'm okay," she said to the paramedic. He shrugged and went back to the ones helping the woman.

After a few minutes of scanning the immediate area, the first officer came back to her. "Are you feeling any better?" When she nodded and rose to her feet, he continued. "Do you remember any unusual traffic or activity in the area tonight?"

Another siren wailed in the distance.

Beams of light from the other deputies' flashlights roamed up and down the riverbanks as the officer continued to question her. Anxiously, she watched the beams moving further and further away. "Do you think they found him yet? Would they call you on your radio —" she pointed to his two-way — "if they saw him, I mean?"

"Ms. Cain, I asked if you saw any unusual activity in the area before you heard the scream."

As the officer spoke, her mind whirled. Would they find him? She hoped so. Sam needed to get back to work. But how could she concentrate on work? "Are y'all gonna check the yard over there? Make sure he's not hiding over there?" She glanced at the truck yard.

And what if he was over there? The pounding of her heart beat in triple time. He could have easily moved down the levee along the edge of the river and then worked his way across the highway and back down to the truck yard without being seen.

"We'll check it out. Don't you worry. In the meantime, until we catch him, I wouldn't work alone over there. You witnessed an attempted killing tonight, Ms. Cain."

A shiver raced across her shoulders and down her back all the way to her toes. She was afraid. There were no ifs, ands, or buts about it. Sam was scared to death. She knew that was her flesh, but right now, she admitted to herself, it was the part doing the thinking. And she was often alone at work. In fact, most nights after the night shift ended at eleven thirty till the morning shift started arriving before seven the next morning. Sure, drivers were in and out at various times but not constantly all night long.

She knew that, later, when she would make her way back to the office and would have time to pray, she would shake this fear. *The joy of the Lord is my strength,* she reminded herself.

A flashing red light on the dash of a small silver car caught Sam's attention. Gravel crunched below the tires as the car jerked to a stop. A man wearing a baseball cap, T-shirt, and shorts climbed out of the car and looked their way. At a glance, something about him looked familiar.

CHAPTER 3

"Glad you made it, Detective Jefferies."

A frown covered the newcomer's face as his gaze slid over Sam.

She was right. Something about him looked familiar, but at the moment she couldn't put her finger on it.

"Langlois. Let's clear the area so no evidence will be disturbed."

"This is my crime scene, Detective. I'm the one who suggested they call you. So mind your manners. The situation is under control. Ms. Cain is a witness. In fact, she helped scare off the attacker, possibly saving the victim's life." The deputy pointed toward the beams of light. "Three of my men are canvassing the area looking for the attacker, and more help is on the way. You want to look around, be my guest, but watch where you step. The crime scene unit is headed this way also." The dour-faced detective glanced Sam's way before walking further up the levee.

Sam gave him a tight smile as she nodded. After a closer look at the detective who had just arrived at the scene and was now walking down the levee away from them toward the deputies, she asked, "You called him Detective Jefferies. Is that Matthew Jefferies, from the 3rd precinct?"

"Yes, ma'am. I asked dispatch to give him a call. This attack could be connected to a couple of high-profile homicide cases he's been working on."

Suddenly three years melted away. Now she knew why the man looked vaguely familiar. He was the man with whom Martin, her husband, had partnered just a few short months before Martin's death.

"Officer Langlois, we're going to take the victim to the Baton Rouge General Hospital," the paramedic said.

"Is she going to make it?"

"She's stable for now, but very weak."

"Could I question her?"

"She's unconscious. You'll have to try later."

The paramedics lifted the stretcher with the injured woman and carried her down to the ambulance. In minutes, the siren screamed to life again.

As the vehicle sped away, another car approached. When the car turned into the truck yard, Sam surmised it was Tim Hutchinson, one of their drivers. In no time, more drivers would be arriving for work.

"Deputy. I need to get back over there. I have work to do."

"Fine. If you think of anything else, please call me." He handed her his card.

Dare she walk over there alone? She hadn't seen any of his men make it over to the yard yet. Sam took a few steps, leaned over, and picked up her mace. Should she ask the deputy to come with her or insist they check it first?

"Langlois! Over here," called a voice in the distance.

They must have found something. Sam glared in the direction of the other deputies. The deputy responded with a hand gesture as if saying he would be right there. Maybe they found him. Oh, how she hoped so.

"Sam," a tall, slim man sporting a cowboy hat called from the foot of the driveway near the street, "are you okay?" Tim started toward her.

"Stay there, sir." The deputy pointed as he spoke. "Don't come any closer." Then he turned toward Sam. "Ms. Cain, keep him away from the crime scene. If we have any further questions, we'll come over there. Go on back to your job. You should be safe. We are right here and will be at your place shortly."

That was probably for the best, to go back to the yard with Tim at her side. But what if the attacker was over there in the yard . . . waiting for her? She rubbed her hands together at that heavy thought. Her hands felt cold, just like the fear in her heart. She shook the thought away.

No one would be waiting for her. She had done the right thing calling for help and then trying to help the woman herself. She had to shake off the grip of fear that was holding her hostage. She knew it was wrong, but she also knew God understood. So much had happened to her in the past.

Had she done the right thing, though? Sam could possibly identify him, and the attacker knew that. What if he decided to come after her? Her son, Marty, was seven years old and needed his mother. And what if he went after her son to get to her? All these thoughts and questions flashed through her mind.

"Thanks. I'll stop him," she said to the deputy, then turned toward the driveway. "Wait there, Tim. I'm coming."

Before going to him, Sam stepped to the

top of the levee one more time and looked in the direction Jefferies had headed to see if she could see anything. Two beams of light still hovered far down the bank of the river, while two others gathered right below her near the water's edge. Maybe they had found a crucial piece of evidence. Hopefully something to help them catch the guy.

Sam sighed.

He probably got away. In fact, it wouldn't surprise her to discover the attacker was hiding right under their noses. She didn't hold a very high opinion of the police, due to her past experience. And her perception hadn't improved over the last couple of years.

Although this precinct was a different group of officers than the ones who had disappointed her a few years ago with the investigation of her husband's death, Sam knew that police, deputy sheriffs — they were all the same in one way or another. It was a brotherhood.

As the memories of three years ago flashed through her mind, she prayed she wouldn't be subjected to the third precinct again or the press. She didn't think she could handle either. Not now. Not ever.

Sam glanced back to the foot of the levee, where Tim stood waiting for her. She took a deep breath. The victim was on the way to the hospital. Everything would be okay. She stepped back down the levee toward the highway.

"Am I glad to see you!" She stopped at the edge of the road beside Tim. At that same moment, another police car and a van pulled up behind the detective's Ford Mustang. A logo on the side of the van displayed a local news station.

"Bloodhounds," she said in disgust. "They catch it all. Let's get out of here." She remembered the media all too well.

"Hey, sweetie. Are you okay?" Tim slipped an arm over her shoulder and pulled her beside him as they started to walk across the street. "What's going on? I saw all those lights when I first pulled up and prayed you were nowhere near any of it. But then I couldn't find you. You had me worried." Tim was talking so fast, Sam didn't have a chance to answer him. "When you weren't in the office, I hollered out back and around the yard for you. You didn't answer. I thought the worst . . . but then I saw you standing on the top of the levee." Squeezing her shoulder and pulling her closer to him, Tim held her tightly to his right side. "At least then I knew you were alive. Fill me in.

Tell me what happened. You are okay, aren't you?"

"I'm fine." She nodded and held on tight with her hand that she circled around his waist. Sam felt safe in the protection of Tim's arm, even if it was short-lived. "I witnessed an attempted murder."

His long stride stopped midstep. He turned her toward him. "A murder? Are you sure you're okay?"

She nodded. "*Attempted* murder. The woman is alive and on the way to the hospital. She has a fighting chance."

When they reached the glass door of the office, he slipped both his arms around her and gave her a quick squeeze. "You scared me, girl. We don't need to lose you. It's bad enough the boss makes you work the night shift. A girl alone, out on the levee road in the middle of nowhere . . . that's unheard of."

"I'm okay. Really. Thanks, Tim," she said, grateful again for the brief hug. "I'm glad you're with me, though."

He pulled open the door and held it while she entered the building. "No problem, kiddo. And I'm gonna stay till someone else gets here, too. I'm not about to leave you by yourself. Not under these circumstances. Is the deputy gonna come over here and check out the yard? Maybe the guy's hiding out back." Tim followed her into the drivers' room.

"My thoughts exactly. He said they would. He must have figured the guy was long gone 'cause they don't seem to be in any hurry to get over here." She shrugged as she answered. But when were they coming?

Sam set her mace down and started making a pot of fresh coffee.

"You sit. I'll do that," Tim said.

"If you don't mind making the coffee, I'd appreciate it. I really do need to get back to work." He nodded as he took over. She grabbed her mace and went back to her office.

Time passed. Drivers started to come and go. Tim got on his way. The sun rose. Glancing out the window occasionally, Sam never saw them bring anyone back in handcuffs nor did she notice anyone cross the way and start checking in the truck yard.

When Pat, her replacement, arrived, she filled him in on everything. They worked to finish the last of the paperwork. Then she gathered her things up, getting ready to head home.

Officer Langlois, followed by Detective Jefferies and a few policemen, walked up as she was heading out the door. "Ms. Cain, we need a few words with you."

Although she had met Matthew Jefferies only once prior to this, she knew his name as well as she knew her own. He was one of a group of policemen who held her to blame for Martin's death.

"Check the building and the yard," Langlois ordered the men. "Make sure he didn't slip back over here somewhere." He turned toward Sam. "Ms. Cain, Detective Jefferies wants to talk to you for a minute."

"You didn't get the guy, did you?" Now that was a stupid question . . . in more than one way.

Before the deputy could answer, Jefferies stepped closer. "I'd like you to come to the precinct with me. I need you to look at mug shots."

"The precinct? The third precinct? Now?" Sam asked, shaking her head no as she spoke. "I can't. I need to get home to my son. I need to get him off to school. Besides, I didn't see the attacker well enough. I told Officer Langlois."

"Don't you realize your life could be in danger? That man is a killer, Ms. Cain, and you saw him."

"Not good," she reminded him.

"But he doesn't know that. You need to come down to the station and try and pick him out of the mug shot books. Or at least give a description so our artist can try and sketch him."

"I'm sorry. I can't help you." No, she couldn't go there. Not to the police station. Not to the third precinct. Not now. Not ever!

CHAPTER 4

The detective followed Ms. Cain home but stayed at a safe distance, not allowing her to see him. Once she was inside her apartment, he found a parking place and backed into it.

Pulling his cap off, he threw it down on the seat. "What was that all about?" he grumbled. Matthew sat in his car with the motor running. He remembered the first time they had met. He believed Martin Cain was the luckiest man alive . . . to have such a beautiful wife. She seemed so sweet and loving, but the truth came out in the end.

So what was she up to? He knew who she was, so why the games? Why pretend to care for someone she didn't even know? Why pretend she had a heart?

Samantha Cain had put on a show just now, and Matthew knew it . . . almost fell for it again. Sometimes her show seemed pretty convincing. He almost believed she raced to save the woman because she cared. But Samantha Cain never cared about anyone but herself, according to her dead husband. If she cared more, maybe he would be alive today.

Maybe she hadn't killed him with her own two hands or even pulled the trigger, but she practically pushed him to his death. That was how all the men at the station saw it.

When Martin died, she tried to make everyone believe she cared about him. She said she wished she could have saved him, but she was too late. And then, like any good wife, she mourned his death. At the funeral, she looked like a walking skeleton covered with a thin pasty layer of skin. Dark circles surrounded her eyes, eyes that stared out into space in a zombie-type state.

The brothers in blue knew it was all for show. Samantha Cain's true identity was revealed day in and day out by Martin's demeanor, by little subtle remarks made by him, by his lack of enthusiasm for life. It didn't take a rocket scientist to see his life was miserable. The Captain suggested Martin go talk to their shrink, but Martin insisted things were getting better at home.

They all knew his wife was the problem, and although Matthew had only teamed up with Martin a month prior, he believed as the rest of them that the wife was the problem.

"Maybe not all of us," he admitted to himself. The supervisors of the department had apparently fallen for her game of charades. She wasn't ever a suspect in Martin's death, according to them.

As far as Matthew and the rest of the patrolmen felt, she staged his suicide. Then, she pretended to be something she was not. She played innocent. It worked three years ago, at least with the ones who made the decisions as to who was at fault. But not today. He didn't buy it. Something else brought her out there. Something or someone, but he didn't know what.

It didn't matter. Matthew had a job to do. For whatever reason, she claimed she saw the killer. If it wasn't for that fact and that there was a slim chance the man was the serial killer Matthew was searching for, he wouldn't be bothered with Ms. Cain now. However, that slim chance existed, and as a cop, he couldn't ignore it.

Somehow, someway, he would drag the description of the man from her subconscious. Matthew needed a break, and he needed it now!

Shaking his head, he raked his fingers

through his dark hair. "I can't believe she even got involved." In his heart, he felt there was another reason she was outside on the levee at that time of night, technically morning, but he couldn't concern himself with that.

For the time being, he was stuck with her, and for his own purposes, he would keep her safe. Using his cell phone, he contacted Officer Shelton, then waited for him to arrive at Ms. Cain's apartment building.

"Keep a good watch on her and her apartment. If she's not inside her apartment, keep her in your sight at all times. If she leaves, follow her. Anyone suspicious hangs around, check him out. Just don't let her get wind you're tailing her."

After leaving instructions with the young detective, Matthew took off. For a brief moment, her image burned in his memory. Her soft innocence touched him somewhere deep.

"No!" he shouted. He would not let her get to him again. She was no good and he knew it . . . even if he had to keep reminding himself.

Matthew put all thoughts of Samantha Cain out of his mind. Before returning to the station, Matthew swung by the all-night diners where the other two victims had worked and questioned the waitresses again. He knew, in his gut, that the latest victim worked at a diner, too, and he would have those details shortly and check there also. Maybe if he asked the right question, he'd get a better answer. Surely one of them saw a person who appeared suspicious, someone with dark eyes.

He was determined to close all three cases if it was the last thing he did . . . and he'd do it before another woman got killed.

CHAPTER 5

That evening, Sam returned to work as scheduled. A hectic pace was set and didn't slow down till way into the early morning hours. But that didn't stop anyone from asking questions, though she didn't take much time to give details. Besides, she wanted to put it all behind her and forget the whole thing — only no one seemed to want to let her. She'd heard several versions of what had happened just from the idle gossip that had spread among the drivers during that day.

Rumors spread fast in the trucking industry. Sam always knew if she wanted others to know something, she need only tell a driver. Not that they gossiped like people claim women do, but between the CB radios and the cell phones most drivers have, things spread. This story spread like wildfire. With each call, the story was embellished a little more than the version before. The guys who knew her told others out of concern, and she loved them all for caring. They were like one big family.

"So you're a hero," said John, one of the more friendly drivers, as he stood at the window waiting for his paperwork.

Sam frowned. Her hands flew over the buttons on the computer as she flashed a sideways glance at him. "Not much of a hero. The woman died, you know. I didn't get help to her in time." That was the first thing Sam had checked on when she woke up that afternoon. "She died before she even got to the hospital."

Sam pressed the ENTER key and stood.

Like a dark cloud, sadness hung over her head as she thought about not being able to save the woman. If Sam had only called right away, maybe the woman would still be alive.

"You tried. That's more than some would have done," John reassured her.

"Thanks for trying to cheer me up. I just wish I had reacted more quickly. But I didn't." Picking up the packet of papers for him, she walked over to the window between the drivers' room and dispatch office.

"You did okay. Don't be so hard on yourself." He took the clear envelope full of his paperwork with one hand, then squeezed

Sam's hand with the other. "Cheer up, sweetie. Ya done good."

She knew he was trying to help her forget her problems, so she hoped her smile was convincing. "For that, I'll make you a pot of coffee." Sam unlocked the door between the two rooms, then started making a pot of black brew the Louisiana way: thick, rich, and strong.

"Thanks." John sat down at the drivers' table and flipped through the papers in his envelope, reading his instructions on his next load.

Five or ten minutes later, after Sam had returned to her office, she heard the slam of John's briefcase, a sign he was about to leave, then the *swoosh* of the glass door being pushed open. At a glance, she saw a stranger walk into the drivers' room, keeping his back to the window, his face turned away.

"May I help you?" she asked, stepping over to the counter and looking through the window out at the stranger.

The man turned slightly, never facing her completely. "The phone. Can I use it?" he asked in a deep, gravelly voice.

She took note of his appearance. The man looked like any other stranger who came in to use the phone — dressed in jeans, T-shirt, and a baseball cap. Most of these guys were workers off the boats that docked on the other side of the levee. In cold weather, the boat workers covered their T-shirts with plaid flannel shirts and usually wore a wooly hat snugged down over their ears.

Although the stranger's face was well hidden by the bill of the baseball cap, she saw the dark stubble on his jaw. He desperately needed a shave. "If you're calling local, you can," she said. "Use line four." Sam turned to go back to the computer, noticing that John had reopened his briefcase, delaying his departure.

Most of the drivers tended to look out for her. They liked playing the protector, and Sam would tell anyone in a heartbeat she appreciated it. Especially now.

She recalled in the back of her mind what the deputy had told her. "Don't be alone." Tonight, she wasn't by herself, only the other worker was way out back on the rack. It wasn't quite what Langlois had in mind.

A few minutes later, Sam glanced up as another driver arrived. When he came through the glass door, she heard the slide of a chair on the bare floor, then the slamming of a briefcase, followed by heavy footsteps.

"See ya later, Sam," John called out as he

was leaving.

"Okay. Have a good night and drive safe." She heard the mumble of words between the two drivers.

A moment later a voice called from the drivers' window, "You can't speak?" The sweet Southern drawl could sweep any girl off of her feet.

Looking over her left shoulder, Sam saw the man's wide smile, bordered on each side with very deep dimples. It was contagious, and his brown eyes lit up the room. "Hey, Jerry, what's happening? You're loaded, heading out, right?"

"Yeah, darling, and you have my bills."

Sam grabbed his paperwork and passed it through the window. Her gaze slid past Jerry to the man on the phone. The stranger sat in the dark corner. Although she couldn't see him clearly, he seemed to be staring in her direction out from underneath the bill of his cap. When she caught a glimpse of his gaze, he turned away and started talking into the receiver.

For some strange reason, the hairs on the back of her neck rose. Then all of a sudden an icy chill ran down her back, as if someone had dropped a frozen cube of ice down her shirt and held it there. Something about this man alerted her. Then, shaking her head, Sam told herself she was just being foolish because of the incident last night.

It wasn't like he was the first stranger to come in and use the phone in the middle of the night. However, she hoped Jerry didn't ask for an advance in front of the stranger. No need to let that man know there was money around. It could entice him to hang around and rob her, even if that wasn't his original motive for walking into the building. Quickly, she motioned Jerry to go around to the locked door.

Immediately Sam unlocked it, giving Jerry access to the dispatch office. Ushering him in and locking the door behind him, she asked in a whisper, "Do you need an advance?"

"You know it, darling."

Stepping over to the drawer where the money was kept hidden, she asked, "The usual?"

He winked in response as he nodded. Sam counted out fifty for him, then had him sign for it. Leaning closer to Jerry, she whispered, "If you have a little time, would you hang around till that guy leaves? I guess I'm a little nervous after what happened last night."

He probably would have anyway, but she was more afraid than she wanted to admit.

51

This was unusual for her. Besides learning how to defend herself, this past year she'd immersed herself in God's Word and learned to depend on Him. But tonight her eyes were on the circumstances around her instead of the Lord.

"I'll go fix a cup of coffee and keep my eye on him." Jerry stuffed the money in his wallet and then jammed it into his back pocket. "Is anybody on the rack tonight?"

"Yeah. Tom's out there."

Sam let him out, then locked the door again. She continued with her work but trained her ear toward the window. Time seemed to move like a snail.

Nothing was said until the stranger finally left.

Jerry stepped over to the window. "Didn't think he was ever going to leave."

"What'd you think about him? Anything?" She stepped over to the counter.

"Strange, very strange." Jerry's lips twisted as his eyes narrowed. "The man didn't speak much for someone being on the phone. It looked like he was trying to wait me out. Maybe he knows you have money in there."

"That thought crossed my mind." *As well as the memory of the man last night,* she thought, but that she didn't say aloud this time. She tried not to give the thought any more credit than she had to . . . but the strange man sure was suspicious looking, lurking around, not saying much.

Jerry's brows drew together in uncertainty. "Maybe you should call the sheriff's office and have them pass by? Make sure that guy's not still hanging around."

Sam's gaze slid to the front glass window as she viewed the exit that let out onto the levee road. The tail lights of a dark sedan disappeared onto the highway, heading east toward the old bridge.

"Naah. He's gone now. But if he comes back, I won't hesitate. Thanks."

On that, Jerry stuck his packet inside his briefcase, picked up his carryall, and started for the back door. "I'm gonna pull my truck around to the wash rack and get a quick rinse, then I'll be on my way. See ya."

"Drive safely."

The rest of the night was uneventful. Sam completed all of her duties. Before the sun started to peek out above the horizon, she grabbed her clipboard to go outside. Locking the back door behind her, she went through the shop and into the yard to make a check of the equipment parked on the yard at her terminal — a daily procedure, one she had failed to do in the excitement of the morning before.

Circling the yard around the building, she noted the number of each tractor and trailer, including the condition of the trailers: clean, dirty, or loaded.

Lester, the mechanic coming on duty, pulled into the gate as she started on the last strip of the yard, the east side. Sam waved in acknowledgment as he honked his horn in response. Passing the east end of the wash rack, she heard the spray of the water Tom was using to clean another trailer. The stench was strong. She wrinkled her nose trying to bypass the odor of butyl acrylate.

The morning held a cool breeze in the air. It wouldn't last long, though. September days started cool but usually, as the full red circle of the sun topped the horizon, the heat would start to build. The breezes that swept through the air gave the false impression that fall was closing in. It was closer, but not there yet. Fall usually waited until October or November most of the time in the South.

People from south Louisiana didn't get to enjoy cool weather very often, not even in the springtime. It was impossible. The humidity thickened the air and intensified the heat. Clothes stuck to the skin as perspiration accumulated in the swelter. People weren't necessarily lazy in the South when they sat on their porch sipping a mint julep, like they showed in the old movies. They were just trying to get through the dense heat of the day.

Sam's eyes flitted from the wash rack to the row of tractors backed up against the fence. When she got to the end and wrote the last number down, she heard a tractor rev its engine, and then turned on her heel at the sound of a unit's tires spinning in the gravel and taking off. The truck was bob-tailed, a tractor without a trailer, picking up speed quickly as it barreled toward her.

Shocked into immobility, Sam watched as it aimed directly for her. Just in time, she dashed for safety between the last two trucks on the row. The smell of burning rubber and diesel exhaust filled her nostrils.

Once she was safely out of the truck's path, she turned to catch a glimpse of the number on the passing unit. It left a trail of dust swirling in the air. The truck was theirs all right. Unit number 2478. But who was driving it?

The unit pulled out onto the highway, never slowing down, not even when shifting gears. Sam took off running for the building. Once inside, her fingers fumbled with the key as she tried to unlock the door. Inside the office, she snatched up the phone and punched out 911.

This was becoming a habit she didn't like. Quickly, she gave the person on the other end the information. The woman promised to send someone over immediately.

After disconnecting the line, she dialed the local intercom. "Lester, Tom, come up front. Please hurry." The urgency in her voice rang through her ears as she dropped into the dispatcher's swivel chair, her heart thumping madly.

Someone had tried to run her down. Who? And why? She hadn't done anything. Why would anyone want to hurt her? She closed her eyes, pressed her hands together, and leaned her face forward, touching her lips to her fingertips.

The killer! Her eyes popped open and her head rose. Her hands started shaking, and she intertwined her fingers.

Maybe it was a truck thief, plain and simple, she thought, *and he was just making his getaway.* A ray of hope slipped in. She had just been standing between the truck and the exit. The cold, hard knot in her stomach slackened ever so slightly.

Tom, wet from washing trailers, and Lester, in grease-stained clothes, came in through the door she'd left unlocked.

"My heavens, Sam, what's wrong with you?" Lester, usually laughing and making jokes, rushed in and moved quickly to her side, then kneeled down next to her. "You're as white as a sheet."

She took a deep breath, dropping her shaking hands to her lap. Lester's expression told her what she wanted to know. "You didn't see anything, did you, Lester?" When he shook his head, she turned toward Tom. "How about you?"

Tom, a new employee who was quiet and shy, never said much . . . until now. "Actually, I saw a truck fly by the bay opening. I thought, *Dang, that guy's driving too fast.* I figured you knew who it was and would report him today. Ain't no sense in it. He could have hurt someone."

Yes. Me. He almost did. "Did you recognize him?"

"Sorry." He lowered his head slightly and shook it. "I didn't get a very good look, and I don't know too many people around here yet. But the guy driving, what I did see of him, didn't look familiar."

"Well, someone just stole a truck and almost ran me down in the process. Lester, did you notice anyone on the yard when you drove in earlier?"

"I only saw you, but I wasn't really looking for anyone either. After I parked my car, I went straight to the kitchen to put up my lunch." Lester rose off his knee, patted Sam on the shoulder, stepped over to the counter, then perched on the edge of it. "Did you call the sheriff? And how about the boss?"

"A deputy should be here any minute." Slowly, she stood, walked over to the big window, and gazed out. "I still need to call Ken. He's not going to be too happy, but —"

The phone rang, interrupting her sentence.

"Liquid Bulk Transport. This is Sam. May I help you?" Her hands trembled slightly.

By the time Sam finished taking an order for a load, a deputy sheriff was standing in her office. Tom and Lester had shown him into the room.

Sam exhaled with relief as she replaced the receiver on the hook and turned to the deputy. "Thanks for coming. Someone just stole a tractor from our yard." She filled him in with the make, model, and the truck company number printed on the side and back of the tractor. Next, she gave him the details of where the tractor was and how she was outside taking a yard check at the time.

"And it almost ran her down," Lester piped in.

"Are you all right, or do we need to call for medical assistance?" the deputy asked as he pulled out his pad and pen.

"No, I'm fine. I got out of his way." She stuffed her hands in her pockets, trying to hide their shaking.

"You said *his*. Did you get a look at him?"

Sam bit her bottom lip as she closed her eyes and tried to remember. "No. I didn't see him at all, but Tom saw enough to know it was a man." She turned to Tom. "I know you didn't recognize the thief, but maybe you could describe him for the deputy?"

"Great." The older man turned his attention to Tom. "What did you see, son? Tell me exactly."

"I caught a glimpse of a man driving the truck. I knew it was a man because he had stubble on his face and a baseball cap pulled down over his ears —"

"There was a man in here earlier tonight fitting that description," Sam said as she interrupted Tom. "He came in and asked to use the phone." She shrugged. "For a time I thought he was going to rob our petty cash."

The officer jotted down a short note.

"Anything else you can think of?"

She shook her head.

"If you think of anything, give me a call. You said he used the phone?" When she nodded, he added, "We'll dust it for prints, but I don't know how lucky we'll get."

Sam pulled a file on the tractor and gave him the details, such as serial and plate numbers. She hoped they would find the truck in one piece, as well as the man who drove it.

The officer called in the info on the stolen truck, and he told them to send someone to take prints. "I'll go have a look around."

Meanwhile, Sam reported the incident to her boss. Ken Richardson told her to fill out the accident/incident report and then stay put till he got there. He wanted to talk to her. She agreed to wait and hung up.

Next, she called the Safety Man from the Houston Office, giving him the details, per standard procedure. Last, but not least, she called Amanda, her neighbor and friend, to let her know she would be a little late this morning. Sam asked if Amanda would mind dropping Marty, her son, off at school. Sam promised to give her the scoop later.

The deputy came back inside. "I didn't see anything out of the ordinary. I did see where he spun the tires, like you described to me. Someone will be by shortly to take the prints off the phone. In the meantime, an APB has been put out over the air, so everyone is watching for a blue and white truck fitting your tractor's description. Maybe we'll get lucky." As he started to leave, he paused. "Aren't you the woman who witnessed that killing last night?"

She didn't get a chance to answer him because Detective Jefferies strode into the room. Her eyes flew open wide as her mouth dropped. "What are you doing here?"

CHAPTER 6

"How did you find out so quickly?" Sam couldn't believe her eyes. Confusion swirled through her mind. How did Detective Jefferies know? No one was attacked or killed, so why would he be here?

He didn't say a word. He only glared at her.

"A truck was stolen. Why did Sheriff Fletcher call you?"

"He didn't. I have my ways of knowing." He looked away from the deputy and scrutinized her closely. "I thought I told you to watch your back. I told you he would be after you."

Irritated, she sighed. "This is none of your concern. I still don't —" She cut her words off as she tried to figure how he knew so quickly. Twisting slightly to her right, Sam glanced out the window and noticed another car parked beside the detective's Mustang. She stole a glance at the detective's face, another back at the other car, then back at him again. The truth glared from his eyes. "You have someone watching me? I don't believe it! I don't need a babysitter!"

"Apparently you do, but unfortunately my man didn't do too good of a job this morning. Otherwise, he'd be where the truck is now, and we'd have our man surrounded."

She closed her eyes and shook her head. It didn't surprise her that Jefferies had someone watching her. Nor did it surprise her that he chose to invade her privacy by having her followed. The detective was just another cop who moved up in the ranks. Did what he pleased, when he pleased, not bothering to clear it with her first . . . even though it was her life. Why argue with the man? She wouldn't win.

Releasing a frustrated sigh, she said, "Detective Jefferies, it was a truck theft — pure and simple. It had nothing to do with your serial killer."

"You don't know that. And I wouldn't be so quick to be sure if I were you." His eyes challenged her. "How often do you get trucks stolen?"

Flinching, she knew in her heart there was a strong possibility of a connection. Why she didn't want to admit it to him, she did not know. Maybe she was afraid if she said it out loud, she'd be relinquishing control to that monster. That she could not do. She had fought too hard to be in control of her life . . . to not be a victim again. Her gaze slipped from the detective to the deputy and finally back to the detective again. Her shoulders slumped. "So we don't have trucks stolen every day of the week. So what?"

"When was the last time a truck was stolen?" he insisted, apparently wanting her to admit he was right. The man was not going to leave it alone.

"Okay, okay." She held up her hands in defeat. "We've never had a truck stolen . . . but it does happen."

"Right. And this just happened right after you saw a killer run away from a murder scene." Turning his back on her and facing the deputy, he asked, "Whatcha got?"

Sam stared in disbelief, fuming to herself as the detective seemed to take matters into his own hands as he turned his back on her. Why ask the deputy? Did he think she wouldn't answer his questions? He was right. She wouldn't, but that was beside the point. He acted as if she wasn't even there. The control thing reared its ugly head.

Holding her chin with her thumb and fingers, she tapped her lips with her forefinger. *What if it was the killer? Maybe I should listen to Detective Jefferies. He could be right. The possibility has crossed my mind a couple of times.*

Sam shook her head. No. There was still a chance it was just a thief. With the poor lighting yesterday morning, she didn't see the killer's face. Only his eyes. So why come after her? Sam doubted she would know him, even if he stood face-to-face with her.

The killer should realize that . . . right?

She closed her eyes. Just then piercing, bloodshot eyes, so dark they were almost black, stared back at her from her memory. Her heart froze. Popping her eyes open again, Sam knew. If she ever looked straight into the killer's eyes again, she could identify him. She had seen those eyes — that cold-blooded stare — an expression she'd never forget.

Quickly she had to rethink her position on the thief. She'd seen the truck thief tonight, the one she believed had stolen the truck anyway, and she didn't connect him with the killer.

"That's not true," she reminded herself in a quiet voice that only she heard. For a second she had thought it could be the killer, but that was out of timing, not out of a visual connection, she assured herself. The man tonight was a thief, not a killer.

Truthfully, it couldn't have been the same man from the night before. She would have recognized the killer's eyes. But then, she only saw a glimpse of the man's eyes tonight. He seemed to make sure of it.

Shaking her head, she grumbled that now she was confusing herself. She didn't know what to believe anymore. Rubbing her face and her eyes, she simply wished it was all over. She was too tired to think.

When she looked up again, the detective was watching her.

"I hope you realize now that it was the killer trying to get rid of a possible witness." Jefferies spoke to Sam, but his gaze went back to the deputy, as if telling him the same thing.

"That thought crossed my mind, too," the deputy said as he agreed with the detective.

"You don't know that for sure," Sam muttered to the detective. It was the timing that convinced the detective. She was sure of it. Of course, it was the timing that made her think of it in the beginning. *But no,* she told herself again. *It's not the same man.*

"Yes, I do."

"So, if you're so sure it was him, why don't you get out there and find him!" she blurted out. Sam was tired of arguing. Tired of worrying. Tired of being tired. She wished she could go home and shut the rest of the world out of her life for now. Her nerves were twisted tighter than a spinning top.

When she heard the slight hysteria in her own voice, she winced. "Okay, I admit you could be right, although I don't believe it. The deputy has everything we know, so get it from him." She jabbed her finger in the direction of the deputy. "Maybe the truck will lead you to your killer." Pressing her hands to her chest, she continued, "But as for me, I have to get back to work. If there are no more questions from either of you, you know the way out."

The deputy glanced at his notes, then shook his head. "No questions at the moment."

"Good." She turned her back on them.

They took the hint and left the office building.

Sam glanced outside the window as all three men — Matthew Jefferies, the deputy, and her apparent babysitter — gathered in the parking lot and talked.

For her own peace of mind, she poured a cup of water, grabbed the report she had to fill out, and sat at her desk to complete it, trying desperately to ignore them.

When she looked down at the preprinted form, though, she saw instead a dark-haired, blue-eyed man with a face that could disarm any woman. It was the detective who had rushed in a few minutes ago and practically accused her of lying to him. Well, not exactly, but close enough. He did ask the deputy for the details, not her.

The same man who only yesterday, she had to admit, had stayed in her thoughts for a brief moment too long . . . until she got her head screwed back on straight. What was it about him? Although she had seen him three years ago, she had never gotten to know him. But she did remember his accusing eyes were the same as the rest of the policemen's.

Enough about the detective. Her thoughts needed to return to the report. It had to be filled out before the boss arrived. Another added distraction. Talking with the boss about anything always gave her the jitters. Somehow she felt sure all of this would end up being her fault.

The stolen truck and nearly being run over was what her mind had to focus on, not her boss's response to the situation or the devastatingly distracting detective and his interference.

Why was she thinking about him anyway?

Since Martin, she hadn't even looked at another man, let alone thought about one.

As she filled in the report, she heard activity in the drivers' room. Someone from the deputy's office arrived and dusted for prints; then the official vehicles all drove away.

By the time the report was complete, an ounce of fear tried to creep into her thoughts again. Idle hands were the devil's workshop. She understood that saying all too well now. Idle hands left her mind free to think about what she didn't need to dwell on.

Finally, she admitted, she needed to face the truth, and the truth was the man in the drivers' room tonight could have been the killer. She believed, down deep, he was the thief, but was that for her own sanity? Had she been by herself, what would he have done?

Her heartbeat grew harder and louder every second — each pulsing throb more intense, more precise, like the pounding of a nail in a two-by-four. The closer the head of the nail got to the wood, the harder the hammer hit, pounding it deeper and deeper into the hardened strip of lumber.

Within the next hour, Ken Richardson, her boss, showed up, and Sam followed him into his office.

Ken pointed toward the straight-back chair perched next to his desk. "Have a seat."

He didn't point blame or give her a hard time. *How unusual. Things must be bad.*

Together, the two decided for her own safety, as well as the company's position, it would be in their best interest if she would take a week, maybe two, of her vacation now. At least until the killer was caught.

After the decision was made, she headed home, occasionally glancing in the rearview mirror. A twinge of fear resting on the surface had her jumping at everything: every sound, every movement, every car. For a moment or two, she thought she was being followed. It could have been the policeman who had been watching her earlier. Her babysitter was probably on her tail but keeping his distance.

Shoving that possibility aside, she remembered seeing all three men — detective, deputy, and babysitter — leave together. Besides which, the bodyguard's car was gold. This one was black. Her mind jumped quickly to the chance it could be the killer following her.

Could it be? She glanced back and forth from the mirror to the highway in front of her. Another glance in the mirror, and the car turned off the highway.

What a vivid imagination she had. Shaking off the tension, Sam kept her mind on her driving. *Come on, Lord. Get these crazy thoughts out of my head.*

In half an hour, she was at home safe and sound, glad to be away from work and what was going on around there. She closed her front door, twisted the deadbolt until she heard a *click,* then dragged herself to the bathroom for a shower. It had been another long night. Thank God for Amanda, who had taken Marty to school again that morning.

When her shower was complete, Sam slipped into a short cotton nightgown and crawled into bed. Picking up her phone, she dialed Amanda's cell.

"Thanks for taking Marty to school again. You are the best."

"No problem. So what happened this time? Not more of the killer, I pray."

"No. This morning we had a truck stolen, so I had to wait for Ken to show up so we could talk. Standard procedure, more or less. Anyway, I'm on vacation now."

"Great! I'll see you tonight, and you can tell me all about everything!"

"That's a promise," Sam said.

Closing her eyes, she sighed. Sleep — that was what she needed after another rough night, and the sleep came almost immediately.

CHAPTER 7

After Matthew reamed Earnie Shelton out for falling asleep on stakeout, Matthew decided to work out a watch schedule. Dumping it on Shelton at the last minute like he had and expecting the man to stay sharp and awake all night after being up all day was bad planning on Matthew's part, but they all had done it at one time or another.

When Shelton had called that morning to say what had happened and admitted to dozing off shortly before the incident, Matthew's stomach knotted in fear for Ms. Cain's safety. Shelton had awakened to Ms. Cain calling for the men working in the back to come up to her office. He had heard the urgency in her voice, then listened from the back door.

No one knew he was there. In that secluded place, there wasn't any protection for those people. How could Sam dare show up for work after all she had been through the night before? Maybe she was stronger than Martin gave her credit for being.

Matthew made a rotating schedule, using Shelton and Davis in the daytime, eight hour shifts each, and took the nights for himself. The detective knew this way he could take a short nap during a portion of the day, as well as follow up on his investigation. This would also leave him free to watch Ms. Cain all night, hoping to catch the killer. He would be back. Matthew knew this.

It was no longer just a possibility in Matthew's mind that the thief was Jane Stewart's killer, as well as the other victims' killer. Why else would this man try to run Ms. Cain down?

This was the break he was waiting for, and he wasn't about to let it slip through his fingers, even if it meant being around a woman he knew in the back of his mind he should steer clear of.

For a minute, he recalled Ms. Cain declaring her independence and expressing she had no need for a babysitter. A smile touched his lips. She needed someone to watch her, all right, looking out for her well-being, whether she liked it or not, and he would make sure she had it.

Sometimes Matthew found it hard to see the woman Martin had described. She didn't come off as a flirt or a tramp when he was around her. She had never flirted with him . . . and, although he wasn't trying to puff up his own ego, he always had women coming on to him. But not her. In fact, she appeared strong and independent, with morals she held to fiercely.

Matthew shook his head. "Who knows?" Besides, it didn't matter now. She was a potential witness who needed his protection, and he needed her cooperation.

As he pulled away from the curb, he glanced at his watch. It was two thirty. *She ought to be getting up about now. Maybe I'll stop by and let her know someone will be watching her at all times . . . and maybe I won't.* His mind battled. How forthcoming should he be with her? Still, he had no trust where she was concerned. If she were anyone else, would he tell her?

He shook his head. *I don't think so.*

Instead he would address the issue of getting a description of the suspect. He needed to see if she was ready to try and describe the killer to a sketch artist. If she would do that, he could show it around at the diners. Maybe seeing a sketch of the killer would trigger the memory of the victims' coworkers. Maybe they knew something about the man that could direct Matthew toward the killer, and they didn't even know it. Maybe the killer paid with a credit card. That would get him a name and an address. If not that, maybe the man had mentioned the kind of work he did. That would point Matthew in a closer direction of where to search. He still needed that break, and he needed it now. Time was running out.

CHAPTER 8

Sam flipped on the television. Her show had already started.

Today she found she was moving slowly, but the minute Remington Steele's face came on the tube in the afternoon reruns of the reruns, Sam thought about the real-life detective, Matthew Jefferies, and warmth spread through her.

As she smiled at the picture on the screen, a thought flashed. Her smile widened a little more.

If my life was on television, I could get the hero. But, unfortunately, my life is real, and Matthew Jefferies was part of Martin's unit. I don't want anything to do with the likes of him.

The doorbell interrupted her notions.

"Not today," she cried.

Sam didn't need any hassles with reporters. They had never called her yesterday and for that, she was grateful. She hoped the police were still keeping her name out of all of it. If not, she would stop the press before they started. She had plans today. This inconvenience was not going to interfere with her life. She and her son would go on as normal.

Killer or no killer, witness or no witness, today she was on vacation . . . so to speak, and she was going to enjoy herself.

These last two days were a thing of the past, and she would put them out of her mind. It wasn't her place to fix things or catch the killer . . . or the thief, for that matter. It was her job to be the best mom she could be. And that was her priority.

She would start fresh today by rejuvenating herself. The gym was going to be her first stop. Sam would then pick Marty up from school and spend the remainder of the day with him. Then, much later tonight, she'd fill in Amanda on all the details of how her life had been turned upside-down in less than forty-eight hours.

Amanda Thompson had been her best friend since grade school. They both knew everything about each other. Sam wouldn't trade her for a million dollars. Amanda would help Sam keep her mind off those things of the past and help her focus on today.

A knock on the door sounded before she

could reach it. *I'm coming. Hold your horses.* She moved a little faster toward the door.

"Ms. Cain, it's me. Are you in there?" Matthew Jefferies' voice called through the door.

She stopped midstep.

"Please. Let me in so we can talk for just a minute." His words sounded more like an order than a plea.

Sam slowly eased over to the door. Her hand clutched the knob. At the sound of his voice, a warm feeling stirred in the pit of her stomach; her heart lurched.

That wasn't the kind of emotion she should feel right now. Aggravation should strike all the nerves in her body. How dare he just show up on her doorstep!

What is wrong with me? Excitement surged inside her, even though she tried to fight it.

Don't get interested in him. He's a cop. Martin's ex-partner. Tell him to go away! her mind screamed, but her voice said, "Wait a minute while I get dressed."

CHAPTER 9

If she was going to see him, the least she could do was look more presentable.

Slipping back into her bedroom, Sam put on a pair of shorts and a T-shirt, then ran a brush through her hair before returning to the door.

Knowing it wasn't smart to talk to him for her own peace-of-mind didn't stop the flutter of her heart at the anticipation of seeing him. This was ridiculous. Why was she feeling like a teenager in the midst of all this turmoil? It didn't make a bit of sense.

The more she thought about him, the more she wanted to see him. Him — a cop, no less — and that confused her even more. She sighed as she tried to control the racing of her heart.

"Now what, Detective?" she asked as she opened the door a crack and blocked his entrance with her body. She didn't dare let her true emotions show, but as her gaze settled upon his face, her pulse quickened even more. Bubbles of joy tingled in her veins at the mere sight of him. It fought against her feelings, but it seemed her body had a mind of its own.

"Good afternoon." Detective Jefferies placed his hand against the door, as if making sure she wouldn't close it in his face. "May I come in?"

She looked at his hand on the door, then back at him. The part about policemen she didn't care for surfaced — the insistence on having things their way. Part of her didn't want to let him into her home, but a battle was taking place from within. Which would win?

Finally, Sam said, "I'd rather you didn't come in. I don't know why you keep coming around. There's nothing more I can say to help you on your case. I didn't see him clearly enough to give a description to an artist. Even if the thief and killer are one and the same, I didn't get a good look at that stranger who used the phone. And again, that's a big *if* he was the thief."

And if you knew what was good for me, you'd stay away and quit making things so difficult, she added, but not out loud.

"Sometimes it helps when you sleep on what you saw," he said calmly. "More comes back to you. I also wanted to see if you gave it any more thought about the guy who used your phone. You say you didn't get a good look, but he walked into the drivers' room and you saw his shape, his size, and his coloring. All of that would be helpful, believe it or not. And if you would be willing to give that information to our sketch artist, it would help him with a composite drawing. They do wonders with computers nowadays."

He dropped his hand to his side, apparently believing she wasn't going to close the door on him after all. "Besides, I wanted to make sure you were still okay. No repercussions from last night or the night before. Sometimes injuries don't show up right away."

Yeah, right. Like he's really concerned for my well-being.

She wished this was true but knew better. Cops, she'd found in the past, were good actors. They let you believe what they needed you to believe so they could get what they wanted out of you. There was no law against that. And, right now, he wanted Sam to believe he was a good cop.

"I didn't get injured either night. I'm fine." She shook her head. "Again, I didn't come up with anything new on his description. Sorry."

Her head knew the truth about Detective Jefferies, but her heart, for some strange reason, was disagreeing.

The battle continued. It was locking on to some goodness somewhere within him. She knew, since her attack and recovery, she had gotten closer to the Lord. By reading His Word, filling her heart with His thoughts, maybe she was becoming more Christlike and was looking for the good in humankind.

But why now? Why him — Detective Matthew Jefferies?

The detective looked at her but didn't say a word. Probably giving her more time to reconsider and invite him in. Cops. They believed too much in the power of persuasion, or maybe it was their power. Either way, she was not letting him into her home.

"I'm okay. I promise."

She squinted as a thought crossed her mind. *They've had all day to find the missing truck. Did they? And did it lead to any evidence?* Tightening her grip on the door, she met his eyes boldly. "Did y'all get anything from the prints on the phone? Did you find the truck?"

Would he tell her if they had?

The detective hesitated only a minute. "The receiver of the phone had been wiped clean. More proof he's a bad guy. Obviously his prints are in the system. Otherwise, why wipe it clean? Only the base had prints, and so far, most prints match those of drivers who are in the new system, and they all work for Bulk. He probably covered his finger with a handkerchief or something. I know you still don't want to believe that the thief and the attacker are one and the same —" his voice lowered to an almost whisper — "but I'm convinced they are. And no, we haven't found the truck yet, but we're still looking."

"I'm afraid you're wrong." That felt good. She noticed when she said it, his eyes widened, as if ready to deny anything and everything.

She could hear his thought. *Me, wrong? Truly you jest.*

Instead, he said, "I promise. We are still looking."

Shaking her head, she said, "No, you misunderstand. I believe what you said — that you're still looking. And I've come to the realization that they *are* one and the same: the thief and the killer. Only I don't believe he was there last night to kill me. I think he was just seeing if I could recognize him — to check out my reaction. But I didn't react. So I don't get why he stole a truck after that. I don't understand his motives, nor can I even speculate, but we already know he's sick or he wouldn't kill people. Personally, I hope you get him soon. I don't want to run into him anywhere. And I don't want him anywhere near my son. That's what scares me the most. I don't like being afraid, either. That was something I had to overcome and, until now, I thought I had."

Looking into the detective's eyes, she added, "I want my life to get back to normal. I'm having to take early vacation because of all that has happened. It's not fair, but I guess I'm ready for a vacation. I need a break from the tension."

Silence hung between them for a minute as they stared at one another. Then finally he said, "Aren't you going to ask me in?"

Her hold on the doorknob tightened, as did a knot in her chest. "I already said no. So I wasn't planning on it. Besides, I don't see the point."

His eyes studied her, as if trying to say something to her without speaking. But she needed to hear him say those words she knew were in his mind.

"How about if I insist?"

"Cops are good at insisting," she said through tight lips. "Why not?" She tossed her hands up in the air, as if giving up, and backed away, allowing him room to enter. "By all means. Come in. Can I get you something to drink?" Sam asked as she turned to head toward the kitchen.

Not that she wanted to be sociable . . . at least not in her mind. Her heart was another matter. She wanted to see the detective again, but not like this. Not because of criminal activities. She wished the situation could be different. Even more, she wished she could get a grip on her heart. He was not for her.

"Coffee, if it's not too much trouble. We need to talk."

Walking through the living room, she glanced at *Remington Steele* on the television, then reached for the remote to mute the sound. *So much for my television hero today.*

Chapter 10

In the kitchen, she put water in the tea kettle and placed it on the burner. "Instant is all I have." Not waiting for him to reply, she turned the burner on, then took down a cup from the cupboard and dumped two teaspoons of instant coffee into it. "Cream or sugar?" she asked, never turning in his direction.

"Black with half a teaspoon of sugar. Thanks."

While waiting for the whistle to sound, Sam poured herself a glass of juice. Better to stay busy than to look at that man. He had a way of getting into her every fiber. What was it about him? His dark hair? His good looks? No. It couldn't be that. She had seen plenty of good-looking men in her life and never had one gotten under her skin this way. It had to be because she was at a vulnerable point in her life at the moment. And, in a way, he came rushing in to save

87

the day . . . kind of like a knight on a white horse, only his was a silver Mustang.

As she waited for the water to boil so she could pour it into the cup, he sat quietly behind her, never saying a word. But she felt his eyes on her back, watching her every move.

She took in a deep breath. Should she bring up the past and get it out of the way? Should she tell him the torture Martin put her through? None of his friends on the force knew about their past. They knew only what Martin had told them. At the time of the investigation, none of them wanted to hear what she had to say. Thank God for people higher up in the ranks who listened and saw the truth. Some truth even they couldn't see, but some seemed to understand.

The hidden scars he left deep within her by his verbal abuse, or the visible scars left by his physical abuse — maybe she should tell Matthew about those now. Maybe she should even tell him how he wounded his own son, scarring him from within.

Martin was a bully and a drunk, but he hid it well from others. He only abused the people he supposedly loved. The police could have helped her, even in the end, had they not ignored the signs.

She sighed. Maybe she should pretend the past never happened? Maybe Matthew didn't remember how they had all blamed her for Martin's death. They judged her and found her guilty without knowing the facts . . . without checking them out. Martin was one of them, so of course he was innocent. Maybe she should just let sleeping dogs lie. What good would it do, anyway? She remembered all too well the pain they put her through after his death.

After the water came to a boil, she poured it into the cup as she thought. No more pain. No more not understanding. No more not knowing the whole truth. It was time she revealed all to one of his buddies.

Ready to confront him, she turned and placed the cup of coffee on the table before him. Then, as she moved to set her glass down and sit in the chair across from him, she opened her mouth to broach the subject.

But he beat her to it. "You seem to be doing pretty well for yourself . . . I mean, since Martin's death. Is there a new man in your life now? And your son — how is he coping with no dad?"

"I don't think that's any of your business or concern."

Now that he had brought it up, she wasn't so sure she was ready to talk about it with him after all, especially from the angle he approached it. She heard the haughtiness in his voice. He thought she was no good then, and he still felt the same way.

He sat in silence, just looking at her. He was either judging her again or didn't care one way or the other. The man was making small talk while waiting to get what he wanted from her. He needed her to help him. Otherwise he wouldn't even be hanging around; Sam felt certain of that.

Finally, she looked him straight in the eyes, as if daring him to deny what she was about to tell him. "I have my son. I don't need anyone else. And Marty is a good boy . . . doing well in school. I believe he is *coping* fine." She stressed that, because if he really was concerned, why hadn't he checked on them a month or so after Martin's suicide? Matthew was his partner, after all. New partner, she admitted, but partner no less. You would think, out of plain decency, he would have checked on Martin's son, especially since they blamed her for Martin's death. But no one did.

"That's good." Detective Jefferies nodded, then picked up his cup and took a sip of coffee. "Tastes good. Thanks."

As much as Sam wanted to straighten things out about the past once and for all, she couldn't bring herself to talk about it, about Martin, about their life. Not now. Not with Jefferies. Maybe she would have another chance later. Maybe not. At the moment, it didn't matter.

Taking a sip of her juice, she decided to get back to the present situation. "Look, Detective. The truck missed me." She raised her hands in the air, glanced down at herself, and then back at him. "As you can see, I'm fine. I ducked between two rigs as the other truck passed." Pensively, she searched his face for an agreement. "The man who tried to run me down got what he was after. If he is the killer, which I agree he could be, he found out I didn't recognize him, so he has no need to fear. So why are you here? I have nothing new to offer."

As if ignoring her words, he asked, "Did you sleep well today? Any dreams . . . or nightmares?"

"I slept fine." She wasn't sure she would tell him, even if she had experienced horrible dreams, recalling things verbatim. It would be a dream . . . not reality.

"Can you recall anything more about the man who used the phone last night? Like I said, you saw him up close in a sense. At least good enough to where you should be able to judge his height and speculate on his coloring. Do you recall enough to give a description of some sort to the sketch artist so he could create a composite of the man?"

"I already answered that at the door."

When he didn't respond, she continued, "I saw him from the back and a slight profile view. John, the driver who was in there when he came in, could probably give you a better description. The man was probably a good half foot taller than John. I did catch a glimpse of his eyes once, but it was only a glimpse, and they were shadowed by the bill of his cap. So I couldn't even say if the eyes were the same as the eyes of the killer, which I admit I got a good look at. The bill covered his eyes last night, casting a shadow over them. Besides, you can't make a drawing from eyes. He made a point of keeping his face away from the light, out of my view. That was another reason I agreed you were probably right about him and the killer being the same man."

The detective listened, never interrupting.

"With the hat pulled down, he hid his hair and part of his face." Closing her eyes, she rubbed them, then raked her fingers through her hair. Shaking her head, she opened her eyes again. "I couldn't see him clearly. However, I did notice the dark stubble on his chin. So his hair is probably dark. Judging by what I could see of his skin, arms and hands, I would say he was a light-skinned man, one who didn't get outdoors too often. He was probably in his late teens, maybe early twenties. The skin looked young, not old — you know, not wrinkled but firm, tight. Also, his body appeared to be in good shape . . . physically fit, I mean."

A strange look darted through his eyes.

He didn't ask what made her say that, but she decided to explain anyway. She could only imagine what he was thinking. "The man's arms looked like they had definition, cuts, you know, as if he lifted weights or his job was physical. I don't know if that'll help or not."

"Every little bit helps, Ms. Cain. It appears you saw more than you realized. Besides, you'd be amazed at what we can do with computers today with only a profile description."

Scraping her top teeth across her bottom lip, she toyed with telling him she may have been followed home this morning. It had concerned her for a bit, but when the dark car turned off, she lost her worry. She doubted anyone would be interested in following her home. If she just left things alone for a while, they would cool off and life would get back to normal. Squinting as her eyebrows drew together, she thought for a moment. She could go in and speak with the artist. If it would help them catch the killer, why not? But would it make her more of a target for him to come after? She had to think of Marty now, not herself. His life, his safety was the most important thing to her. She could endure anything for her son . . . if it meant keeping him safe. *But have I really seen enough to give them a description?*

"You do realize now, even though you didn't get a good look at him, he saw you." Matthew's words rang in her head. "Up close, I might add. Twice in fact. And the second time, he studied you."

"All right, all right, yes," she admitted as she envisioned the man hiding in the shadows. "I could tell he was watching me when he was on the phone. That's why I thought the man was there to rob the place."

"You need to be careful. Be aware of what is around you at all times. He could be following you."

Now was the perfect time to tell him, but the car had turned off. Besides, she would sound paranoid. She didn't need to add more things to his list of bad things about her. "But that was at work, almost fifteen miles from here," she said. "And I won't be

94

going back there for some time. I should be fine here at home. He doesn't know my name, so he can't find out where I live."

A short silence fell between them.

She didn't like the quiet, so she filled the silence with thoughts that had bothered her for some time. "I don't understand why some people do what they do. If all of us would just work hard for what we want, instead of taking from others, preying on the weak, this world would be a much better place to live in." She looked straight into the detective's eyes. "I guess now that you're a detective, you really get to know more about what makes these people do the things they do, like thieves, rapists, killers, and even serial killers." She shuddered. "I guess you deal with all sorts of people now. What makes people act so bad?"

"Serial killers do what they do usually for physical gratification. To them, each killing is like a sexual peak. Other killings, random killings, are usually from greed or for power. Sometimes done in the heat of passion, but usually well thought out, premeditated. For thieves, there are many explanations." He shrugged. "Some people are sick and can't help themselves, while others are lazy or greedy. Some are in a bad situation in life, while others are just in the wrong place at the wrong time."

Shivers ran unimpeded all over her body as a sick feeling consumed her. "I couldn't deal with those kinds of people day in and day out. I don't know how you do it." Maybe that was why Martin changed so drastically, but Sam had a hard time contributing it all to the job. Martin hadn't been a policeman for that long a time.

Matthew reached across the table and covered her hands with his.

Warmth crept through every fiber as silence hung between them. Sam knew she shouldn't respond this way just from his touch, his compassion — even if it was sincere — but she couldn't stop herself. Sam looked up from their hands, and her gaze lingered on his face. A soft dark lock of hair had fallen across his forehead, and Sam wished she could reach out and brush it back.

Then Matthew swiftly pulled his hands back and jammed them in his jean pockets. He looked anywhere but where Sam sat. Before he spoke again, he seemed to gather his thoughts. But Sam waited for him to speak, afraid her words wouldn't sound right even if she tried to speak them.

"It's a job. And somebody has to do it." He turned his gaze back upon her. "Back to the subject at hand. I believe someone has fixed his sights on you. Maybe I'm wrong, but what if I'm not?"

Swallowing the lump in her throat, Sam realized she had to take his words more seriously than she had so far. He could be right. Maybe she could describe the man well enough for an artist to sketch. Glancing up at the detective's face, she knew if she could keep her mind off his blue, penetrating eyes and his soft, dark hair long enough, she might be able to do it. She would at least give it a try.

Boldly, she said, "You're right. I'll try to describe the man who used the phone to your artist."

"I'll bet if you close your eyes right now and take your time, you could probably see him better than you think." His words were soft-spoken, encouraging.

For the next few seconds, she closed her eyes and thought about the man coming in to use the phone. Focusing on him, she looked past his build, concentrating on the face under the brim of that hat, and honed in on his expression when his eyes clashed with hers. Yes. He had seen her, too. Now there was no doubt in her mind. Not only could she see the cold-blooded stare she had seen the night before, but she realized

97

the awareness in his eyes as he glared at her.

"Dark. Almost black," she whispered as she shivered slightly. "No. That was the light, or lack of it, the shadow on his face. But his eyes were dark, dark brown. Like rich coffee grounds. And sick . . . oh-so sick. The thoughts that must go on behind those eyes scare me. Wait." She looked deep into the remnants of her mind. "I've seen eyes like those before."

Chill bumps raced down her arms as she trembled. Tears welled up in her eyes as the memory that rested in the back of her mind tried to come forward. Blinking twice, she reached her hand up and wiped away the tears. She shook her head no, not ready to give in to that memory. Her conscience fought it as her mind tried to recall. Where had she seen that look before?

Her eyes popped open. The answer came quickly. She sucked in a quick gasp of air and then closed her eyes again. She laid her face in her hands as she shuddered. *No, Lord, please don't let me think on it. Don't let me go back there.*

The thought frightened her as she recalled who had that look. Her husband, Martin, the day he scarred Sam for life . . . the day he killed himself. It had to be the anger, the hate in his eyes.

"Oh," she groaned as the icy fingers of fear slipped around her neck, clutching, holding on tight. No. He was dead. It had been three years. She refused to let it shake her so.

"It's okay. I'm here with you. No one's going to hurt you. Where have you seen eyes like those before?"

It had been a long time since she had trusted the police. Slowly, she opened her eyes. Adjusting her gaze, she focused in on the detective. *Could she trust the police? Could she trust him?*

As she questioned herself, with her fingertips she reached up under her bangs and touched the thick, rough skin on her forehead. She rubbed the disfigured skin gently out of habit. A scar left by her husband, a trusted friend, someone she loved . . . a cop. A quick reminder of where trust had taken her before it left her cold.

Dare she trust again? *No.*

"You wouldn't believe me if I told you."

CHAPTER 11

"Tell me," he repeated. "Where have you seen those eyes before? Who are you remembering?"

Sam shrank back in her chair, afraid to speak the truth. He wouldn't believe her. Everyone at the station believed Martin was a great guy. Why bother wasting her breath? Besides, could he be trusted with the truth or would he turn that around to hurt her more? The truth was something she had always lived, so why change now? "I'm not sure I can trust you."

"Of course you can trust me. It's my duty to protect you."

"Why?" She raised her brows in question. "Because you work for the police department?"

"Exactly."

"Sorry. Not good enough." History could not and would not repeat itself. Other than Marty and Amanda, she had learned not to trust anyone except herself and the Lord. No other human. Especially the police. "Past experience keeps me from believing that to be a good enough reason to trust you. Three years ago, you all blamed me. But I was the victim. Marty and me. Martin was the guilty one. None of you could see that. You didn't believe me then, and I doubt you would believe me now."

"Let's put the past behind us and leave it there. Concentrate on today." As he spoke, his eyes probed deep within her soul, it seemed, stabbing at her heart.

"No!" She wished she could trust them . . . him . . . but she couldn't. "I mean, yes. I mean, I wish I could." Frustrated, she shook her head and then her fists in the air. She raised her voice. "I don't know what I mean! Just leave, please. Why don't you leave now! I can't help you."

"I can't leave. I need your help. Think of the victims the man has taken. Please try . . . for their sake. For the sake of future victims. I'm sure you can remember more if you would just try. Start by putting the past aside. Try to forget it."

She took in a deep breath, then continued in a calmer tone, "I don't want to forget the past, but I need to. I've forgiven the past — well, Martin anyway — but I have to remember what I've learned. I've tried to forget the pain, but it keeps coming back to haunt me. Especially now. Don't you see? Can't you understand?"

When he didn't respond to her question, she threw her hands up into the air. "I give up. You don't know what I went through." She jumped to her feet, snatched up her glass, marched to the sink, and rinsed her glass out. Slamming it down in the sink, she turned and faced him. "The past doesn't really matter, because it has no bearing on what happened yesterday, so let's drop it. Or like you said, forget it. Put it behind me . . . at least in connection with you today."

The detective watched her. His expression showed he was puzzled.

"Never mind," she finally said. "I'll come by the station while I'm out today and get with the artist. That's the best I can do."

Turning her back on him again, Sam changed her mind about more juice. Her dry mouth needed some. She picked up the glass again, poured the water out of it, snatched open the refrigerator door, pulled out the jug, and opened the lid. "I'm refilling my juice. Do you want more coffee?" she snapped.

Her fingers tightened further around the

glass as she heard the strain in her own voice. She hoped he would turn the offer down. She wanted him to go. Samantha needed him to leave so she could get her senses back.

"I'll pass."

Why so much emotion? Why try to convince herself there was nothing to fear, when deep down she knew she had a lot to be fearful of? Well, not fear itself, as much as she needed to be aware of the facts around her? First off, someone was possibly after her. Secondly, the man's cold eyes looked like none other than Martin's eyes right before he attacked her. Surely, that was only because Detective Jefferies had brought the past up to haunt her. Thirdly, Marty's life could be in danger. And last but not least, the police were back in her life, and she appeared to have a fascination with this detective whom she had no business being attracted to in the least tiny bit.

All of a sudden, the room seemed to be shrinking. Sam found it hard to breathe. She didn't know why, but she knew she had to get out of that room, and fast. He drew too much emotion from her.

She took one big swallow of the juice, then set the glass down on the counter. *Escape. I have to escape.* Turning, she darted out of the room as she said, "I have to go, so you need to get out of here. Now, please."

Leaving didn't help. He followed right behind her into the living room and stopped within an arm's reach. He needed to go. She needed him to go, get out of the room, out of the apartment, out of her life.

"I didn't come here to upset you or bring up the past. I came here to get a description from you and make you realize the danger you're in. I'm here to protect you. That's my job."

"I don't need protection!" She stepped further away and then wheeled around to face the detective from a distance.

He stood in the archway dividing the dining room from the living room.

"Especially from you!" she said as she jabbed her finger in his direction. As quick as she said it, she wished she could take it back. "I can protect myself. I've trained in self-defense classes. I made sure I could protect myself. I refuse to be a victim again." Covering her mouth with her hand, she stopped herself from saying anymore. She tried to gain control of her emotions and figure them out at the same time.

Why fuss with him? Was she blaming him for the past? Was she blaming him for her being caught in the middle of her present danger? *Why? Why? Why?* she screamed in her brain. The words pounded inside her head. *Help me, Lord. Please take control of this conversation.*

In seconds it hit her like a Mack truck, or maybe an answered prayer. It wasn't Detective Jefferies who upset her. She started getting upset when she tried to envision that man, the man on the phone, the man who tried to run her down. Not so much the man, but the look in his eyes. Intense fear had grown inside her. She had lost control.

That was it! That was the problem. Someone else was in control of her life . . . again. *Let me be your strength, your protection.* She knew she should be turning her situation over to God totally; no one was greater than Him. But right then, her flesh was in control — and scared to death.

Her bottom lip started to tremble. Control was the key. The man after her was in control.

But why take it out on Detective Jefferies? Why should he suffer for her uncontrollable feelings of terror? He hadn't done anything, except to make her wake up to reality. She was helpless *again,* and that frightened her, more than she cared to admit.

Sam's hands shook as she dropped on the couch, then cradled her head in her hands.

She shuddered from head to toe as tears flowed softly down her cheeks.

Once the feelings had swept through her and settled in the pit of her stomach, she leaned back against the couch, wiped her face dry with the back of her hands, and then dropped them to her side. "I'm sorry. You're right. I'm venting my anger on you. I thought I was past all these feelings. I didn't know I could still feel so much fear . . . so much anger, so quickly. I didn't even know I was this upset. I truly thought the past was in the past."

"It's okay. I think you're more scared than anything." The detective walked over and sat next to her, looking as if he wanted to offer her comfort but not actually offering any.

Holding her hands up, she kept distance between them. She didn't want or need his pity. "You're right. I'm so used to hiding my fear, covering it up, I just couldn't see it. I work a man's job, so I can't afford to show my fear there. I have to be tough. If I showed fear, the drivers would run all over me."

"A little fear is good for you. If nothing else, it'll make you more cautious."

Cautious, huh? Like I'm not cautious enough. Sam had wrapped herself and

Marty in a cocoon, guarding and protecting them from the pain of the outside world. Yes, she had learned her lesson all right, the hard way, and it had left her with a lot of emotional baggage, as well as physical scarring. She dare not let anything else happen to her son. She would protect him with her life. Her whole life, her whole world was Marty.

Since the "accident," she didn't go to parties much or out with friends. She never dated, although she had been asked by several men. Sam worked and came home. She overprotected Marty and restricted his playtime and his friends. The two of them visited Amanda, but she lived across the hall. It wasn't too scary to walk across the hall. Sometimes Sam would take Marty, and they would go visit her mom and dad, but that was the extent of her social life.

In fact, when Marty got out of school today, she was going to bring him to her parents' home to stay for a few days for his protection. She hoped that was all it took to keep him safe. Of course, she still had to clear it with her parents, but when they learned what had happened, they'd encourage both Sam and Marty to stay with them. She couldn't chance bringing danger into their home, too, so her staying was out of the question.

Another thing she did for her own enjoyment was to take time for the health club on her off days while Marty was at school. Staying in shape, preparing physically in case of another brutal attack, was her whole life, aside from Marty. Obviously she wasn't prepared enough since she had not escaped the clutches of the attacker. Not that he had attacked her per se, but, she told herself, she had never prepared for another mental assault. That was what she was experiencing now by letting the past haunt her and un-nerve her while she waited to see if this man would come after her.

Sam had to face it, so she better start preparing herself all the way. Looking at the detective, she saw concern in his eyes.

"No need to worry about me now, Detective. Remember, I'm on vacation as of this morning. No more going to work until the man is caught — or at least until the excitement dies down. The boss and I both decided it was for the best."

"When they find the truck, maybe we'll know more. Just remember, he missed you this morning, but he may come after you again."

Through tight lips, she said, "Thanks for those encouraging words."

When he didn't say anything, she added, "Don't worry. You've done your job. I'm scared now, and I'll be watching constantly, so you can go."

"Sorry, but somebody had to make you see it." He paused. "I'm just glad you didn't get hurt."

"Me, too." She stood and showed him to the door. All her energy and emotion had been zapped. "Thanks again."

At the door, he stopped and turned. Reaching into his pocket, he pulled out a card and handed it to her. "Here are my work and cell numbers. Call me if you think of anything or need anything."

She took it and slipped it in her shorts pocket. "Thanks."

"Remember, be extra careful. Do you have a gun?"

"Men! Yes, I have a gun, but I don't carry it. I'd be more danger to myself than to anyone else. I haven't shot it in years. Besides, guns scare me. Trust me, I'll be okay." Sam reached for the knob to open the door and let him out.

Before he left, the detective extended his hand toward her face, but stopped halfway. His eyes studied her; then he appeared to look deep into her soul. Suddenly drawing his hand back, he said, his voice soft and tender, "Take care."

A lump caught in her throat. If she didn't know better, she would almost think he cared. "Sure," she murmured.

Sam watched him walk away, down the breezeway, till he reached the stairs on the other side and started descending one step at a time.

Confusion filled her as she thought about the emotions he stirred within her. What happened to make her react this way to this man? Why the physical attraction? Sure, he was very handsome, but looks weren't everything. She'd learned that a long time ago. If for no other reason than he had been Martin's partner, she shouldn't be finding herself attracted to him.

Sam leaned against the doorframe and smiled. It didn't matter what she told herself; her heart didn't seem to listen. It didn't have to know him to experience the feelings he awakened in her, feelings that had been dead for over three years. That was why it was called a *physical attraction.*

Stepping inside her apartment, Sam closed the door and locked it. She glanced into the living room at the TV and noticed the end of her show. With a flick of her brows, she admitted to herself that Matthew Jefferies was worth missing Remy over. *Enough of that.* She sighed. *It's past time for a workout and to fix my mind on the here and now.*

CHAPTER 12

Dressed in form-fitting workout garb, Sam grabbed her athletic bag, tossed in a towel, swimsuit, hair supplies, and a change of clothes, prepared for a trip to the gym. Next, she packed a bag for Marty. In it, she packed enough clothes for a whole week's stay at her parents' — not that she believed it would take that long, but it was best to be prepared. Closing the case up tight, she headed out of his room with her gym bag on her shoulder and Marty's case in her hand.

She grabbed her purse and keys off the side table and headed toward the door. Glancing at the clock, she saw she had three hours before she had to pick Marty up at school. Could she do a quick workout and slip by the police station to give a description to the sketch artist all in three hours? She may have to skip the sauna. She would make it happen.

As she pulled the door to close it behind her, the phone rang. Sam started to ignore the ring, then thought better. Someone from work could be on the other end with a question, or her parents could be calling to check on her. It could even be the school about Marty. Pushing the door open, she raced to answer it.

On the third ring she snatched up the receiver. "Hello."

Silence hung on the line, but it wasn't a dead line. Whoever called was still there. His heavy breathing was loud.

"Hello," she said again.

The breathing continued, sounding hot and heavy. She didn't need practical jokers at a time like this in her life. Taking a deep breath, she prayed it was a practical joker and not *him.* Slapping down the phone, she headed out the door and slammed it shut.

As she was locking the deadbolt, the phone rang again. Her hands started to tremble. No. She would not let this frighten her. Quickly, she walked along the breezeway toward the stairs.

Although she tried to fight it, apprehension stirred strongly. She slowed at the top of the stairs and glanced around. *Remember to watch your back,* she heard the detective tell her. She could do that. She had to do that.

Nothing looked suspicious, but nonetheless, she continued to look around, making sure no one was lurking in the bushes or behind cars.

Reassured with a dose of phony confidence, Sam rushed down the stairs toward her car, threw the bags in the trunk, climbed in her Toyota, and fired up the engine. The gym was near her apartment, so she didn't have far to drive, but she watched her surroundings the whole time, staying aware and alert.

"And don't forget to go by the station after the spa," she reminded herself again when she recalled her promise to Detective Jefferies . . . *Matthew.* "No," she told herself aloud. Her mind wanted to wander, but she focused on her driving.

The drive was a short trip she took often. On most of her off days, Sam would go to the spa for a workout. If time was against her, she would settle for a jog to the elementary school and back, a four-mile trek that took a little over an hour. Sometimes she did it as Marty was getting out of school, so that slowed her down a little on her return. But either way it was a good workout. Marty didn't like it so much.

He would rather her pick him up in the car every time.

Upon arrival to the health club, she pulled open the glass door. Music blared. The large open room behind the check-in desk had several people lined up moving this way and that to the beat. Aerobics — her favorite. The next room was filled with equipment. There were free weights, Stairmasters, treadmills, and electronically weighted machines that made a workout easy. Every woman there appeared to be doing her best to get in shape.

After dropping her bag in a locker in the dressing room, Sam did a quick warm-up routine, then joined the women in the weight room. Next she planned to go upstairs to the track for a jog. To join in aerobics, it was best to start on time at the beginning with the slow warm-up moves before the workout and stay through the cool-down. Her timing wasn't right this time. Maybe tomorrow she'd do better.

Before leaving today, she planned to catch a swim and maybe even treat herself to a relaxing time in the whirlpool.

An hour and a half later, Sam left the spa feeling relaxed and rejuvenated. "This is the way to start a vacation," she murmured to herself as she drove home. Her skin tingled.

She felt so good, she forgot to worry, forgot to feel fear. Forgot to go by the station and give a description to the artist.

Unlocking the deadbolt, she turned the knob on her front door, pushed it open . . . and froze.

CHAPTER 13

The room had been turned upside-down. Stepping back, she closed the door quietly.

He knows where I live, she thought wildly. *And he could still be in the apartment!*

She wasn't about to chance it. Amanda wasn't home from work yet, so Sam ran next door to use Mrs. Gabriella's phone.

Sam knocked but not loudly. She didn't want to make the intruder aware that she was back. Mrs. Gabriella came to the door. "Hello, dear. What can I do for you?"

"Someone has broken into my apartment. I need to use your phone and call the police. They may still be inside," she whispered.

The old lady hurriedly ushered Sam in, double-locked the door, and led her to the phone.

Sam didn't have the detective's card, so she dialed 911 again. They said someone would be there in a few minutes, to stay in the neighbor's apartment.

No problem there. Sam didn't feel like trying to be a hero. No one in her apartment needed saving. Here the two of them should be safe.

Sam hid in the shadows of the curtains as she peered out of her neighbor's window, watching for the cops. While waiting, she noticed a medium-sized dark car, maybe a Ford, parked against the fence across the way. In it a man crouched down, as if hiding. Her hands started shaking. *What if it's him?*

She prayed silently that the police would hurry. Should she call Detective Jefferies? Oh how she wished she had memorized his number or even had his card with her. No. She had set it on her dresser at home and left it there. How stupid could she get?

She studied the man as she kept hidden behind the curtain. It could be someone waiting for a friend to get home, but why was he ducked down low in his seat?

Mrs. Gabriella talked nonstop. Fear does that to some people.

Sam couldn't watch any longer. Her nerves couldn't take it, so she started pacing. Back and forth she walked, as she tried to answer Mrs. Gabriella's questions. Occasionally she glanced out the window. Time dragged by. It seemed like half an hour, but in all actuality, it only took ten minutes for them to arrive.

A strange thing happened, though, as the police car pulled into the parking lot. The man who had been hiding slipped out of his car and met the official vehicle when it came to a stop.

"What the heck?" she said aloud, the corner of her mouth twisting with exasperation. "He had someone watching me. I told him I could take care of myself. A babysitter! And a lousy one at that!" She was furious at Jefferies.

In no time, the two uniformed policemen raced up the stairs while the stranger rushed back to his car. Sam met the men in the breezeway. She put her anger to the back of her mind so she could concentrate on the moment, the here and now.

"I'm Officer Wiley and he's Dixon. Go back inside your neighbor's apartment while we take a look around yours," the young officer ordered her.

"No problem. I left it unlocked."

They disappeared inside while she waited, but she waited in the breezeway. She found herself watching the stranger in the car instead of worrying herself sick about the inside of her apartment. The man was in his own car talking on what looked to be a CB radio. Immediately, Sam knew he was calling in to report to Detective Jefferies. It had to be.

She shook her head, fuming under her breath. *It won't be long before the great detective himself shows up at my doorstep.* Although on the outside she was perturbed with him, deep inside she fought a smile that tried to form.

Did this make her happy, the thought of seeing him? She swallowed hard, trying to make that flicker of joy disappear. Then she reminded herself that she had wanted to call him almost immediately. She just didn't have his card. So, in a way, this was doing what she wanted to do all along. But she still didn't feel the need for a babysitter. At least one she didn't know about. Why couldn't he have told her he was leaving someone to watch out for her? That would have made her feel better and maybe even safer. But no, he didn't tell her a thing. So, in short, he lied to her.

"You can come in now," called the older policeman from the front door, snapping her preoccupied mind back to the situation at hand. "You should have waited inside your neighbor's home as you were told."

"Sorry, I couldn't," she said. Looking up at Officer Dixon as he waited for her to enter the apartment, she hesitated before taking a step toward the door. When would this all be over? It had to be the same man. The one at work and the man who broke in . . . didn't it? The one who wanted to hurt her, or see her dead, and now had entered her home. Her security. Her safety net. She felt dirty and violated. How could he? Her insides were as tossed and turned as her living room.

"Look around and see if you're missing anything," instructed Wiley.

It didn't take long to discover the small bank on her dresser was gone.

"I've been robbed," she said a little too enthusiastically. "My bank that sits on my dresser is gone. I had close to five hundred dollars in bills and rolled change." Sam breathed a little easier. It *was* a normal break-in. A thief — not the one who wanted to hurt her.

Did she really believe this, or was she trying to convince herself? The thought that it wasn't the same man excited her. It made her feel a little less stressed, a little more at ease. It allowed the tensed muscles in her back to relax somewhat. But was she kidding herself?

"The burglar must have been looking for ready cash. He didn't take anything of value to pawn, since your television and stereo are both still in place." Dixon made another note in his small pad. "I doubt very seriously we'll find whoever stole your money since all he took was the cash. Nothing to trace. You might want to get a better lock on your door, though, one that can't be picked so easily."

A slow grin spread across her face as she found her head and heart agreeing in unison that it was the work of a burglar. That mattered more than anything right now. Then she overheard Wiley tell Dixon something that wiped the smile off her face immediately.

"With what Davis told us a minute ago, don't you find it a bit strange for someone to come in and tear up one room, then take some ready cash from the other room?" Wiley pushed his hat back slightly on his head, then scratched his forehead. "This could have been a warning to her. Maybe letting her know he can get at her whenever he wants."

"We go by the facts, Wiley. Cash was stolen. That's it." Dixon turned back to Sam. "We'll file a report. Again, I suggest you change that lock on the door."

After they left, she was more confused than before. Wasn't it locked when she got home? She knew she used the key. Maybe it wasn't locked, and she couldn't tell when she turned the key.

She sighed. Was it the guy or not? What Wiley said made a lot of sense to her, but Dixon, the older policeman, didn't seem too concerned. She grabbed the gold knob, twisted the lock, and slid the chain into the slot.

"That should do it for now," she whispered. "I will have another dead bolt installed . . . maybe two."

Turning around and leaning against the door, Sam realized she was slightly disappointed Detective Jefferies hadn't shown up by now. Part of her had been looking forward to him coming there. After seeing the man in the car who had been watching her, she had a spark of hope that the detective actually cared about her well-being.

Shaking her head, she tried to erase that thought. It was just a job to him. She was his job. She was a witness. Besides, didn't her babysitter watching from the car prove she couldn't trust the police? The cop downstairs didn't stop the break-in. What good was he? She could have been lying on the floor dead, and he would have never known it. Of course, she realized in the back of her mind that her "tail" had probably been at the gym with her, waiting outside in the heat the whole time.

"So much for protecting me," she grumbled. A big mess waited for her, so she might as well get started in cleaning it up. Taking a step toward the bathroom to get the cleaning supplies, her mind flashed on her grandmother's diamond broach that she kept hidden deep in her dresser drawer. The thief had been in her bedroom. That was where the money bank had been. Practically running, she rushed to the bedroom and yanked open the drawer.

She stood in shock as she stared in the drawer. Scrawled in dark red on a piece of paper she read, *I can get to you anytime, anywhere.*

A bloodcurdling scream reached her ears. It came from her lips. Fear, stark and vivid, streaked across her face, reflected in the mirror attached to the dresser.

CHAPTER 14

She was about to break down and cry like a baby when she heard wood splinter as her front door crashed to the floor.

No time for tears now. Searching around the room, she looked for a weapon to protect herself. Her reflexes started working. Her blood pumped ferociously. *Nothing sharp!* Sam rummaged through the drawers and around the room for something, anything, with which to protect herself.

Footsteps rushed down the hall toward her. He was coming quickly. She was running out of time. She grabbed a can of hairspray, ready to spray it in the assailant's eyes. With her finger on the button, she stood, feet slightly apart, ready. Distraught, she took aim.

As the bedroom door flew open, Detective Jefferies filled the frame. Sam's eyes widened. "Oh! It's you."

"Samantha, are you okay?" He grabbed

one of her arms as he slid his gun in his holster, then pulled her body to his and wrapped both of his arms around her. "I heard you scream and thought he had come back for you. You scared me to death."

"I scared you?" Sam wanted to laugh. His body trembled as he held her close. Or was it hers? She couldn't be sure. The warmth of his touch spread as his hands stretched across her back, holding her close. This gave her comfort. For the moment, she was safe. She closed her eyes and relished the way his warm breath felt against her cheek.

Maybe the trembling wasn't from fear, but from an aching need that consumed her at his touch. She needed protection. She needed someone she could depend on for help. She needed someone to care for her. She was tired of having to be strong and take care of herself and Marty. Yes, she had the Lord, but maybe He was giving her help.

His fingers caressed her back as he held her tight. For a few minutes, neither seemed to know what was going on between them. It was like a safety net enveloped them, keeping them from the world for a moment in time.

Suddenly, she froze in his arms, knowing this was wrong.

His hands stopped. Reality must have

replaced physical reaction as he dropped his hands. They both stepped apart, leaving a space between them.

It took all the strength she could muster to move away. She wanted to feel his arms around her again, feel the safety, the warmth, the tingle, the joy.

Instead, they stared at one another, not saying a word. Sam didn't have the power to breathe, to look away, or speak. All she could do was gaze into his warm blue eyes. She watched fear, confusion, and concern flash through them but knew he felt the same thing she had.

Finally, he broke the silence. Of course, being a man, or maybe it was because he was a cop first and man second, nothing was said in reference to their moment of weakness. That was okay.

"Why did you —" Matthew didn't finish his question. He didn't have to. His gaze looked down at the open drawer and saw what had caused her to scream. "I knew it! I knew it was him!" The detective pulled out his flip phone and punched in a phone number.

As her brain took in the conversation the detective was having, her heart concerned itself over the physical reaction she had just experienced and the desires that still burned within. The need to feel his arms around her again consumed her. She wanted to tremble in his arms one more time.

Sam had never felt that strongly before. Not even with Martin. How could that be?

When Matthew slapped his phone closed and jammed it back into his pocket, she jumped. Immediately, her mind returned to the present and listened for what he had to say.

"I'm not gonna sit back and watch that nut move in on you. The captain is coming around slowly, but too slow. The note gives great credibility to the *possibility* you are being stalked by the serial killer, so he said we could keep a watch on you . . . that we are already doing. It's not enough. We tried a tail and it didn't work. *Twice!*"

He fixed his eyes on her and clamped his hands around her forearms. "You know it wasn't a simple burglary here. Right? It was the man who is after you, the man you saw kill someone. Everything has been him, and it's you he's after. You know that now, don't you?" With each sentence, his grip tightened as he shook her ever so slightly, displaying the urgency he felt as he spoke.

Point was taken. She nodded.

"The crime scene unit is coming out for prints and possible evidence." He dropped his hands and started examining the room for other signs the perpetrator might have left. "After they get here, I'm gonna take you out of here for a time. We'll go get a cup of coffee, maybe even a sandwich if you're hungry."

Again Sam nodded.

"Great. We'll have to try to figure out what we can do to protect you. There has got to be a better way." He glanced at the drawer again. "Come on. Let's get out of this room."

Sam did as she was told. She hadn't said a word since he rushed in to help her. Maybe she was in shock, she didn't know. But talking was not on the top of her list of things to do at the moment.

"Your phonebook. Where is it?"

Sam pointed to the drawer below the phone and watched as he flipped through the pages.

Matthew pulled out his cell once again and punched in the number he had found. After a brief conversation, he hung up. "Someone will be here shortly to put up a new door for you. Sorry I destroyed it."

Sam couldn't help but smile. He had kicked the door down to rush in and save her. Her heart skipped a beat as the warmth he'd shared with her only moments ago enveloped her again.

"It will be okay," he said as he stepped near her and rested his hands gently on her shoulders. "I think you're in shock. I haven't heard you say a word, but you will be fine. Trust me."

Trust him? She believed, right now, she did trust him. If he'd known the sensations that raced through her when he touched her, she didn't think he would be touching her so readily, but he appeared oblivious to his power over her. Had she gone crazy?

"Whoever is after you is one sick man. We're going to play this a little differently from now on. Whoever is scheduled to watch you will be with you, not down in a parking lot watching from afar. That won't work anymore."

The men from the crime scene unit arrived, and Matthew told them about the note in the drawer and who he had called out to put up a new front door, then he led Sam out the opening. Quickly, he drove them to a nearby coffeehouse but watched constantly to make sure no one was following them.

The aroma of the dark roasted brew filled her senses as they walked into CC's. Matthew ordered them each a cup before they sat down. He turned with his back against the wall. He eyed everyone who came in the front and side door.

"I'm gonna run this by the shrink at work. See what she thinks about the way he is acting with you. This guy is playing games for some reason. It doesn't make sense. The doc will know, though."

Sam sat with her hands on the table as the waitress brought the two cups of coffee to them. Matthew rested his hands on hers, then squeezed slightly. "It will be okay. Sip your coffee. You're too quiet. You're starting to scare me a little. I promise you we're going to help you."

She smiled. "I'm ready for the help," she whispered. "I'm ready to trust you."

His gaze flashed on Sam for an instant then turned back to his hot brew. Sam could tell he was amazed when she didn't argue. Maybe it confused him more than astonished him.

CHAPTER 15

Matthew pretended to be relaxed, but inside every one of his nerves was on fire. Here he was trying to keep his mind focused on protecting her, and she had to go and say something like she trusted him. Sure he wanted her to trust him, but not get too relaxed. Her life was in danger. She had to stay sharp. Up until now, she had done wonderfully.

He kept a keen watch on the side and front doors. His jacket hung loose, giving him easy access to his gun. Although his body stayed alert, ready for action if necessary, she kept his mind going in circles. He couldn't get over how Samantha managed herself through this whole ordeal. He saw the uncertainty in her eyes but was amazed at how she pushed past it, ready to face the problem head-on. Fear didn't slow her down.

Somehow through this whole thing, they

seemed to be carrying on a pleasant conversation. Things were different somehow. She almost appeared to enjoy his company. That was a first, and he decided he liked it. Is this what trust did to someone?

They sat for a while as he quietly asked questions about her life. Maybe this would give him some kind of lead on the case. Probably not, since she was a witness turned to the killer's next victim if that sicko had his way.

"So, besides work, where do you go? Who do you see? Name some people you come in contact with on a daily basis. Anyone who might have a grudge against you? We'll work this thing from a different angle to prove the only person after you is the serial killer." Matthew took notes of every name she mentioned, though there weren't many. She lived a very closed existence, it sounded. Again, it was nothing like the picture Martin had painted when he talked about her.

The list covered people at her work, at the health club, her best friend and neighbor, and her family. In fact, it sounded like everyone who ever had come in contact with Samantha in the last few years of her life . . . every person except Martin's family, for that matter. *I wonder why that is?* Why weren't Marty's grandparents involved in their grandson's life? That made no sense at all. Maybe she didn't mention them, assuming that was the only part of her life he already knew about, so she had no need to mention them. Or maybe because that had been over three years ago? For some strange reason, he found he was glad Martin's family had no contact with Samantha.

Matthew decided to avoid the subject of Martin. That added a strain when he was mentioned. Martin's past was something they both had in common. It wasn't a pleasant memory for him, either. That was even more a reason to bring it up, probably, but he liked the pleasantries between them at the moment and didn't want to blow it. He'd bring up Martin and his past with her later.

In the middle of her sentence, she slammed her cup down on the table. "I almost forgot. I need to pick up my son from school." Glancing at her watch, she added, "Like five minutes ago. In all the commotion . . ." She jumped to her feet. "We've got to go."

He had forgotten all about her kid being in school. "You know, it's not safe for him to stay around through all of this. He could get hurt . . . or even worse. This sick man could use him against you." He tossed his cup in the trash as he led her out the door, the whole time looking around, making sure no one was watching them.

"I know. I've already thought about that. I packed a bag for him to go stay with my parents for about a week. I hope this can be solved soon." Suddenly she stopped, and Matthew ran into her. "I left the bag in the trunk of my car."

"No problem. We'll get it."

She bit her lower lip as she reached out and touched his arm. "I'm praying you get this guy very soon."

"You and me both." He winked. "Let's go get Marty."

CHAPTER 16

Marty was a smart kid. Matthew watched the way he looked at his mom. He knew something was up as they drove toward his grandparents' home.

Although he listened to the interaction between mother and son, Matthew kept his eyes peeled, taking a lot of extra turns, watching for anything suspicious or a possible car following them.

"But Mom, I want to stay with you. I know you need protection. Something is going on. I could tell by the way you and Aunt Amanda were talking. Please let me stay with you."

Samantha was turned halfway around in the front seat as she spoke to her son. "I need you to be my strong boy and stay with Granny and Papaw while the detective helps Mommy find the bad guy and gets him arrested. He needs to go to jail for what he has done."

"But, Mom," he pleaded.

"I packed your slacks so you can go to church with Granny and Papaw. While you're there, pray special for me, would ya?"

Glancing in the rearview mirror, Matthew saw the boy grin at his mother. "I love you, Mommy."

What a smart boy she had raised. The boy knew something was wrong. Matthew could hear it in his voice and see it in his face, but he also had sense enough not to upset his mom. He knew when to stop begging. He seemed to be protective of her. It was almost like he was the man of the house.

The love from mother to son was obvious, too. She wanted to protect him. All the things Martin had said about Samantha were being proved wrong over and over again. How could he and the other guys have been so blind?

"I love you, too, Marty. You mind Granny and Papaw. And don't go outside without them while you're there. It won't be long. I promise."

It took a lot of convincing to get him to agree to that, but it worked. They dropped him off without any problems. The grand-parents understood the dangers and begged the detective to take good care of their baby.

Matthew and Sam left to head back to her

apartment.

By the time they returned, the door had been replaced, and extra locks had been placed on the new door. The CSU had come and gone.

Matthew had radioed ahead for a policeman to meet them at her apartment. He brought in one of the plainclothes officers, Officer Brent Davis. Davis pulled evening relief on this surveillance assignment. After giving him new instructions and introducing him to Samantha, Matthew said, "Now we will stick to her like glue. No more keeping our distance." The detective's main concern was to keep Samantha safe and alive. There would be no more screw ups. He was going to make sure of it. Sam could tell.

Sam eyed this Brent guy closely. He appeared young. She wasn't sure she could trust him. She had only just learned to trust Detective Jefferies. Sam also didn't know if she would like having strange men, especially policemen, staying at her place. But given the situation, she had no choice.

She didn't want to be a victim of a homicide. Maybe this time would be different. Maybe the police would do a better job of protecting her. Detective Jefferies seemed to take his job seriously.

After Jefferies left, Sam cleaned the apartment while Brent Davis stayed out of her way. But no amount of scrubbing and cleaning would take away the fear the stalker had instilled in her by letting her know how easy it had been for him to get into her apartment. He was still in control, and that was what he had been telling Sam with the strategically placed note he had left behind saying, *I can get to you anytime, anywhere.* With a guard on duty twenty-four hours a day, she hoped things would be different.

She even cleaned Marty's room. That was a feat in itself. She smiled as she realized it was probably all that nervous energy getting her apartment so clean. Well, at least something good came out of it.

She hated to admit it, but part of keeping busy was also a way to keep from thinking about the way Detective Jefferies made her feel.

After folding the last basket of clean clothes, she heard a knock at the door. Officer Davis rose immediately, drawing his gun as he moved close to the door.

It wouldn't be the killer. He'd just break in. Her hand touched the top lock, about to turn it. Thinking twice, she paused. "Who is it?"

"Me. Amanda."

"You can put that thing away," she told the officer. Unlocking the top two deadbolts and removing the solid gold bar that locked over a piece on the doorframe, Sam opened the door. "Hey girl, come on in."

"How many locks did you put on your new door? What happened here?" Amanda stared at the door and the new gold shiny pieces. "What are you protecting, Fort Knox? You even have one of those things like you see on hotel doors. Girl, this is getting serious."

"You don't know the half of it. Come in. Have a seat."

Amanda hugged her friend. "You look a little pale. I'm glad I stopped by. I think you need what I'm about to suggest. We're going to shake things up around here. Cheer you up. Get your mind off of your problems." Amanda, with her short, curly, blond hair and bubbly personality, bounced into the room. "Whatcha got planned for tonight? Any —" She stopped short. "Sorry. I didn't know you had company." Her sweet smile revealed two deep dimples.

"Hi," Officer Davis said. "Name's Brent." He extended his hand.

"Hi. I'm Amanda. Nice to meet you, Brent." She placed her hand in his for a second or two. "Oh, Samantha. You've been holding out on me." Amanda grinned from ear-to-ear as her eyes twinkled.

"It's a long story." Sam sighed as she headed toward a chair in the living room. "If you've got a few minutes, I'll fill you in."

Amanda plopped down on the sofa. The officer took the opposite end.

As Sam told her story to her best friend, she wished she was more like Amanda. Petite and cutesy, a blue-eyed beauty who never let personal problems, no matter how devastating, get in the way of enjoying life. Unfortunately, Sam, the plain Jane type, short, full-figured, with brown hair and green eyes, let her problems control her life . . . more than she should. She'd basically stopped living three years ago just to feel safe. But she knew that wasn't the answer. And now she was trying to lean on the Lord totally. The devil had a way of stepping in right when she thought she'd gotten it together.

Although Sam had forgiven Martin, she still couldn't shake the attack, the injury, or the pain. She would be the first to admit she'd left it at the cross many times, only to take it back again. She didn't want to. She prayed for strength to leave it. Still did. But she hadn't totally let go of the fear yet. Until she could do that, Sam knew she wouldn't move forward in her life.

"So, all-in-all, things haven't been too great," Sam said.

"Well, we're going to change things right now. I know you never go out anymore, but tonight is going to be different. Where is Marty?"

"At my parents'."

"Perfect. And I won't take no for an answer. You'll have your —" she winked at the policeman — "personal bodyguard. What harm could come to you? Mark Roberts just opened up a new club a couple of weeks ago. I know you don't go to bars. You don't have to drink. Besides, Mark is an old friend from school. It wouldn't hurt to show your support."

"I don't know."

"I promised him I'd twist your arm and make you come with me tonight. One night won't hurt. Besides, it will take your mind off of what you've been going through."

Mark was a guy they had gone to junior high and high school with. Even though it had been ten years, a lot of the old gang still lived locally. Only a few had gone on to other places and other things in their lives.

Sam took a seat in the chair. "I don't think I can." Part of her knew she shouldn't. She had no business going out during a time like this. She was making herself an open target.

"Well, I need to, and I need you to go with me. Since Charlie and I broke up, I haven't done much myself, and I'm about to climb the walls. Come on. It'll be good for you and me both. Whatcha say?"

Sam rubbed the back of her neck. "You miss Charlie, don't you? I thought by now you two would have patched things up."

"I did, too," Amanda confided, pursing her lips as if to pout. "I still love the jerk, but until he's ready to settle down and make a commitment, I don't need him around. He'll grow up one day . . . I hope."

Sam decided she did need a little diversion to take her mind off all the things that had happened. "Going out might do me some good."

If nothing else, it might help her quit thinking about that handsome detective. She glanced at Officer Davis. When he didn't say she couldn't, Sam said, "I guess okay. What time?"

Amanda squealed. "All right! I can't believe you gave in. Oops." She covered her mouth. "Did I say that out loud? Didn't mean to. Anyway, I think you'll enjoy it. I'll pick you up around eight thirty."

The policeman was young, so maybe the idea sounded good to him, too. Besides, Sam saw the way he had been watching Amanda. She could have her pick of men, but she had always loved Charlie.

Sam hoped Charlie wouldn't change like Martin had. People did that . . . changed. She'd learned that from firsthand experience, but it was not something you could tell another person. Everyone had to learn it for themselves.

After Amanda left, the policeman called in and gave an update on her plans and where they would be.

"My relief comes at eleven. I needed to leave word so he knows where to meet me."

Sam smiled. "No problem." She was surprised Detective Jefferies didn't say no. That was what she had expected him to do. Maybe it wasn't such a bad idea after all.

CHAPTER 17

Shortly after nine, Sam heard Amanda knocking on the door. "It's me. Let's go." Amanda was never on time.

Letting her in, Sam said, "I'll drive if you'd like."

"Great."

"I'll follow in my car," said Officer Davis.

"Fine, Brent," Amanda said. "I don't plan on explaining you to any of our friends. Right, Sam? We'll introduce you as a new neighbor." Amanda looked to Sam for agreement. She nodded.

"That would be for the best," he said.

With that straight, the three headed out the door and down to the cars.

When they arrived, the place was jumping, and by ten it was packed. The people were shoulder to shoulder, and the room filled with thick smoke. That was another reason Sam didn't like coming. Besides, she preferred staying home with Marty. He was her life.

Sam and Amanda ran into some old school friends just as expected: Brad, Mike, and Terrie. Later Sally and Dan joined them. Mark came by their table and thanked them all for coming to his club. Much later, Charlie slipped into the crowd. Before Sam knew it, they had a couple of tables pulled together full of people.

Eventually, Sam started to dance, but she stayed near their table so the officer could see her at all times. She danced with a few of the guys in their group, which helped her keep from thinking about the past forty-eight hours . . . and the detective.

Davis fit in well. He seemed to be having a good time, but every time Sam glanced his way, the policeman's eyes were upon her and her surroundings, keeping a close watch. She had to give him credit. He seemed to be doing his job. Not like the policemen in her past experience.

Around ten thirty, Sam was dancing a slow song with Brad. He was a good bit taller than Sam, all six-foot-five of him, but they danced well together. The two moved slowly with the music, keeping perfect rhythm.

"It's been a long time since we've danced like this," Brad whispered in her ear as he leaned down slightly to compensate for the difference in their heights. He had been her best friend in high school. Secretly, she had had a crush on him but told no one. In their college years, everyone told Sam to watch out, warning her that Brad had a crush on her. By then, though, Martin had already won her heart. About five years ago, everyone had even joked if Martin found out Brad was still carrying that torch, he would have punched Brad's lights out.

"It's just like old times," he continued.

Sam laughed lightly. "Yeah. Great, isn't it?" In a flash her mind whispered, *But wouldn't it be nicer if it was Matthew I was dancing with?*

Her eyes flew open in surprise, and she pulled slightly away from Brad. Her thought had even called him by first name. *Too forward. Too easy.* She had to get Detective Jefferies out of her mind, but every time she closed her eyes, his blue ones came into clear view, making forgetting him virtually impossible.

Think about the here and now, she told herself as she closed her eyes one more time. *Think about Brad and the good old days. Think about anything but Matthew Jefferies.*

Sam opened her eyes when Brad released

his hold on her. The vision in her mind appeared in the flesh. There, cutting in on the dance floor, stood Matthew Jefferies. Her breath caught in her throat. She had to force herself to take in air. Blinking twice, she made sure she wasn't dreaming. As his blue eyes stared deep into her soul, he nudged Brad out of the way and pulled her into his arms.

"Sam, do you know this man?" Brad's narrowed eyes and frown showed his aggravation.

"Sure." She nodded. "Everything's fine, Brad." But everything wasn't fine. Yet she couldn't stop herself from stepping into Matthew's arms willingly. Her hands trembled as her stomach fluttered.

"What are you doing here? Trying to get yourself killed?" he said through tight lips. The words were spoken close to her ear. So close, his hot breath covered her neck. His words were meant for her ears only. "When I found out what Davis called in, I couldn't believe it. If I'd been at the precinct when he called, you never would have come."

So that was why he hadn't protested this excursion. He didn't know. Sam listened to the detective scold her for her own protection. She knew he was right, so she didn't stop him. Besides, she enjoyed being held close in his arms. She relished it way too much to protest against his words.

At the end of the song, when the last note held on, Matthew stopped scolding long enough to ask, "Where is your purse? We're getting out of here."

When she pointed, he took her by the elbow and walked her toward the table. Officer Davis was already on his feet, waiting for their return.

Sam stopped midstep. A chill rushed over her as she spotted a familiar . . . it wasn't a face so much as a familiar pair of eyes in the crowd.

"What's the matter?"

Sam turned to Matthew and swallowed hard, then looked back in the direction she had seen those familiar eyes. The face disappeared. She must have imagined it, someone who looked like that guy from the other night.

"I guess nothing," she said. "I thought I'd —" She shook her head. "Never mind."

They made their way to the table, her friends still crowding around it.

"I —" Before Davis could offer words of explanation, Detective Jefferies cut him off, saying, "We'll talk later."

Amanda and Charlie's heads were huddled together in deep conversation, oblivious to what was going on around them. Sam hated to interrupt, but she had to. The detective's grip on her elbow had not relinquished. "Amanda, are you about ready to leave? I'm kind of tired."

The couple looked up. Love seemed to be glowing from their faces. "Charlie will bring me home. If that's okay with you."

Sam nodded. "Sure, no problem."

"You'll be safe . . . won't you? He'll follow you home?" she asked, directing her eyes toward Davis.

"I'll be fine," Sam said as her gaze darted to her side at the detective hovering close.

Amanda stood and hugged her friend bye. As she did, oblivious to Sam's situation, she whispered in Sam's ear, "I think Charlie's going to ask me to marry him. He told me he realized how much he loved me once I told him to get lost. It just took him awhile to work up the courage to tell me."

Sam squeezed Amanda's arms. That explained where Amanda's mind was and why she hadn't noticed Detective Jefferies holding on so tight. "That's great. I knew you two would work things out. See y'all later."

Charlie joined them, slipping his arm around Amanda's waist. "We'll see you later, Sam. Come on, baby. Let's dance."

Saying good-bye to the others at the table, she picked up her glass of Sprite to take one last swallow to wet her dry mouth and saw scribbling on the napkin. The paper had stuck to the bottom of the glass. Her hand froze as she held the glass in midair, almost afraid to read the note, but she knew she had to.

Slowly, she peeled the napkin off the bottom of the glass and lifted it slightly to look closer at the scrawled handwriting.

I'm watching you, she read. Glancing around, she scanned the room for that face again. Matthew must have seen her actions, because he leaned close and read the napkin over her shoulder.

He reached under his coat for his hidden revolver. Sam dropped the napkin back on the table as her hands started to shake. Using another napkin, Davis picked up the one she had dropped, and the glass, too. He dumped the drink in another almost-empty glass. He, too, had noticed the reaction and knew it was important. After covering it carefully, he slipped it in his jacket pocket.

"Let's get out of here. Now!" Jefferies said.

She yanked up her purse and scrambled toward the exit with Davis in front of her and the detective on her heels. She shivered as she stepped into the night air even though it was hot and humid outside. Apparently, it had drizzled for a short time, and now steam was rising from the heated streets and sidewalks. Another warm September day followed by an afternoon sprinkle had led to a warm, steaming night. Perspiration gathered across her forehead and at the back of her neck as she took in short, quick breaths.

The detective said to Davis, "After we get Ms. Cain safely out of here, I want you to take that evidence back to headquarters. Have them check for prints, and have them put a rush on it. The glass was probably wiped clean, but with today's technology they might lift one off of the napkin. We might get lucky."

Sam's icy fingers wrapped around the keys. She walked faster and faster to her car with Matthew on her heels. Alarm had overtaken Sam completely as she unlocked the door and climbed in. Her pale face stared back in the rearview mirror.

"Samantha. Listen to me." When her eyes turned toward the detective hovering at the side of her car, he continued. "Put on your seatbelt. I'm gonna lock you in. Give me a second to start my car. Officer Davis will stand right here until I get behind you. I'm just a car over. I'll follow you home."

She nodded. Fastening her seatbelt, she started the car and waited. When she saw Matthew's car come to a stop slightly behind her, she pulled out of her space. The officer climbed in his own vehicle. The three cars pulled out of the parking lot, forming a single line.

As the music played, she tried to take her mind off the fear growing inside. Glancing in the mirror, she saw Matthew's car following close behind and Brent Davis behind him. Without realizing it, she ran a yellow light. The detective slowed for only a second, flipped on his flashing light, and continued through the red light. A short distance separated them.

Looking down at the belt across her chest, she laughed. That was strange. Now she knew just how frightened she was, because she never wore her seatbelt, even though it was the law. Sam always had nightmares of being trapped in one and not being able to get out. Yet when the detective told her to buckle up, she did exactly that.

It wasn't long before she reached the curving road that her apartment was on. *Almost home. Matthew Jefferies is right behind me, so I'll be fine. Safety is right around the corner.*

As she made the next curve, a black car pulled out in front of her. She slammed on the brakes, throwing the car into a tailspin on the slick road. *Turn your wheel,* her mind screamed. *Which way?*

Sam couldn't remember if it was into the spin or against it. Making a snap decision, she went with it. It was either the wrong way or too late. Her car spun off the road, hit a pothole, and flipped. Her hands clutched the steering wheel tightly as the airbag released and expanded.

Her head spun like a Ferris wheel. She tried to stay focused but couldn't. The car lurched to a sudden stop as it hit a tree. Her face smashed against the bag. Unconsciousness covered her like a blanket.

CHAPTER 18

Slowly, Sam opened her eyes to absolute whiteness; curtains, sheets, ceiling, everything. Where was she? As her blurred vision focused, she realized she wasn't alone. With a start, she tried to sit up.

"Where am —" Her question cut off as a knife jabbed into her skull . . . at least that was what it felt like. Then a hand gently restrained her from rising.

"Don't move, Ms. Cain," the nurse said softly. "It's best if you lie still. You've had a terrific injury to your head, and any sudden movement will only make you hurt more. I suggest you move slowly."

"You're right about the pain. Where am I?" Turning her head slightly, she winced.

"You're at the Lady of Mercy. You were in an automobile accident."

The curtain was pulled back. The detective entered her cubicle and rushed over to the other side of the bed. "Samantha. I mean, Ms. Cain. You're awake. That's a good sign, right, Miss Williams?"

"Right you are, Detective," the nurse said.

Detective Jefferies leaned forward slightly. "Do you remember what happened? When I came around the curve, your car was spinning. I didn't see what caused it."

Her mind scrambled. Thoughts, images, flashed through her mind at lightning speed. "I'm not sure," Sam whispered in a raspy voice. "It's all a blur. Not clear." She winced.

The nurse took her pulse as the detective tried again to get her to remember. "Relax. It'll come to you. The doctor will be back shortly. He talked like you'd be okay. No internal injuries, just surface wounds. One of the uniforms is in the waiting room so he can take a statement from you as soon as you're up to it." He touched her hand and squeezed it gently as his eyes seemed to search her face for the answers he was looking for. "Still no memory?" he asked.

"Sorry." Looking around, Sam realized she was in an emergency room where curtains hung on three sides of the bed and overhead the fluorescent lighting went on and on. In the distance, she heard other soft voices and an occasional ding of a bell, like the sound of an elevator stopping or an intercom system coming on or going off. Everything was in hushed tones.

Sam closed her eyes. All of a sudden, her mind's eye watched in slow motion what had happened earlier. "I remember! You were right!"

"I knew you would," he said as he leaned closer. "Hold on one minute." He rushed past the curtain and, in less than a minute, he returned with the policeman who was there to take her statement. "Go ahead. Tell us what happened."

Closing her eyes, she rewound the vision and replayed it in her mind. "I was driving home and as I turned the curve, a dark car pulled out in front of me. It was . . . it was like it was waiting for me to come around." Sam opened her eyes and looked at Detective Jefferies in disbelief. "The car was black, like the one that seemed to be following me the other night from work. Anyway, when it pulled out in front of me, I hit the brakes and my car went into a tailspin until it crashed against something, then I hit my head."

"A car followed you — never mind. That's good."

"Can you tell me the make or model of the car?" the policeman asked.

Reaching for her forehead, she winced

when her fingers brushed against a bandage. An old injury splashed suddenly into her mind, and her head started spinning like a merry-go-round. Closing her eyes again, red flooded her vision.

No! She couldn't relive that now. That was then. The past. Leave it alone! She squeezed her eyes tight until the bloody mess faded into a memory. As it did, she opened her mouth to speak again but couldn't. It was too dry.

"Water . . . can I have some water?"

The nurse obliged Sam's request, then went back to writing down notes in her chart. When finished, she left the small area.

"Can you remember the make or model of the vehicle?" Matthew encouraged Sam. "Did you see the driver's face?"

"It happened so fast. I'm sorry," Sam said as her eyes were getting heavy, burning badly. She didn't want to remember. She wanted to sleep. She wanted the pain to stop. Her fluttering eyelids closed, but she fought against the sleep that called her name. "Maybe. I'm not sure. Sleep. I need to sleep. Can I rest?"

"If she remembers anything else, you'll let me know, right?"

"No problem," the detective said.

The lids of her eyes grew so heavy, she

couldn't hold them open. She couldn't stay awake, but she wanted to. She wanted to talk to the detective, not the police officer, and not about the accident. She wanted to forget that. Her memory snatched a vision of them dancing, a slow dance. She wanted to talk about that. It had been heaven. Why couldn't she stay awake and talk to the detective about that? A sigh escaped her lips as she drifted back to sleep. . . .

When she awoke, Amanda was at her side. She had no idea how long she had been sleeping, but she noticed immediately the detective was nowhere around. It was probably for the best.

"Hey, sweetie. How are you feeling? Charlie and I left shortly after you, so we saw the ambulance taking you to the hospital. Poor baby." Amanda leaned down and hugged Sam lightly. "You've been through so much. It's not fair."

"I'll be all right. Would you call my parents? Let them know what happened but tell them not to tell Marty. Let them know I'm okay. Tell them I'll call as soon as I can."

"Sure. Don't you worry. Oh, by the way, who is that cute guy you left with? He's at the nurses' station down the hall stirring up all kinds of trouble . . . about you. He's been on his cell phone for quite a while yelling at everyone, trying to get something done. The man seemed very interested in your condition and what happened to you."

Sam smiled. He was still there. "Matthew Jefferies. Detective Matthew Jefferies."

"Oh." A wicked smile covered Amanda's face. "Where have you been hiding him?" she asked as she wiggled her eyebrows.

"Be real! He's a cop! The detective on the case I was telling you about." Though she had found herself interested in the man, she didn't share it . . . not even with her best friend. Especially her best friend. Amanda knew everything Martin had put her through, and she wouldn't want to see her go through that again. Sam felt sure her friend would convince her to remember the pain Martin put her through. She'd remind her not to get involved with a cop, of all people. But right now, Sam didn't want to hear that.

Amanda scrunched her nose as she frowned. "Oooh. Misunderstood. Sorry." Shrugging, she added, "Well, all cops can't be bad. Maybe this one will be different." Amanda gently rubbed her hand. "By the look on your face, I do believe I see a little interest there . . . no matter what you're saying to me."

A doctor pulled the curtain back slightly

and came in, followed by the nurse. Amanda backed out of the way, not giving Sam time to respond.

"Ms. Cain. How are you feeling?" After Sam's murmured response of not being sure, he continued. "I'm Doctor Clifton. You suffered a severe blow to the cranial, and you have a slight concussion. There is a gash a little over an inch long that runs along your hairline. It took six stitches to close it."

Another scar to add to the old one. *Just call me Frankenstein.* Oh well. At least she was alive. Maybe this one wouldn't show. Sam knew she had the worst headache of her life. It seized her head in a viselike grip and squeezed. If the pressure could just let up, she would feel better.

"I've prescribed you a mild sedative, and we'll let you go home."

"Great," Sam said, feeling a little groggy.

The doctor made a few notes on the clipboard. "I'll leave the prescription with the nurse. You'll probably feel a little sore tomorrow. By the next day you'll feel a lot better, but I suggest you take it easy for a couple more days. A little bed rest, and you'll feel as good as new. Go see your primary doctor in ten days to have the stitches removed."

"We'll give you a ride home," Amanda volunteered as soon as the doctor and nurse left the cubicle. "Charlie's in the waiting room. I'll go let him know."

"Thanks."

"No problem. That's what friends are for."

CHAPTER 19

When Matthew saw the blond come out of Samantha's cubicle, he rushed back in. He was worried sick about her but worked hard at convincing himself it was because she was in his protective care at the time she got hurt. He kept telling himself he had no feelings for this woman. He barely knew her. So she had been his partner's wife and he had met her only once; he knew what Martin Cain had told him about her. The man put his wife down at most opportunities, if Matthew recalled correctly. This alone should warn him not to let his attentions wander in her direction.

Martin had said a lot of bad things about her over the short period of time they had been partners, but in these past few days Matthew had seen a totally different woman than the one Martin Cain had described three years ago. That he could not explain.

It was just a case, he reminded himself,

trying to dismiss the direction his mind had taken him. He cared about all of his cases. He wanted to solve them. Give all the families peace of mind . . . a safe feeling . . . nothing more.

"Ms. Cain, we need to talk. Do you feel up to it?"

Pushing the button to raise the head of the bed, she nodded ever so slightly.

He didn't want to scare her, but by now she should have already figured things out for herself, so the best approach was straightforward. "The man we presume to be the serial killer got within killing distance again tonight. We're not sure if he was out to kill you, or if he was just toying with you some more. It's like he is playing a game. He's a sick man. He hurt you bad, but I think if he had been trying to kill you, he would have. Or if he meant to, when he finds out he missed, he's going to be mad, and he'll be back with a vengeance. And next time he won't miss."

Matthew watched her eyes change from confusion to understanding before he went on. "But we won't let that happen. I'm not sure what's going on in his mind, but our psychologist believes he has twisted things up inside his head and now, instead of continuing in his normal MO, he's turned

164

to stalking you and tormenting you. A power game. A game of control. The doc thinks the killer didn't really try to kill you with the truck, just scare you a little, letting you know he's around. Then what he did in your apartment — the note he left you — was another way to scare you and let you know he was in control. The man has a fixation on you and a need to control you. But we're not sure how long that will satisfy him. You're in grave danger."

She frowned. "My first look at him wasn't really that good. By him coming by work, he gave me a second chance at seeing him. Maybe he wants to be identified. You think?" She paused, as if thinking about what she had just said. "I hate to say it, but it didn't help — that second look I mean. Not much anyway, but when we started off the dance floor I could have sworn I saw his eyes, then his face. It was just a glance, but enough to make me think of the guy who had used the phone. Does that mean I could describe him to your artist now?"

"Yes. That would be great. I'll get you with our composite artist as quick as I can, while the killer's face is still fresh in your mind." He squeezed her hands. "Maybe he's made his first mistake . . . actually second. We got two partials off of the napkin and glass that match, so now we are running it through CODIS, hoping to get a match . . . and hoping it's not the bartender's print. If it is the killer's, his second mistake was, when you didn't recognize him, he started playing games with you, and just maybe that will work in our favor. You now have a visual in your head." Matthew stood and started pacing. "This time we'll get him."

"So now what?"

Stopping at the side of her bed, he looked her in the eyes. "Round the clock protection somewhere other than your place. I'll put you where he can't find you."

"He could be waiting outside the hospital, ready to follow me home or even waiting at my apartment."

"I know, but I have a plan, and it's already in motion."

The blond came in, and Samantha introduced Amanda to Matthew. She smiled at him, then turned her attention to Samantha. "Okay, hon, they've finished the paperwork. The nurse will be bringing in your release papers and prescription, and then we'll take you home."

"Change of plans," Matthew intervened, glancing from Amanda to Samantha and back to Amanda. "She's going with me, and it won't be back to her place."

He saw Samantha's eyes widen, but what else could he do? He had to control the situation. Not let the killer do it. That sicko was out to hurt her, and the only way Matthew knew how to keep that from happening was by keeping her with him. He had planned to take her to a safe house and guard her 24-7, but when the captain wouldn't approve the expense, since he hadn't given them anything but speculation and theory so far, Matthew decided to hide her out at his place. Marie Boudreaux, his friend and a cop, agreed to help him out. She would stay at his place, too, so the woman wouldn't feel threatened by only the two of them being there. It was for the best. Now he just had to figure out the best way to tell her without spooking her. He wasn't sure he liked it any more than she probably would, but he had no choice. He couldn't let the killer get to her again, and Matthew would take whatever means necessary to prevent that from happening.

"For what? Is she under arrest? It was an accident," Amanda said, apparently not in full knowledge of the danger her friend was in.

"She's not under arrest. It's for her protection. Her life is in danger."

"Oh." Amanda's tone softened. "Sam, are

you sure you want *police* protection?"

Now that was a strange question. Who wouldn't want police protection when they were being stalked by a killer? He watched a flash of fear in Samantha's eyes as she listened to her friend's question, then Sam glanced at him. Her eyes softened, then she looked back at her friend. "I'll be all right. Thanks for being here for me, Amanda." Sam reached out her hand to her friend.

"Well, you know my number if you need me. Call, and I'll be there." Grabbing her hand, Amanda leaned down and kissed Samantha's cheek.

When Amanda gazed at him, he could feel her sizing him up. *What is it with this woman?*

"You had better keep her safe," Amanda said in a determined voice. "She doesn't need any more pain."

"She'll be fine," he assured her. "I'm gonna keep her safe from the maniac who's been terrorizing her. Trust me."

The blond's brows rose. "I hope we can."

When Amanda left, Matthew asked, "Are you ready?"

Samantha slipped her feet off the side of the bed. "Where are you taking me?"

"To my house."

"To *your* house? Ah-ah, b-but," she stammered, "I don't think that's a wise decision.

I could stay at my friend's apartment, or go to my parents." Then she shook her head. "But I don't want to put anyone in danger."

He saw fear in her eyes . . . or was it frustration? Maybe she didn't understand the gravity of her situation. "Your life is in danger. He wants to kill you. Don't you understand? This is the best answer. It'll be a safe house for you to stay at. I'll have a policewoman stay there with you. I'll be in and out. When I'm gone, she'll still be there, plus I'll have guards posted outside. It's for your safety."

She sighed. "Okay, I guess that would work. But what about the composite artist? The one who can take my information, put it in their computer, and come up with a picture?"

"You're understanding it right. And we'll do that . . . soon. I promise. First things first, and that's your safety. Don't you worry."

CHAPTER 20

Sam watched the detective as they traveled toward south Baton Rouge. *Matthew.* She liked his name. It fit him. The name was strong, masculine, independent, and self-assured, just like the man. Although in the beginning he had reminded her of a fictional character, a television hero, he was now a very real person with a warm, caring side that both surprised and scared Sam at the same time.

Could she trust him? He was a cop. She had learned a long time ago not to trust them. Where were they when her husband physically attacked her? Where were they when Martin committed suicide? Worse, they blamed her. After his death . . . never mind. She didn't even want to go there.

And this policewoman — who was she? Did this woman know Sam's history with the force? Would staying at his place be protection enough for them to get this killer without him getting her first?

The short of it was, in her past experience, cops had proved to be unhelpful. Yet regardless of her past, and now with her present, Sam found herself being physically and emotionally drawn to this man, this policeman. She couldn't understand it.

She couldn't help but study his rugged profile; it drew her like a magnet. Her gaze traced the contours of his face, starting with the notorious single lock of jet-dark hair that religiously fell across his forehead. She then continued her gaze down his profile to his perfectly straight nose with the slightest hint of freckles and paused momentarily at the fullness of his firm lips.

The pounding of her heart mounted. Squeezing her eyes shut, she forced that image away from her mind. The jolt of pain in her head from an action as simple as closing her eyes helped her lose concentration on him for a moment.

They were together for one reason, and one reason only. That was what she needed to keep at the forefront of her mind. She felt an additional comfort in knowing that policewoman would be at his place, too. Thoughts of him had no right in her mind, she vowed, and she would not allow them to come forward again.

He was a cop. That was all she had to remember, and she would be okay. She would repeat it over and over in her brain if necessary, but she would not — she could not — think of him in any other way.

Sam shifted her view as she fought to regain her self-control. The car turned off South Acadian onto Lakeshore Drive, following the curved road around the University Lakes.

"So what is the big plan you have in motion?"

"Another policewoman, dressed in street clothes, wearing a brown wig matching your hairstyle, was led out of the cubicle next to yours in the emergency room. Two uniformed officers took her to a police car and slowly drove her home. All three went up to your apartment. They'll wait awhile and then she'll change back to uniform. She'll pack you a bag of your clothes and bring them to the station. Officer Boudreaux will bring your bag with her when she comes."

"Pretty smart. Maybe he'll fall for it . . . if he's watching, that is."

"Oh, he's watching."

After various twists and turns, he slowed the car down and eased into a narrow driveway. The house wasn't as large as the neighboring homes, but it was pretty. It resembled an Acadian cottage: white, trimmed with green shutters framing one big window in the front that overlooked a wonderful view of the lake. The driveway led them around to the back of the house.

When the car stopped, Sam climbed out, ready to escape the close proximity. She shouldn't have moved so fast. It made her dizzy. Her head pounded, but that didn't slow her down. She had to get away; she needed some distance between her and the detective. Turning the corner, she headed toward the front of the house.

"Samantha. Wait." He caught up to her. "Stay out of the view from the road. We'll go in the back door. I'm sure we weren't followed. I was watching, but it doesn't hurt to be cautious."

He stopped her just in time, because she had intended to put some major space between them. She had planned to take a very close look at the lake, like at the water's edge. Sam had momentarily forgotten she was in hiding. Slipping back behind the house, she followed him inside.

It was cool in his house, although the afternoon sun had heated the temperatures outside to over 90 degrees. Perspiration had gathered near her hairline, at the edge of the stitches, under the bandage. The cool air against the wetness sent a chill through her body. She shivered slightly.

"Is it too cold for you in here?" Matthew asked as he placed Sam's bag of medicines and papers on the counter in the kitchen. "I think it feels good in here, but I can cut the air down . . . uh . . . up, I mean."

"I'm fine. Thanks."

Turning on the tap water, he started to fill a glass. "Want one? Or something else, maybe? Juice or tea? I could even put on a pot of coffee if you would like. Maybe that would warm you up some."

"Water is fine," she said as she took in the view of the kitchen with its white countertops, cabinets, floors, and mini-blinds. Everything was white except the black appliances and cabinet doors. This impressed Sam. The room was immaculate. At a glance through the two doors exiting the kitchen, the rest of the house appeared to be just as clean. Another positive quality.

"You do live here, don't you?" she asked as she reached for the glass of water he handed her.

Matthew scratched his chin. "Hmm. Maybe we're in the wrong house," he said with a touch of humor. "Of course I live here." He chuckled slightly. "This is my home. Why do you ask?"

Her gaze swept around the room one more time. "Sorry."

"Oh, I get it. Because I'm a guy, you thought the place would be dirty. Maybe trashed with dirty clothes thrown around, or crusty dishes stacked in the sink. What can I say? My father taught me to be neat. You might even call me a neat freak." He turned and headed for the hall door. "Come on. Let's get you settled so you can lie down for a while. I want you to make yourself at home, but there are a few rules. You can't go outside. Can't make any phone calls to your parents or Amanda or work . . . he could have tapped into their lines. I doubt it, but we want to be careful. That's about it. Other than that, make yourself at home."

"Whew. After all those instructions, I could use a nap. You wore me out," she said trying to make things light as she smiled. "No, really. I could use a short nap. I'm feeling a little lightheaded." She followed him to a corner room.

"This is the guest bedroom. It has a bathroom connected to it. In there you'll find a new toothbrush, toothpaste, soap, shampoo, and various things you might need. Boudreaux should be here soon, but for the time being, you can sleep in your clothes or use one of my T-shirts."

"My clothes are fine for a nap, but I might take you up on the offer of a T-shirt tonight for use as a nightgown, if she doesn't think to grab my nightclothes."

"No problem. I'll give you time to settle in. I hope you find everything you need. If you don't, let me know." As he started to leave, he turned back. "One more thing. Keep the blinds pulled down on both windows. Marie's taking the bedroom next door to you."

It was late morning, and Sam was very tired. Sure, she slept at the hospital, but it wasn't the same. Besides, the doctor had told her to rest. She thanked him and then looked around the bedroom. Upon closer examination of the windows, she found they were locked. "I'll be fine. Thank you. Do you mind if I take a shower? And then maybe the nap?"

"No. But if you're going to stay up a bit longer, I could put in a call to the station and have you talk to the artist. When you're through, he'll fax us a copy and you can make any corrections or additions to it. We need to get that out of the way, if you're up to it. If not, we'll do it after the nap."

"We can try." As he left her alone, she told herself, "I guess the shower and nap can wait." Sam settled for splashing cool water on her face and washing her hands. Afterward, she ran a brush through her hair, taking it slow near the stitches. Those few things took a little more energy than she thought they would, but she felt better for it. Feeling a little more refreshed, she joined him in the kitchen again.

The next half hour she spent on the phone with the artist, and then Matthew went from an office, which he'd set up in one of his rooms, to the kitchen and back again, checking out the fax as the artist made the necessary changes until it was right. By the third copy, it was what she saw in her mind when she closed her eyes. A slight chill slid down her back. The image was too close for her liking. "I think now I'll go take that hot shower. And the nap will probably be more like a half hour to an hour. I'm really tired."

"Help yourself. You need your rest. Think you could eat a light lunch before your nap? I could fix it while you are showering, if you're hungry that is. Or again, it can wait till after."

Even with an empty stomach, she didn't feel hungry, but she said, "That would be great. Thanks." The nap could wait awhile longer. Who knows? If she waited long enough, it would be nighttime and maybe she would just sleep the night through.

When left to herself, she closed the door that led to the hallway, stepped into the bathroom, and removed her clothes. The only clothes she had were the dirty ones on her, so she hand-washed her undergarments and left them draped over the shower rack to dry.

As she stepped into the shower, she thought about how much she already missed her son and the freedom to come and go as she pleased. "But I'll make it, Lord, as long as You lead me," she prayed as she adjusted the water flow and the temperature. "Keep the detective sharp and objective, so he can catch this man before he hurts anyone else, including me. Keep Marty and Mom and Dad safe, too, and don't let them worry about me." That was the good thing about prayer; it was talking to God. She could tell Him what was on her heart, and she knew He was listening. "In Jesus' name I pray, thank You."

And she was alive. She was blessed. Her life had taken her through tragedy, but the Lord had seen her through it then and He would again.

After a warm shower, Sam slipped her jeans and blouse back on . . . all part of making do. She had wrapped her hair in a towel to keep from getting it wet. That was one thing she couldn't do for the time being. Those stitches needed to stay dry. Removing the towel, she let her hair fall around her shoulders.

No need for shoes. Maybe he would loan her a pair of socks.

She sighed. How long would she be hiding out in Matthew's home? It was a beautiful home with a peaceful feeling. She liked that. Although it was neat and everything was in its place, she felt a warm glow. It was a true home, not a clinic, where you weren't allowed to touch a thing. But she wanted to go home, to bring her son home. Go back to her cocoon.

What if it took more than a day or two for them to catch the guy who was after her? Could she stand being cooped up any longer than that? Being away from Marty that long? And would she get along with Officer Boudreaux?

Sam didn't think she would last long. For one thing, she had her daily routine, and she hadn't noticed any treadmill or workout equipment in his home. Of course, she hadn't seen every room.

Secondly, and the most troubling concern, was: Could she handle being shut up in one place with this good-looking man — correction, cop — whom she found herself attracted to? Even with someone else in the house, he would still be there most of the time, she presumed.

With the greatest of care, she covered the new bandage with her bangs, which in turn hid her old scar, too. Sam had always considered her old scar ugly and cringed at the thought of what waited under the newly bandaged area. She'd know soon enough.

Walking down the hall, she zigged when she should have zagged and ended up in the living room. That was okay by her. Before going to the kitchen, she wanted to see the view of the lake. At night, she presumed it would be beautiful with the moon glistening on the water.

An afternoon view was pretty in its own right. Small sailboats glided across the lake. People were having fun. Wouldn't that be wonderful? Sighing, she turned and found her way to the kitchen. At the door, she smelled something good but couldn't guess what it was. A growl from deep within let her know she was hungrier than she cared to admit.

"What is that? It smells delicious."

Matthew stood at the stove with his back to Sam. "Broccoli and cheese soup. Have a seat." He ladled two bowls of the hot liquid and then carried them to the table. Already on the table were two empty saucers to set the bowls on and a platter with several small cut sandwiches.

"Aren't you the perfect little chef," she exclaimed. "What an amazing guy you are. Are you sure I can't do something to help?"

"No. You take it easy. I hope this is enough food. The turkey sandwiches have sweet peppers and Philadelphia cream cheese on them."

Sam made a face. "Cream cheese?"

"You don't like it?"

She laughed. "I don't know, but I'll find out. I just figured out I'm ravenous." After blowing on the hot liquid, she sipped a mouthful of soup. "Mmm. This is delicious. I'm not a soup lover either, but I like this," she said as she washed it down with a swallow of iced tea.

"I hope you found everything you needed. It will be better when Marie gets here with your clothes." Glancing at the clock, he added, "That should be in the next hour."

"I admit, I miss fresh clothes after a shower. I can live without my makeup, but not clean clothes."

"I'm gonna give you that T-shirt I promised you, to sleep in. Just in case."

"Thanks." She wasn't too sure it would be

wise to sleep in his clothes. It might bring on some unwanted dreams — or some wanted dreams, for that matter. Either way, she wasn't looking forward to it.

At the table, Matthew kept the conversation light, which pleased Sam. She didn't feel like facing all the problems that surrounded her. Not yet anyway.

She loved the tang of the sweet peppers mixed with the cream cheese, as well as the stories Matthew told of his early days of being a cop. Nothing like Martin's early days. Martin had found nothing pleasurable in them, whereas Matthew found the joy and the thrill of good conquering bad. And the stories about his dad and his partner, Greg, kept her amused.

Taking another bite, she asked, "What is the funniest case you recall working on as a uniformed policeman?"

Matthew thought for a moment. "I know. There was a stolen horse rumored to be in hiding in Louisiana . . . of all places. I helped track him down. The jockey suspected of tampering with the horse before each race was believed to have arranged the horse's disappearance.

"The horse was our only proof. We had to find it. Besides, it wasn't just any old horse. This one had won several races, and the owner planned to race her in the Kentucky Derby. Like I said before, they had tracked the horse thief to Louisiana — to be more precise, Baton Rouge — and thus the case entered our department. The thief didn't give up easily. He went down fighting, venting most of his anger on me. I ended up in a pit of fertilizer, thanks to him."

Sam watched as Matthew made a horrible face, recalling the incident. She didn't know talking about things involving policemen could make her smile, but somehow the detective did that very thing.

"Luckily for me, it ended well. The thief helped us put away the jockey. So everything, including the way I smelled, was worth it. I laugh about it now, but at the time, trust me, it wasn't funny," he said as he shook his head. "I didn't think I'd ever get the stench out of my hair and my skin. It took several baths. In fact, the odor was so deeply imbedded in my pores, I had to soak in a tub of vinegar and water." He laughed. "And my clothes, yuk. I gave up on them totally and threw them out with the trash."

Sam burst out laughing. "Oh. Ow. Oh," she mumbled between the bouts of laughter. She couldn't stop herself. Tears streamed down her face. "I can't believe it. Did the owner offer to repay you for your loss?"

A shocked look swept over Matthew's face. "I didn't tell him and dared the other guys to say a word to anyone." He laughed some more. "Besides, it was all in the line of duty."

Once the laughing faded, she stood and started clearing the table. "In the line of duty," she whispered more to herself than aloud.

Matthew stopped laughing. "Unfortunately, the work we do is not always funny; in fact, very little of it is. Sometimes you see a lot of death. Some cases more gruesome than others. That was hard at first." He helped clear the table.

And policemen turn hard and cold . . . and vindictive. Martin did.

"Some handle it better than others," he said.

That was for sure. Of course, Sam knew Martin's problem went deeper than the typical reaction of a burned-out cop, but that didn't make it any easier to accept. It made it easier to forgive, but not easier to accept. According to his mother, his problems went back to his childhood. His father was an abusive man.

Enough of that. She didn't need to be thinking about Martin or her problems in the past. The past needed to be forgiven and forgotten. She had been working on it. She was sure she had forgiven, but the forgotten didn't seem to be happening. Now was a perfect time to lay them at the foot of the cross and leave them there. For Marty's sake, as well as her own, she needed to do that. And with her life in danger, she needed to be concentrating on the here and now.

"You are so right," she agreed.

CHAPTER 21

"You go make yourself comfortable in the living room. Maybe you can take that nap you've been wanting, or go to your room for the nap. I'll do the dishes," he said as he stacked the few dirty dishes on the counter near the sink.

"But I can help."

"Go. You've done enough. Remember, you're the one who was hurt. Try and rest so you can get your strength back. It's probably time to take a dose of your medicine anyway, and it will probably help you sleep," he said as he opened the container and dropped two pills in his hand. He then handed them to her and picked up her glass of iced tea. "More tea, or would you rather have water to swallow them down with?"

She didn't argue. "Tea's fine. Thanks." It wouldn't have done her any good, and she knew it. She took the pills and then made her way to the living room. In there, she snapped on the television set. Perfect timing. With two flips of the remote control, she locked the set on *Remington Steele.*

Sam sat on the couch, leaving the recliner for Matthew, guessing it to be his favorite chair. Not realizing how exhausted she was or how quick the medicine would work, she nodded off while watching another rerun of Laura and Mr. Steele solving yet another case together.

When she woke, the room had darkened. She found herself covered with a light blanket. *How sweet of Matthew.* In her mind she called him by his given name, but then corrected herself. *The detective.* Slowly she sat up and listened for a noise in the house.

Nothing. Without making a sound, she got up and wandered around from room to room. The kitchen was empty. Cutting back through the living room, she strode down the hall, and then turned to the left this time. A light shone from the far end. She heard voices coming down the hall also, although they were kept low. She couldn't make out what they were saying, but she knew the policewoman had arrived. As she came closer to the light near the end of the hall, she noticed a clacking sound as well.

"So there you are," she said as she stepped inside. "Hi," she added, speaking in Officer

Boudreaux's direction. The policewoman was sitting on a chair near a tabletop that looked almost like a sketching table but had various pictures and notecards strung across it. She immediately started turning the pictures facedown but kept her eyes on Samantha. At a glance, Sam noticed the woman was long and slender . . . petite in a way. How could she help protect Sam and Marty from this lunatic? But under closer scrutiny she saw the strength in her arms and the assuredness in her stature.

Matthew introduced the two. After turning over the last picture, the officer extended her hand. "Please call me Marie."

When the woman faced her, Sam also noticed the wisdom in her dark brown eyes. Her hair was short but stylish. In her line of work, it had to be easier to deal with. "Thanks for coming, Marie. This is strange for me, to be staying in a stranger's home . . . away from my son. And I'm taking you from your home. I'm truly sorry."

"Make no apologies. I'm here to serve and honored to be able to help."

Samantha thanked her before turning her attention to the detective and his room. "What are you working on?" she asked as her gaze darted around the room. His office at home looked organized — everything in its place. Not one thing appeared out of order. Behind him was a bulletin board with eight-by-ten pictures in two separate groupings. One had several pictures of women . . . dead women by the looks of them. The other group had a young girl in the middle, and other pictures circled around the one with notes below each picture.

Matthew stopped typing on his keyboard and looked toward the doorway. "We're going over the evidence, and I'm typing up a few notes."

Answering the question, yet not giving details. Good way to avoid answering her question. He seemed good at dancing around the questions. Then he tossed out a couple questions of his own. "How are you feeling? Did you get enough rest?" His fingers pressed two buttons, and the screen went black. Switching it off, he stood and walked toward her. "Can I get you something? A glass of tea? Cookies maybe? Let's all go to the kitchen."

She shook her head. He wasn't going to get out of it that easy. She wanted to know. "I'm fine. Thanks. I don't need anything. What exactly are y'all doing?" She took a tentative step into the room toward the drawing table. The notecards were still turned up. Maybe she could read a couple of them.

"Like I said, we're rehashing what we know on the serial killer . . . what evidence we do have. Noting a few observations that fresh eyes see. Since Officer Boudreaux — I mean, Marie — is going to be working closer on this case, I wanted to familiarize her with what we do have. Get her up to par on the case. And this is my work room at home. Work doesn't stop just because I'm not at the office. I keep the same pictures and notes up on my boards at home as I do at work so I can keep my mind on top of everything."

Pointing toward a wall of pictures, he continued, "This is another case I'm working on right now. A young girl was murdered, and I'm closing in on the killer. The way I work, putting everything out in front of my eyes, helps me solve the case, but please don't get close to them. You don't need to be seeing some of this stuff. Even the pictures involving your case. Let us do our job, and you just get well."

"Go back to whatever you were doing, and I won't bother you," Sam said. Glancing around, she wondered what all he had on that serial killer. What had he learned about him through the other crimes? Did he have anything on the man who had been following her? She knew that, before her, no one had lived to give a description. But had they found other fibers with DNA, like the crime shows on TV talked about?

She saw a copy of the description she had given the artist in view on the board with the dead women. Dread swept through her. Turning away, she realized she really didn't want to see anything in relation to her case right now.

"That's okay. We need to take a break anyway." He yawned and stretched as he rose. Quickly, he walked Sam away from the room and steered her down the hall. Marie followed closely behind them.

"There is something I learned today that I need to share with you, but I've been putting it off."

Did she want to listen, to hear something on her case? She took a staggered breath. Yes. She wanted to get her life back, and if he found more to get her life back to normal, she was ready. "Great. Let's sit in your living room. Okay?" She liked the comfort of his sofa. She'd sit there and hold the blanket across her knees. Maybe she could hold on a little longer to that feeling of peace as she listened.

"Great." They made their way toward the living room as he said, "One of my snitches told me he heard a guy at one of the bars bragging about chasing some woman and putting the fear of God in her. He said the man wasn't very old himself and claimed to be taking out some kind of revenge on her. My snitch says his whole face lit up with pleasure as he spoke about it."

Sam stopped midstep as nausea threatened her. Spinning on her heel, she said, "How sick! He brags about it?" It would take more than a comfortable sofa and a warm blanket to feel safe from that sick man.

"I showed him our sketch of the guy." Matthew touched her shoulders lightly as he turned her back around and eased her again down the hall toward the living room. "My snitch said it could be the same guy."

"You left for a while today?" She had slept thinking she was in his safe protection, and he wasn't even there.

"Not even an hour. And it was after Marie arrived. Your nap was almost four hours long. And don't worry; the house was watched, front and back. You were safe and sleeping like a baby." His eyes searched Sam's eyes. Worry crossed his face as he glanced in Marie's direction.

Maybe it was a sign from him for her to leave the room because almost immediately she said, "I'm going to take you up on that offer and go pour me some tea, if you don't mind. Either of you care for any?" Both Sam and the detective shook their heads, so she left them alone in the living room in pursuit of her tea.

For some reason the fact he had left bothered Sam. Since she was staying at his house, she presumed they would be together constantly. She presumed when he said he was going to be protecting her, he would be around her all the time. But of course that couldn't happen. The detective wouldn't be able to do his job if he stayed with her constantly. Besides, he had told her that was one of the reasons Officer Boudreaux was staying there. The other, of course, was because he was a moral man or at least knew she would feel better with another woman around. Anything to keep her safe from that sicko.

She grimaced. She didn't even want to think about that crazy man or her situation anymore. Not now. Not at this moment anyway. She shivered as she walked over to the big picture window and gazed out upon the peaceful lake. She needed a change of thought, a change of scenery, to disperse the coldness she felt inside, to combat the fear that threatened to consume her. *Give me peace, Lord.*

"It's pretty impressive. The view that is," he said softly as he stopped directly behind her.

With low lighting in the room, she felt safe and out of sight. The scene displayed in front of her took her breath away. It was better than she had imagined earlier. The moon sparkled on the water, throwing a pathway of diamonds in front of her. It was quiet and serene, allowing peace to settle over her. An answered prayer.

Maybe she could put her trust in this cop, this man, and in Officer Boudreaux. Marie didn't seem to have prefixed feelings of dislike for Sam. Maybe the woman hadn't been around three years ago and didn't know Sam and Martin's history. *Lord, You brought them into my life for a reason, and I'm going to trust them because I trust You.*

"Do you like it?" The detective's question came almost in a whisper.

She nodded without turning her head. "It paints a picture of serenity. In your type of work, dealing with crooks and killers, the bad side of life, I imagine it helps you to stop along the way and get your bearings."

"This view was the reason I kept the house after my father died. When I'm stuck on a case, I find myself standing here thinking, and before I know it, pieces start to fall together. It puts my mind at ease, helps me get my sense of direction."

"I wish it would give me the missing pieces right now. The who and why." She sighed.

"We'll figure out the who. The why is because you saw enough to put him away for a long time."

They both stood a moment or two in a comfortable, compatible silence. Then she broke it. "If I didn't know better, I'd say the world was at peace at this very moment. Too bad it can't last."

Matthew laid his hands gently on her shoulders. "It is, for now anyway, but you probably shouldn't stand in front of this window."

Marie walked in, clearing her throat at the time. "Sir, Ms. Cain, you sure neither of you want some of this tea? There's more hot water in the kettle. I can go make another cup or two."

Sam shook her head.

Matthew said, "No thanks. Let's sit." He led Sam to the sofa, and Marie sat at the other end. Matthew took the recliner but didn't lay back in it. When they sat, he asked, "Tell us about your job. What exactly does a dispatcher do? Shouldn't a man work the late shift?"

Her claws threatened to show themselves, an automatic reaction of hers, especially when the question was asked in the tone he used. She glanced at Marie. Surely she, as a woman, had dealt with these same caveman feelings before. Men are big. They handle the tough jobs. "Why? Do you think a man would do a better job?"

Marie smiled but said nothing as her eyes rested, amused, on the detective. It was like she couldn't wait to see how he handled Sam's question. Good. Marie was on her side. Sam had figured as such.

"No, not a better job. I just thought at night like that, with the creeps in this world, it might be safer if a man worked that shift."

Marie interrupted. "I think Ms. Cain has been through this type of discussion before. Am I right?"

"Yes. And please, call me Sam." Her claws slid back into place as she said reluctantly to the detective, "Possibly true, but you won't get me to admit it. Besides, I've worked the night shift for a couple of years now and haven't had a problem I couldn't handle . . . until now," she added.

"I believe that. How about you, Boud . . . uh, Marie. I'm gonna have to get used to calling you by your first name. Sorry. But

Samantha, I didn't mean to offend you. I'm a cop. That's how I think. I believe people should always do things a certain way, and of course," he glanced from one woman to the other and then finished his sentence, "that way is my way."

They all laughed.

Shaking her head, she backed off on her attitude. "I'm sorry. I don't mean to get so defensive. I've already argued this with Martin in the beginning, my parents, and with several drivers who believe a woman's place is in the home."

"For the record, Marie, her husband was a policeman. He died a few years ago."

"Sorry. I didn't know." Marie smiled apologetically in Sam's direction.

Matthew leaned back against the chair. "So you don't think a woman should be at home, playing Mama?" He tossed his head slightly in the policewoman's direction. "She probably agrees with you."

Sam shrugged. "I didn't say that. But no, I don't think that's where a woman has to be. Sure, at some time in her life a woman might choose that, but while she's working, she should do whatever she wants to do. If she can manage a family at the same time and wants to, great. But most homes today need the woman to work."

"She got you there, sir." Marie laughed. She was clearly enjoying watching them volley remarks back and forth.

"Think about this. If a man had been in the office the other night, right now you wouldn't be in danger, and you wouldn't have to hide out here to be safe."

"Back at you, Sam. He's right there." Marie's grin seemed to be growing by the minute.

Sam looked away as her mind stated, *And I wouldn't have gotten a chance to know you.* Immediately she shook that idea out of her head. "It would just be him instead of me."

"I doubt that," Marie said.

"A man wouldn't have even noticed the scream, or if he had, he would have thought it was a cat fight and forgotten about it," said Matthew.

Marie shook her head in agreement with the detective.

"We don't know that for sure. Besides, it was your idea for me to hide out here," Sam reminded him quickly. "You're the one who said I needed protection and decided to take it on yourself. I don't have to stay." Her whole body stiffened. She wanted to get up and run out of the room. The last thing she wanted to be for anyone was a burden.

"That's not what I'm saying. I know

198

you're not here because you want to be. What I'm saying is that if you hadn't gotten involved, you wouldn't be hiding out, and it wouldn't be necessary for me to keep you safe. Why did you go across the levee? Did you truly think you could save her?"

"Well, yes and no. Although I've taken several self-defense classes, I knew I couldn't hurt that big man, but I thought I could slow down the process at least long enough for help to get there. And as far as you having to keep me safe, nobody asked you to become my protector." She jumped to her feet; her head spun slightly at the sudden movement. "I can take care of myself," she threw at him as she stumbled around Marie's feet, then fled the room. Sam didn't need his help — or anyone else's, for that matter — nor had she asked for it.

By the time she reached the bedroom, Matthew was right on her heels. "I think you misunderstood me . . . again."

"I think I read you loud and clear," she said as she stepped into the bathroom. Sam snatched her underthings off the shower curtain rod, balled them up, then stuffed them in her pants pocket. Her bag was on the bed, so she grabbed it. Now to call for a taxi.

When she turned to head to the kitchen, the dizzy sensations tried to overcome her. She spared not a glance at him as she started to walk around him, standing in the middle of the bedroom that was to be hers for the duration of her stay. Maybe Marie would take her home. She'd ask her.

"Samantha," he pleaded as he took her by the shoulders, stopping her from leaving the room. Turning her to face him, he slipped her hands in his to prevent her from pulling away. "Look at me. I wasn't complaining." His expression had softened, but that was beside the point.

She looked down, trying not to take in the emotion she saw in his face. "You could have fooled me. It sounded that way." She kept her eyes averted to the floor, not ready to look him in the eyes, especially this close.

When she didn't look up, he dropped her hands and lifted her chin toward him. Cupping her face in his hands, he said, "I'm glad you're staying here. I know I shouldn't admit that, nor should I say it. But had it not happened when it did, we would have never met . . . I mean, gotten to know each other better. I'm just sorry your life had to be put in danger." Lowering his voice to a whisper he added, "I'm also scared something could happen to you. I don't want that."

Sam didn't say a word. He was doing it again. Her pulse raced. The throbbing at the base of her neck was about to explode. His clear blue eyes flashed silver sparks. Had his words been a slip of the tongue, or was he really glad they had a chance to get to know one another?

What did it matter? She had to quit being sidetracked by his looks, his personality, and his so-called concern for her.

"You do realize the guy may be ready to end your life? Sure, he's toying with you now, but death could be at the end of his plan." His eyes seemed to caress her as he moved ever so slightly closer. "I can't let him get near you. The next time you might not be so lucky."

Sam swallowed hard. Her gaze darted to his eyes, then to his lips and back again. Her mind had been heading in this direction for the past couple of days . . . and now it was there. She wet her lips. She wanted him to kiss her. Her breath caught in her throat as she waited what seemed like an eternity.

Gently his hands cradled her face; his thumbs brushed her cheeks. "I shouldn't . . . I shouldn't be doing this."

She closed her eyes.

"But I want . . . I want —" His lips came down on hers.

The wonderful pressure of his mouth against her lips weakened her knees. She couldn't resist and kissed him back.

What was she thinking? She didn't do this. Kiss a man she barely knew. Kiss a man period . . . let alone a cop. Then it hit her. She was scared, scared for her life.

As if he heard her question, Matthew stopped kissing her and pulled away slightly. "I'm sorry. I shouldn't have done that. I'm supposed to be protecting you, not taking advantage of you."

She looked him in the eye, swallowed hard, but didn't say a word.

He couldn't tell her she had been a distraction to him from the first moment he'd laid eyes on her. Sure, he knew who she was and what she was supposed to be like, but nothing she had done since they met backed up anything Martin had told him over three years ago.

His thoughts flashed on what might have happened, had he not stopped them. What if Martin had been telling the truth? What if she was setting him up? He exhaled. He didn't know the truth. Confusion twisted in his gut. He shoved his hands through his hair again as he remembered what had become of Martin. He didn't need to get involved with this woman. He only needed to protect her so he could get close to the killer. So why tempt fate?

"You're right. This shouldn't have happened. I haven't even kissed a man since Martin. I'm sorry. It didn't mean anything. I know that. I've been so scared these past couple of days."

He thought for a moment. If Martin had been telling the truth, it meant something. It meant she was up to something, trying to manipulate him just like she had done Martin. "All that matters right now is that I'm on a case, and my job is to protect you, not become involved with you."

He looked deep into her eyes, watching, wishing he knew what she was thinking. Was the past the truth? Or was she a different person than Martin had painted? Matthew just couldn't be sure.

But he did know that he had a job to do, and that was what he had to keep first and foremost in his mind. "I'm a cop. Let me do my job," he said, backing away slightly.

Matthew's words brought Sam back to reality, like a slap in the face. It was just a kiss. What had gotten into her? She thought earlier it was fear, but she wished she knew.

"Good idea. Go do your job."

He reached out and touched the side of her face. "Don't worry. You're safe. I'm not going to let anything happen to you. And I won't kiss you again. Sorry. That shouldn't have happened. It sounds like Marie turned on the television. Let's go watch a little TV. Then maybe you'll be able to get some more rest. I'll go get your medicine. It's time to take some more."

She turned away, putting space between them. "I'll get my medicine. You just do your job."

His words had sounded sincere, but down deep she knew they were not the words she really wanted to hear. As much as she told herself she didn't want a cop around, didn't need a cop, she knew, this man, this cop, had moved into her heart, and there was no getting him out now, whether she wanted to or not.

CHAPTER 22

The next morning, Matthew left Samantha with Marie so he could check with Jake, another one of his informants, and see if he picked up on anything new. Matthew had officers staked out in the front and back of his home, still making sure no one could enter. She would be safe.

Driving slowly through downtown and along the river, Matthew watched for any sign of Jake. It wasn't long before he found his snitch begging on the streets.

"It's always women you beg from Jake," Matthew mumbled under his breath as he eased into a parking spot along the curb. Maybe his informant believed women felt more pity, which was probably true. And his looks and youth didn't hurt when he turned his charm onto these older women who visited the city.

Matthew didn't wait for Jake to finish panhandling as he bumped his horn a few times, catching the snitch's attention. When Jake gave up and walked over to the car, Matthew pushed the passenger door open. "Get in. Didn't mean to interfere with your work," he said with a touch of sarcasm.

The snitch pulled a handful of cash from his pocket, spread it out, and waved it in front of him like a handheld fan. "That's okay. I'm doing good today. Whoever said the South was full of friendly people knew what they were talking about." Jake slipped the wad back into his pants pocket. "I guess you're here to find out if I got any information for you."

Matthew nodded.

The bum wet his lips in anticipation and, with a greedy glint in his eyes, rubbed his forefingers against his thumbs. "So, what's in it for me?"

"As long as people continue to give you handouts, you're never going to try to get back in the game of life, are you?"

Jake smirked. "Why work when you ain't got to?"

Matthew realized Jake found his new life too easy. In fact, it wasn't even new anymore. The man had been on the streets for two years. Matthew almost felt sorry for his snitch but knew deep down the man had quit caring. He had lost his job, his home, and then his wife and children. Swallowing what little pity he had left for the man, Matthew said, "Tell me what you found out, and I'll pay you what it's worth. I've always been fair."

The bum shrugged. "Okay. It's like this. The guy you're looking for stays at one of those run-down motels a few blocks from here. Not sure which one, though. Rumor is, he has family here but for some reason doesn't associate with them. His boat is scheduled to pull off at the end of the week, but last night he claimed he had unfinished business to tend to before he left town again. Sometimes the guy hangs out at the bars downtown. That's where he's been mouthing off anyway, at The French Door and The Moonlighters."

"Why didn't you call headquarters when you saw him last night?" Anger started to burn within Matthew at the missed golden opportunity.

"Wasn't sure how long he'd stay and whether I had time to leave and go call you. Besides, I didn't have a quarter. I made all that money you saw today."

Squeezing his fingers around the steering wheel, Matthew tried to control his temper. Once he felt he had it under control, he continued. "What did he look like? Can you

ID him? Did you find out his name or what boat he worked on?"

Scratching the stubble on his dirty face, Jake said, "Last night they called him Buddy or Bobby. Something like that. I'm not sure." He shrugged. "Never got a good look at him. The bar was dark. He's bigger'n me. I saw that."

That wasn't saying much, because Jake was small for a man. "How much bigger is he?"

The snitch shrugged. "About a head and a half taller. He's probably about six foot. But that's a guess. Could be more. And the boat he works on, who knows? There're so many. All I know is, he's gonna do something before he leaves Friday night."

Matthew wished Jake had more information, but at least he could have the two bars staked out and check the ships scheduled to leave at the time Jake had said.

"Okay, Jake." Matthew pulled out two twenties and one of his cards. On the back, he jotted down his cell number. "If you hear anything, I mean *anything,* or see him, call me right away. If I'm not at the station, you can reach me by my cell. Here's a couple of quarters. Don't spend them. Save them to call me. Time is running out."

Jake's eyes widened at the two twenties.

"Sure. Thanks." He stuffed the money and the card in his shirt pocket, then dropped the coins in his pants pocket. As quick as he could, he opened the door and jumped out of the car.

Matthew watched as Jake disappeared around the corner. Rubbing his jaw, Matthew thought about his next move: finding Freddy, the derelict, who slept in front of the old motels downtown. Sometimes, the bum even found a way to slip into one of the rooms for a full night's sleep. Maybe Freddy knew more than Jake.

As Matthew drove around slowly, looking for Freddy, he remembered bits and pieces of last night. The confused look on Samantha's face focused clearly in Matthew's mind.

"Oh, Samantha," he murmured.

Once again he tried to fight his attraction to Samantha. He reminded himself what she had put Martin through and where he had ended up. If Matthew was smart, he wouldn't want the problems that came with knowing that woman . . . that is, *if* what Martin said was true. Doubt jolted through him.

He tried to brush off his attraction to Samantha Cain as pure physical attraction, but he knew it was more than that. Every time he turned around, something about her touched his heart. The way she handled herself with the drivers. The way she cared for the woman over her own well-being. The way her friends rallied to her side. That was the kind of woman a man could fall for easily. If he let himself . . . but he wouldn't.

Not him. Even if Martin had totally lied about her, look at her. Her life was in jeopardy now. Three years ago it was a mess. She could be the one causing all the problems in her life. She was the one who ran out and straight into trouble. How many people run toward a scream? Most run away. And even if she wasn't causing the problems, Matthew reminded himself, if he focused on his feelings for her, he would be putting her and her son in a constant state of possible danger. And that would be his fault. That was the reason he steered clear of serious relationships with women in the past. Why change now?

Closing his eyes, he realized he couldn't bear it if something happened to Samantha. Not now. Not ever. He could tell himself until the cows came home that Martin knew her better than he ever could, but Matthew knew that wasn't true. Knowing how he would feel if something happened to her told him something he didn't want to know

— or admit. He had already fallen for her.

What did it matter? He knew he wasn't good material for any woman looking for a serious relationship anyway, because his job was such a dangerous one, plus it had the odd hours. No woman in her right mind would get mixed up with a cop. Not much free time. No regular hours. Go whenever the case demanded. Basically, he was on twenty-four hour call.

This morning over breakfast they had eaten in strained silence. The only one who had really talked was Marie, and she tried to force conversation throughout. None of them had spoken of what had happened the night before. Marie didn't know the whole situation, and Matthew would keep it that way. As for him and Samantha, they probably needed to talk, but right now that couldn't be his number-one concern. Now he needed to concentrate on keeping her alive and catching the man who was after her, the man who had already killed three women . . . three that he knew of. There could have been more elsewhere. He was checking into that, too. The guy could have started these attacks years ago and worked up to murder. Who knew? That was what he intended to find out.

"Safety," he said. "That is what I'll do

today. I'll take her to the firing range. Let her practice shooting."

He caught up with Freddy at the old Capitol-Heights Inn, which was closed down, badly in need of repairs. With the casinos on the riverfront, old hotels were being remodeled and made like new. It was only a matter of time before this one would be fixed up as well.

Freddy was in one of his drunken stupors, so he was of no help. Next, Matthew ran down some information on another one of his cases, then slipped by the station. He managed to get more copies of the sketch made and passed around at the station. Every once in a while he caught himself looking back at that sketch. Something about it, about *him,* felt familiar.

Matthew discussed the new developments of the case with Davis and Shelton. After much deliberation, he and the two assisting officers arranged a stakeout at each of the bars downtown and organized a follow-up on the boats to interview the deckhands scheduled to leave port on Friday at midnight. With the aid of a computer, they ran a comparison of those boats with the dates of the incidents and determined which ones were docked at the time and which weren't.

A list of workers scheduled to go out on the boat, along with the sketch of the assailant, would give them a list of possible suspects, and then a team of officers would be dispatched to pick up and bring them in for questioning. In that group, they should find the pervert.

Satisfied he'd done all he could for now, Matthew headed home, watchful of his surroundings, making sure he wasn't being followed. Pumped and alert, his adrenaline soared. Each moment drew him closer to catching the killer. Time was near. His nerves tingled with anticipation. He was about to catch his killer. Matthew couldn't wait to get the crew members in for interrogation. The rap sheets alone could probably single out the man.

"Probably not," he corrected himself, mumbling. The serial killer had been very careful so far.

Matthew turned into his driveway, still scanning the neighborhood for anything out of the ordinary. *Nothing. Good.* Using his cell, he checked in with both officers and relieved them so they could go back to the station.

The back door was locked, so he unlocked the door and let himself into the kitchen. Intense quiet filled the room as an odd feeling crept over him. He set his briefcase down on the counter.

Samantha, where are you? And Marie, where are you? Your car is still here. He wanted to scream their names out loud but restrained himself. Instead his eyes sharpened as his gaze darted around the room, and his ears honed in on the slightest sound in the house.

His training and experience took over. Quietly he slipped his gun out of his shoulder holster and released the safety. Without making a sound, he slipped in and out of each room, searching them quickly. Had she taken off? Decided she couldn't trust him after all? Or had the nutcase found her? Fear ate at his gut. How could his men not have seen her slip out, or the killer slip in? No. Marie wouldn't have let her. This made him more nervous. What if the killer had slipped in unnoticed? Taken Marie down by surprise? He would have Sam to himself. He could be toying with her now, torturing her. Matthew took a deep breath. This killer was sick, not smart. He wouldn't have been able to slip in unnoticed, Matthew told himself as he continued from room to room.

The rooms were empty. No noise came from any part of the house. No television sounded, nor did he hear a stereo playing. He didn't even hear the sound of running water.

In her room, the bathroom door stood open a good foot or two. No one was in there. His senses heightened, he glanced in Marie's room. It appeared to be in order.

Down the hall, Matthew peeked into his office, thinking maybe she was snooping around at his notes and the pictures while Marie studied the case file more. He wouldn't like that, well the part about Samantha looking into the case more . . . seeing the brutality the killer used on those women, but he almost prayed that was what she was doing. It beat the alternative.

Nothing. His anguish intensified. Where were they? Quickly, he glanced in his room as he passed it. No one was in there either. He moved to the back room of the house. Opening the door slowly, he peered around the doorframe, then breathed a sigh of relief.

There they were. Samantha was exercising with earphones covering her ears and Marie was walking the treadmill with pictures spread across the front. Her eyes darted up, and her hand drew her Glock instantly. He clicked the safety back into place on his own weapon and then slipped the gun in its holster.

Marie lowered her weapon. "Gheeze, Louise. You took a chance coming in so quietly. Why didn't you say something, sir? I could have blown you away."

He shook his head, thankful nothing had happened to either of them. "Samantha!" he bellowed.

She stopped midstep, her face flushed. "You're back early," she said as she removed the headphones from her ears. "I thought you said you'd be in late this afternoon. I hope you don't mind. I borrowed a pair of your gym shorts I found on top of the dryer. Marie didn't know I'd be up to a workout so she didn't bring any of my workout clothes."

"She said the doctor told her she could go back to her routine activities if she felt up to it. I hope you don't mind we helped ourselves to your workout room."

Words caught in his throat. He wanted to yell and scream at both of them, especially Samantha for scaring him so badly, but couldn't. No words formed. Mixed emotions stormed within. Glad she was safe. Well, glad they were both safe, but angry that they had put him through unnecessary worry, unnecessary torment — not that Samantha had even known what she had done. Marie, on the other hand, had seen him enter with his gun drawn and probably read the look on his face. But not Samantha. He would keep her in the dark as far as how she made him feel.

"What's wrong?" she asked as her eyes searched his face. "You look as if you've seen a ghost."

Matthew swallowed a lump in his throat before speaking. "I thought for a second or two you had gone. Decided to protect yourself." He didn't tell her any more than that. Didn't let her know the real fear he had felt and hoped she couldn't read his emotions.

The look on her face, an expression of guilt, told him more than he wanted to know. He realized immediately she had thought about leaving. That thought was like a sharp stab in the heart, but he didn't try to understand why. He didn't want to know why that knowledge hurt. He pushed that reality, the fact she wanted to leave, to the back of his mind.

Suddenly, looking at her standing there, glistening in sweat and perspiration, another thought took the place of his last one. She might have thought about leaving, but she didn't.

That touched him, but he didn't dare let her know. No. Some things he had to keep to himself. He had to get a handle on his feelings before even a hint of what he might be feeling was made evident.

"I got through early and decided we are going to the firing range if you're up to it. Obviously, if you're exercising, you must feel pretty good."

"Working out helps me think clearer." Sam wiped the sweat off her neck and face and then tugged at her bangs. "Besides, it makes me feel better. I promise, I'm not overdoing it. You'd be amazed how much energy was zapped out of me. By the way, I made a long-distance call. I'll —"

"What? You're not supposed to let anyone know you're here. You're hiding out, remember!" Anger started to build in him as his fists tightened into two balls. Was she trying to get herself killed? Why couldn't she follow simple instructions?

"It was my folks. Don't worry. I didn't tell them anything, only that Amanda and I were heading down to New Orleans for a couple of days so they wouldn't worry about me. And I didn't stay on the line but a minute. I remembered what you had said. Marie, tell him. I did it the only way she would let me."

"She did good, boss. Don't worry."

"Oh." He ran his hand through his hair.

Maybe no harm was done. He hoped. Scratching the back of his neck, he added, "Do you feel up to practicing your shooting?"

"I learned how to shoot a gun a long time ago. My daddy took me out to the country and made me learn. However, I believe a gun is dangerous in the hands of those who don't know what they are doing. So I keep mine in the top drawer of my dresser, tucked out of sight."

"Well, I'm going to see that you know what you're doing," he said as he arched his brows. What was he going to do with this woman? "You may not care to use a gun for protection, Samantha, but with your job, as well as the odd hours, it wouldn't hurt to know a little bit more about how to protect yourself with a gun. At least enough to feel confident with a gun."

"Besides, it could come in handy in the situation you are in now. Wouldn't you rather know you could protect yourself if you needed to?" Marie asked.

"I can defend myself." Sam turned the radio off and placed it on the shelf behind his weight table. "I've taken courses to be sure I could. Maybe not with a gun, but —" She couldn't continue. Turning worried eyes upon him and lowering her voice to a whisper where only Matthew would hear, she said, "Truthfully, I'm afraid of guns. Martin killed himself with his own gun. Since then, guns are something I make a point of staying away from."

Choosing to ignore the remark about Martin, he said, "I didn't think you were afraid of anything. Well, no problem. I can help you overcome that fear. I'm going to take you to the firing range." He turned his back on her and walked down the hall.

"I guess that means we're going. You're in charge, and I follow your lead." There was a slight sarcasm in her voice, but only slight, Matthew felt sure.

"Hey, boss. While y'all go there, I think I'll run over to headquarters and finish up some paperwork I need to do . . . if that's okay by you."

"No problem, Marie. That should work out great. I'll give you a ring when we get back to the house. Do either of you want lunch first?" he called over his shoulder. "All that exercise should have built up an appetite."

"I'll catch a sandwich at headquarters."

"I'm not hungry, but I do need to clean up first," Samantha said.

The old Sam was back. He heard it in her

voice. He liked the fighter in her, and right now she needed to stay that way.

CHAPTER 23

In no time at all, they were at the public firing range. Very few people were there, probably because it was the middle of the day. That was fine with Sam. She didn't like guns or the noise they made, but she could use the distraction. The range master took their money and handed them ear protectors.

"Wear these," Matthew said as he put his on. "Your ears will thank you later. Let's go." Matthew led the way.

Placing two guns down on the booth in front of them, along with ammunition, he said, "We're going to start easy and refresh your memory on how to shoot with this .38."

He showed her the proper way to hold a gun, how to aim, and then squeeze the trigger. "Take your time and you can hit your target. Squeeze the trigger slowly." Matthew set up a human silhouette as her target.

"Are those legal?" she asked. "I can see a deer maybe, but a human?"

He gave her a disgruntled look, then placed the silhouette fifteen yards away.

That didn't seem too far to Sam. She shouldn't have any trouble. Sam had seen people shoot on television often enough. It seemed fairly simple when she had been a teenager, although time had passed slightly by since then. She had hit the can her father had set on a tree stump. Of course, it did take about six tries, if she remembered correctly.

She held her arm out straight, took aim, then squeezed. Her hand jerked upward. Sam knew immediately she had missed the target entirely.

So much for what it looked like on television. They practiced for the next couple of hours. By the end of that time, at least she was hitting the flat piece of cardboard. Sam knew of one more thing she hated about guns — the smell that lingered in the air. Gunpowder left a stench that was hard to describe, but one thing was for sure, it stunk worse than a cap gun.

"I'm going to move it in to ten yards now."

Sam read his lips more than heard his words but understood what he told her.

For another hour, she practiced. Only this

time, he didn't let her take aim. Instead, he had her hold the gun by her side, safety off. At the drop of his hand, she was to raise the gun, fire three times at the chest, and then they checked to see if she reached her mark. Matthew set up a new silhouette for this exercise.

When he brought the silhouette to them for the last time, he said, "You're getting better. Not bad, in fact."

Matthew's words brought a swell of pride to her chest. It didn't last long though. His next words ruined it.

"But if you had to use the gun right now to save yourself, I'm not sure what the outcome would be."

Her brows drew together as a frown formed on her lips. She didn't mean to pout but couldn't help herself. "I thought you just said I was doing good?"

"Not bad, really. But we'll have to come back for more practice. Can't learn it all in one day, you know." With thumb and forefinger, he raised her chin and added, "Don't worry. You'll be fine. I'm not going to let anything happen to you." He hesitated as he looked deep into her eyes. "I promise," he whispered.

Sam bit her bottom lip as it started to quiver. His touch alone was enough to make her fall apart, but for him to sound concerned over her well-being, and that voice, so deep and sincere — it was more than she could bear. She thought he had made himself perfectly clear the other night. She wished he would quit confusing her.

Matthew dropped his hand. "You've watched me fill the clip and change it; now I want you to do it." Matthew dropped the clip and emptied the few bullets that were left in it. Handing the empty clip to her, he said, "Give it a try."

Grabbing the black piece of hard plastic and several small bullets, she attempted to do what she was told. By the time she had slid five bullets into the clip, she found it becoming harder with each one. After filling the clip, Matthew showed her how to load it into the gun and remove it. Next, he pointed out the safety and explained the purpose. He taught her to load the first bullet into the chamber. She had to pull the slide, and it automatically fell into place.

To practice this, he had her drop the clip, remove the bullet from the chamber, and start over. After several practices, she did it one more time, set the bullet in the chamber, then put on the safety.

Matthew and Sam picked up their spent casings, then Matthew put the guns safely away into the holsters. Sam watched as he paid the man for the extra targets they used, then turned to her and said, "Let's go."

Sam rode in exhausted silence as Matthew drove toward his home.

"Stay in the car till I signal you to come in. I have to be sure no one has gotten into the house."

She watched as he checked for the tiny piece of thread he'd left in the door at knee level. Matthew had told her about it as they left to go shooting. He said no one ever thought to look down low for something that really wasn't visible. If it was still in place, no one had been there. However, if the thread was missing, someone had opened the door.

In an instant, he whipped his gun out of its holster and glanced around the back yard. It didn't take a genius to read his expression.

"Not again," she cried out to the empty car she was sitting in.

Quickly, with the gun pointed downward, he ran back to the car. "Look in that case on the backseat and pull out the .38. Remember it's loaded."

She nodded.

"Take the safety off and wait. Somebody went in my place, and they might still be here." He peered around the back yard.

Fear rose in her chest. She only hoped it didn't show in her eyes.

"You'll do fine," he reassured her. "Just hold on to the gun while I'm inside checking things out. Do you remember how to hold it?"

She nodded.

He saw her innocence mixed with fear and hated to leave her by herself but had no choice. He never should have let Marie go back to the station. "Good girl. Don't forget to take the safety off and just sit tight while I look around." He leaned through the window and gave her a quick kiss on the lips. Why, he didn't know. "Just don't shoot me when I come back out." He tried to give her a smile of encouragement. On that, Matthew headed back to the house.

As quietly as possible, he opened the door and moved silently from room to room. Nothing seemed disturbed. Matthew checked all the closets, the shower stalls, and anywhere else someone could be hiding. Nothing. Great. Maybe Marie had come back. Maybe she had forgotten something. He'd give her a call and find out.

After a quick phone call to the station, he found out Marie had been there the whole time. "Well, someone came in to the house while we were gone. I'm going to have to move Samantha. I'll give you a call when we settle, and you can come to us. But when you do . . . make absolutely sure you are not followed. Do you understand me?"

"Yes, sir. No problem. I'll be waiting for your call."

Returning to Sam's side, he said, "Come on. You're going to throw your things in your bag and I'll pack some of mine. Grab a change for Marie, too. We're going to go somewhere else to stay the night."

She didn't question him, just did as he said. The fear was still strong in her eyes. Her enlarged pupils pulsed as she searched for hidden answers. Her head darted this way and that, not trusting a soul. He wished he could remove the fear from her eyes . . . from her heart.

Before leaving, Matthew grabbed his charger for his cell phone and packed it, too, just in case. He didn't dare miss Jake's call.

When they were both packed, he put the bags in the trunk and got the two of them out of there fast. He drove around, making sure they weren't being tailed.

After riding around for twenty minutes, Sam finally broke the silence. "It looks like we're going in circles. Where are you taking us?"

"I'm making sure we're not being followed." Matthew pulled into the parking lot of a bank and, using the drive-thru ATM machine, withdrew some money from his savings account. Her eyes were full of questions as she watched him put all that money in his wallet.

Before she could ask, he answered her unspoken question. "We don't know how long we'll be staying at a motel, and I don't want to charge the room. That's too easily traced . . . in case he's smart enough to know you are with me."

His eyes continually glanced to the left, to the right, then to the rearview mirror. "I'm making sure no one is tailing us, especially a small black car."

She didn't like seeing the concern in his eyes. It meant she was in danger. He was, too, but she had put him there. It wasn't fair. Automatically, Sam slid down in the seat, and her eyes darted around, looking for any sign of that black car. How long would they be driving around? *Please find us a place soon. I feel like a sitting duck.* Sam knew Matthew would drive as long as he deemed necessary to keep her safe. "I'll pay you back the money you are spending," she assured him.

He flashed his white teeth at her in a re-assuring smile, yet never taking his eyes off the road or their surroundings. "Don't you worry about it. The department will reimburse me."

"If not, remember, I pay my way, and since this is all for me, I will pay back every cent."

He finally pulled into the parking lot of the Red Roof Inn. While he went in to get the rooms, Sam stayed low and waited in the car, again holding the gun as he'd instructed her to do.

He was back in minutes. "Our room's in the back. That way no one can sneak up on us."

She started to question *our room,* but he didn't give her a chance. Nor did she get to ask if Marie would be joining them.

"You'll be safe. No one can trace us here. I signed us in as Mr. and Mrs. Tom Jordan. I told them we would be here for a couple of days."

She wanted to ask why he didn't get each of them a room, but he'd parked the car and was exiting it before she could form the words.

He unlocked the door to the room, and they went inside. *Good.* Her gaze fell on two double beds. At least it wasn't as bad as she thought it would be at first. But in this small room, with no other place to go except the bathroom, could she keep her distance? Surely she wouldn't want to be rejected a second time by this man she had no business even thinking about to begin with.

Yes. Of course she could handle it. She had no choice.

CHAPTER 24

The minute they were in the motel room with the door closed, Sam found she didn't have to worry about Matthew's intent. He immediately pulled his cell phone out of his jacket, flipped it open, and started punching numbers.

Apparently, making advances toward her was the last thing on his mind. He also made sure she couldn't overhear his conversation by turning his back on her and keeping his voice low.

"Humph," Sam mumbled under her breath as she made a face, shrugged, and turned away from him. Why couldn't he let her hear? It was her life that was in danger.

She sighed. Maybe it wasn't about her. He was the professional. Leaving everything in his hands, she decided to go get cleaned up. It was going to be a long night.

She scooped up her shampoo, conditioner, underclothes, one of Matthew's T-shirts and her robe, and took them into the bathroom with her. He'd told her to stuff some of Marie's clothes in her bag, too, so the policewoman must be planning to join them. That was good. It would give her someone to talk to, because right now she didn't feel like being sociable to the detective. Turning the hot water on, she waited for the steam to rise before adding cold water to adjust to a perfect temperature.

"A good hot shower. I need that tonight." As the water blasted, she directed the stream of water on the lower part of her face, careful not to hit the stitches. *Yes. Rinse away all that pain and the problems I seem to have in my life. Let me go back to those boring days I used to complain about.*

What she wouldn't give to be living that old routine of life again. But, if she were back into her old life, she wouldn't have gotten to know Matthew Jeffries, nor would she have felt the tingle of excitement that rushed through her when his voice called her name. She would have hated to miss the sparkle in his eyes when he spoke of his work. Sam loved the dedication he showed in his job. Matthew was everything she dreamed a good man would be. Everything she had hoped Martin would be. Sam had stopped believing one existed . . . until now.

The past few years had tarnished her view of men. First Martin and the pain he put her through, then his fellow men in blue and what they had put her through, suspecting her in his death. And, she had to admit, there were a few men she worked with who lived for the day, never worrying about tomorrow. That wasn't what she believed a man or woman should do. Not that she would worry, but she would plan, work for a future for her and her son. God's Word said to worry about nothing and pray about everything. Those words had gotten her through many a tough week.

The problems of today are large enough to worry about, she thought, *but I won't. I'll trust the Lord.* After all, He had sent Matthew and Marie into her life to help save and protect her. Matthew had a good head on his shoulders, and Marie seemed to be in better shape than Sam had given her credit for. She'd noticed when they were working out, Marie had strong biceps and her legs were taut with muscles. She would trust the Lord — and trust Matthew and trust Marie.

Matthew Jeffries seemed different than all those other men. He lived every day to clean the crime out of the city and make tomorrow a better, safer day for the citizens. He believed the world was worth fighting for.

She sighed. Slowly, she washed her aching limbs with soap and water. Pain shot down her arms to the tips of her fingers every time she moved. It was bad enough the headache she already had from the accident, but now, due to all that practice today, her whole body hurt.

Sam didn't remember her hands and arms hurting like this when her father first taught her how to use a gun. But then, she realized, it hadn't been a matter of life and death. When her dad showed her, it was just the basics, and he wasn't worried if she perfected her aim. However, the aftereffects from today left a great deal of strain and pain in her body. Hours of practice had done that to her, but at least now, if necessary, she felt confident she could pull out the gun, fire it, and hit what she was aiming at.

Sam stayed under the spray of water until it turned cold. The time had come to climb out of the shower and face the detective. Better yet, she would face her attraction to Matthew Jefferies. She should face it and fight it. Yes. She would fight it . . . she hoped.

After drying and dressing, she wrapped the towel around her hair and marched out to face her fate. To her surprise, he wasn't there. Only Marie. Her heart sank. So much for good intentions. But that was a good thing. "Where did he go?"

"He just left. He said he'd be back in a few minutes. Of course, I just got here myself," Marie said.

Frowning, Sam toweled her hair as dry as possible, then started combing the tangles free.

"How did the shooting go? Did you learn more?"

"I think so," Sam said. "I know I hurt in my arms and fingertips. But I'm sure that will pass soon enough."

Marie laughed. "Yes. You'll feel better by morning."

They talked about hair next. Marie told her how she used to leave hers long and hanging, but once she became a cop, she had started braiding it. But it was such a hassle that last year she'd whacked it off and never looked back. She said it saved hours of combing, drying, and fixing. She called it her wash-and-wear do.

By the time the last tangle was out, Sam heard a key turning in the lock of the door. Her heart stopped. She froze. She didn't even try to run for cover in the bathroom. There wasn't enough time. Besides, Marie was right there, and she had already pulled her gun out and had it aimed straight at the door. The woman was fast.

The door opened, and Matthew stepped in. Marie slipped her gun back into her holster.

Sam blew out the breath she had been holding. "You scared me to death." As she started to fuss, her stomach let out a big growl, and her nose knew instantly what was in the bags in his hand. "Food. All right!"

Marie laughed. "You change your moods faster than anyone I know."

Matthew closed the door, locked it behind him, then set the two bags on the dressertop.

"Oh, that smells wonderful. I'm starving."

"I'm glad to see your appetite is back," Matthew said with a smile. "I wanted to wait and see what you wanted to eat, but you took so long in the shower, I gave up and decided to please myself. Marie ate earlier so she's not hungry like us, so she said anything would be fine. I hope you like Popeye's fried chicken."

"Perfect." Sam smacked her lips in anticipation as she sat down on one of the beds, waiting for him to pass her a bag of her own. "Let's eat."

He pulled three boxes from one bag and

passed her one, and then Marie. Next, he reached in the other and pulled out a couple of drinks. "I hope you all drink Coke. Forgot to ask you, Marie, before I left. Sorry."

She shrugged. "Fine by me."

Before he sat down with his food, he took a moment to place his cell phone in the charger on the nightstand next to his bed. Seconds later he shrugged off his sport coat, revealing his shoulder holster and gun. He removed them and laid them next to his cell phone. Last but not least, he got his box of food and drink and sat on the side of one of the beds, with his gun in reach.

Matthew turned on the television and started flipping channels. About the time Sam figured out what show they were watching, Matthew changed the station.

"Make up your mind, would you?" she said.

"Yes. Please. You're making me dizzy changing it so fast," Marie said.

"What do y'all want to watch?"

"I don't care. I'm going to take my shower when I finish eating." Marie bit into her chicken without another word.

"It doesn't really matter to me either, but if there's a good cop show or detective . . . never mind." They probably had no desire to watch what they lived every day. "Anything is fine. A comedy. Whatever. Just make a decision, please."

CHAPTER 25

Matthew hid a smile. She was something else. The more Matthew was with Samantha, the more he liked her, no matter how hard he tried not to. Martin must have had something wrong with himself. Everything the man had ever said about Samantha was proven over and over again to be untrue. She was open and honest, always trying to be fair with everyone around her, even though it was *her life* in danger.

"Here," he said as he tossed the control to her. "You pick. I have some things to go over when I finish eating anyway." He watched the expression on her face change instantly.

"What things?" she asked as her eyes grew big with curiosity. "If I can ask, that is."

Matthew took a bite of a biscuit and washed it down with Coke before answering. "I got word that the sheriff's office called today with some results. They found the truck that was stolen from your yard and lifted some prints." He took a bite of his chicken and started chewing. "Mmm-mmm. Popeye's. They make the best chicken. Spicy . . . just right."

"Don't change the subject. So they found the truck?" All thoughts of food seemed to disappear as she pushed her food aside and rose from the bed. "Great! So now what?"

He hated seeing her get so excited. There was news, but no leads to the perp yet. "The prints matched the set they lifted from your apartment connecting the two crimes, just like I had thought all along. They are all one and the same: the attacker, the thief, the stalker, the psychopath killer we're trying to catch. We have probable cause to get a search warrant requesting fingerprints of the boat workers from the local shipyards, the two that are scheduled out Friday night. If they keep prints of their employees, maybe we'll get a name and a face so we can catch this guy. Apparently, he's not in the system. It doesn't mean he's never done anything wrong until now. It only means he's never been caught. But we will get him."

"Great," she said quietly, then dropped back down on the bed. The enthusiasm left her voice as color drained from her face, and her eyes glazed over.

Which was worse? Too much faith in believing everything was coming together, or finding out the police didn't seem to be any closer to catching the perpetrator? "Finish eating. We'll talk about it when we're through." Matthew watched her as she stared right through him. What was she thinking?

"He didn't look like a killer, you know," she mumbled. "I mean, the guy who had been at work the other night. I didn't really see him good, but you know what I mean. How could I have been so close and not known?"

"The majority don't look like killers," Marie said. "But who is to say what a killer looks like?"

Matthew frowned at Marie and then said to Samantha, "Eat. We'll talk later."

"I think I've lost my appetite."

They sat in silence as Matthew tried to eat his dinner. Marie finished her meal and threw away her empty box and cup. He noticed Samantha was true to her word, because she didn't eat another bite.

After he finished, he cleared his mess and set Sam's aside. She seemed to be in a trance.

"I'm going to shower." Marie disappeared

behind closed doors.

When Matthew finished washing his hands, he walked over to the side of Sam's bed and sat across from it on the other one. "Samantha," he spoke, his concern strong, "you've known all along they were one and the same — the truck thief, the burglar, and the killer. I've been telling you that from the beginning. Now we're getting closer to proving it. That's all. Nothing has changed, except we are getting closer."

She sighed but didn't say a word.

"You have to be brave a little while longer. Don't give up on me now. We're going to catch him. I promise."

Sam's bottom lip quivered as she ripped out his heart. *She is so strong . . . so warm . . . so loving.*

Her green eyes looked up at Matthew. "But what if you don't? I can't spend the rest of my life running. I have a son to raise. And I need to be with him." Tears rimmed her eyes. "I can't believe I didn't know. That man sat in the driver's room watching, waiting. Why didn't he do something to me then? He had opportunity. Why put me through torture now?"

Matthew shrugged. "I think that's all part of his game. Who knows? Or maybe there were too many people around?"

A single tear trickled down her cheek. Matthew did the only thing he could do. He wiped it away with his thumb, but then another followed. Feeling compelled, he moved to her bedside and pulled Samantha to his chest and wrapped his arms around her. Holding her tight while she cried, he said, "I'm glad he didn't, 'cause he could have killed you." Matthew ran his hands gently over her back, trying to comfort and reassure her. "We won't let him get you. I won't let him," he whispered. "I promise." He rocked side to side, holding her close.

Tears streamed down, soaking the front of his shirt.

"Now that the chief is finally in full co-operation with us, we should be able to close in on him quickly."

"The more I think about what this man has done, the more confused I am. If he knows where I live, why only tear my place apart?" Her voice choked back sobs as she questioned the man's motives.

He wished he knew. The man had plenty of opportunities to kill her; had he wanted to do so, she would be dead.

"Why didn't he wait for me to return and . . . kill me? Why?" Her breathing was jagged, her words broken. "Why?"

"He's a sick man who enjoys making you

afraid and delights in your fear." Tightening his embrace, Matthew wished he could console her, make her forget the killer was after her.

Samantha's body shook in his arms as her sobbing grew stronger.

"With the other women, our psychologist believed he was taking out his frustrations against his mother. But when I told the doc I suspected him of following you and making attempts on your life, she said that was a bad sign. Once a psychopath changes his normal routine of doing things, it only gets worse. I know you don't want to hear that, but the good thing about it is that's when they start making mistakes. And he's done that. And we will get him. I promise you that." Gently, he ran his hands down the softness of her hair. "I'm sure it gives him some sort of sick perverted pleasure, scaring you like he has."

She didn't say anything else. Samantha settled into a soft, steady cry, and Matthew didn't try to stop her.

Finally, her crying abated, and the short gasps of air softened to a steady rhythm. Matthew noticed the evenness of her breathing.

She puts on a good tough fight. But where does this woman get her strength? Her body has worn itself out. Maybe she'll rest well tonight. He continued to stroke her hair gently.

He wished she wasn't a target. He wished he wasn't committed to staying unattached. It would be easy to fall in love with Samantha, but he couldn't. Mostly for her sake. He had to be strong. He had to do what was right, what was best for Samantha and Marty.

When Marie came out of the bathroom dressed in sweats and her hair sticking out all over her head, Matthew looked up. "She got scared and started crying. First time," he whispered. "She cried herself to sleep."

"That's a good thing. I noticed she was always trying to be tough through this. Crying means she has truly accepted her situation. We'll get him, sir. I know that."

"You're right, Boudreaux. We will. Do me a favor, and pull back her covers," he said as he scooped Samantha up in his arms.

Marie pulled back the covers and fixed the pillow, then slipped out of the way.

He settled Samantha into the bed and pulled the spread over her. Before turning the light out, he glanced at Marie. She had her back to him, facing a mirror combing her hair. Quickly he bent down and gently

pressed his lips against Samantha's.
"Sweet dreams," he whispered.

CHAPTER 26

The next morning, the sun peeped through the curtains and woke Matthew. He had slept in the chair all night. Well not much, but some. He had dozed off about an hour before the sun rose. Since he had given the other bed to Marie, it didn't leave him much choice but to sit up all night. He had done it before and could do it again.

As he turned his attention toward Samantha, he found she was sitting up in bed. "How long have you been awake?"

"Not long," she said softly.

"Do you want some coffee now, or can you wait for breakfast?"

Marie started to stir as Samantha said, "I can wait."

Throwing back the covers, Marie climbed out of bed. Her sweats were crumpled, but she looked comfortable as she said, "Well, I can't. I have to have my morning coffee. I'll start the pot," she said as she marched over to the counter in the dressing area. There sat an empty coffee pot, unopened cups, and a pack of coffee grounds.

"Good. Make you some coffee. Samantha, maybe you could get dressed while I go take a quick shower."

"Matthew. I'm sorry about last night. I mean, the crying. I don't normally do that. Air my emotions like that."

Matthew noticed the smile that touched Marie's face before he turned back toward Samantha. "Don't worry. I think you needed it. I'll be ready in a few minutes."

When he returned to the room, Samantha was combing her hair as best she could and Marie sat in the chair he slept in the night before. "I'm almost ready," Samantha said.

"Where do you think you're going?" It wouldn't be safe for her to be running around the city this morning. He couldn't let her go. He wouldn't take that chance.

Samantha's eyes opened wide. "I'm not staying here. Besides, you were very careful, remember? No one followed us. And I'm hungry. You said breakfast, remember."

Matthew slipped on his shoulder holster, secured it, and then covered it with his lightweight sport coat. The look in her eyes betrayed her. She wasn't going to give up. He glanced at Marie for help in persuading

Samantha to stay put.

"Don't look at me. I'm hungry, too."

He sighed. "I guess we can go right across the street to McDonald's." As a warning, he added, "But we sit with our backs to the wall, as hidden away as possible. Do you have a pair of sunglasses, Samantha?"

Looking in her travel bag, she pulled out her purse, dug deep, and held up a pair of sunglasses. "No problem."

"She's a woman always prepared, boss." Marie winked at Sam.

"You sound like you feel better today." Her eyes looked a little puffy from the good cry she'd had last night, but he wouldn't mention that. Matthew watched as she slipped on the glasses and stared at her reflection in the mirror.

"I can still see your eyes. You have a pair she can wear, Marie?" As the woman shook her head, he said, "I guess those will do."

"Good. Then I'm ready, 'cause I'm hungry!"

"Me, too," Marie echoed as she headed for the door.

Matthew stepped behind Samantha. Their reflection in the mirror shone like a family snapshot. Their eyes met, and Matthew winked at her, "That's my girl." He liked her *nothing can get me* attitude. "Let's go

250

get something to eat," he said, grabbing his phone and sticking it in his pocket. Marie had opened the door and headed out and down the stairs. He stepped out the door and saw Marie scanning the area. He looked around for his own peace of mind, then let Samantha leave the room.

"Stick close to me." They walked around the backside of the motel and crossed the street to McDonald's. When their order was filled, they took the food to a corner table in the back where they would be unobserved. Marie and Matthew sat facing the room, and they had Samantha sit with her back to everyone. During breakfast, Matthew and Marie constantly looked around, making sure no one watched them, but they did it very nonchalantly.

"So what's on our agenda today?" Samantha asked between mouthfuls.

Matthew almost choked on his coffee. "Excuse me? Did you ask what *we* were doing today?"

"It's not like we're at your house where I can move around, work out, watch television. You know. Keep myself occupied. The motel room is small. Marie and I can't stay tucked up there all day. I'd rather be a sitting duck at home."

"You're not going to change my mind.

There is no 'we' today. 'We' aren't doing anything. I am. You two are going back to the room and wait." He took a bite of his eggs.

"I thought this was my case," Samantha said with a pouty expression.

He saw Marie hide her smile behind her coffee cup.

"I mean, I'm the prime target now. Even your chief admits it. And you're going to leave me and Marie in a room with no back exit? Doesn't sound like much safety in that. No offense, Marie, but I know I won't feel very safe. I know you know your job, but what if he comes through the front. While you're trying to stop him, I won't be able to run for my life. No back way out. What I am to do?" She shook her head and said, "Not safe at all."

She was trying to get his pity. That was a card she hadn't played before. In the time he had known her, she'd usually played that tough guy role.

He took another bite of his eggs, trying to ignore those eyes, that voice. He was not going to give in to her. Seeing this side of her almost made him laugh, and he would have, had it not been such a serious situation. Of course, that didn't stop Marie. She laughed out loud but tried to cover it with a cough.

Samantha leaned over the table, moving closer to him, practically putting her face up next to his. In a firm, hushed tone, she questioned, "Why can't I go with you? I don't want to stay in the small motel room. Please," she begged.

Matthew wiped his mouth with a napkin, took another swallow of coffee, then sat back against the booth. Looking at Samantha in all her innocence, he was so tempted to reach out, pull her into his arms, and protect her from the ugly world outside. But he had to resist.

He shook his head as he waved her back. "No. You almost got me," he said, pointing at her. Shaking his head, he said, "But no. Sorry. You can't go with me. Marie will be with you in the room, and I'll have a man right outside your room, only you won't be able to see him. He'll watch your room like a hawk. You'll be safe inside. I promise."

She stuck out her bottom lip, pouring on the pity-me picture.

"Don't think that's going to change my mind. Samantha, you can't go with me. Right now, you'd be safest if you stay put, out of harm's way."

Samantha took a deep breath, then said,

"Whatever you say." She turned her attention back to her breakfast.

That was too easy. Matthew didn't like that quick answer, nor the tone in which it was spoken. It probably meant he should handcuff her to the bed if he wanted her to stay in the room, but he couldn't do that, although the thought was very tempting. Marie would see to it she didn't leave the room. He could trust her to take good care of Samantha.

After breakfast, he saw them safely back to the room. Looking out the window for the officer assigned to protect Samantha, Matthew said, "I see him now. He's out in the parking lot dressed as a telephone repairman. It's Guidry," he said to Marie. "If you need him, just signal or call the station and they will send him in right away." Looking at Samantha, he added, "Just stay in and watch some soap operas or something. That shouldn't be too difficult."

Samantha rolled her eyes. "You don't know me at all."

Anger permeated her face, and Matthew knew she was agitated with him. He hated leaving her like this, but he had no choice. Quickly, he closed the door behind him.

In no time, Matthew was whipping in and out of traffic, making good time to the station. He knew the sooner he started talking to the boat hands, the faster he could get back to them.

Johnson met him at the interrogation room. "We narrowed it down to two boats and pulled in ten men who fit the description. Unfortunately, the ship had no prints of their deckhands. We're checking to see if the search warrant covers taking these guys' prints as we question them. In the meantime, the sketch eliminated four of them. There are still a couple of the men we couldn't find. Davis and a couple more of our men are out looking for those guys. Do you want to split this group of men in half for interrogation, or both of us cover one at a time?"

"Quicker if we split the job. Did you pull a rap sheet on any of them?"

Johnson nodded. "Two of the six had a record."

"Fine. You take those. I'll take the other four." Matthew saw Johnson's brow furrow, trying to understand his reasoning, but he knew better than to ask. Sam's assailant's prints were not on file, therefore, Matthew wanted the possible suspects with no prior record.

Matthew took one from his group at random and Johnson took one from his.

Each pair went into separate interrogation rooms.

The questions asked were basically the same, and their answers were being recorded. They asked each: "Where were you on the dates of the killings? Can that information be verified? What about family? Do you have any? And are they still living? Is there any special woman in your life?" And they watched each man's response.

By the time they finished questioning all of them, Matthew and Johnson met at Matthew's desk to go over the results. They each concluded that neither found a prime suspect, but to be safe, Matthew instructed a couple of uniforms to follow up on each person's alibi, making sure they could be verified. Besides, none of them had those dark eyes that Samantha described. Sure, they all had brown eyes, but not *dark*.

"We need to find those other two fast! I feel it in my gut, one of those guys is our man," Matthew snapped as he pushed his hands through his hair.

"We're working on it, sir." Looking wearily at Matthew, Johnson swiped his eyes. "I'm tired. Last night was a long one. It took several hours to find the ones we could find. The night ended pretty late." Glancing at his watch, he said, "Why don't you bring

Ms. Cain back with you this afternoon. We should have the others by then. That way, while we ask them questions, she could be looking them over and give a positive ID."

He didn't like the thought of Samantha coming down to the station where the killer could see her. He refused to take that chance. "She's hidden away for a reason," he snapped. Matthew's voice had a curt edge to it.

"Okay, okay! I just asked. I thought it would be a good idea. We'll find those two. We'll page you and meet you back here, okay?" Johnson said as he headed for the door.

"When we have the killer locked up, with no chance of seeing her, or following her, then and only then will I bring her in to identify him."

"Got it."

Matthew closed the folder on his desk as Johnson left the room. Nerves were on edge around here and Matthew knew it. Everybody was working nonstop to get this maniac before he struck again. Matthew stuck the file in his desk drawer and got up to leave.

A familiar voice said, "Well, where the heck have you been?"

His gaze jerked in the direction of the

voice. "Greg, you old son of gun." His father's old partner, Greg Singleton, came in and plopped down in the chair next to Matthew's desk. Matthew slapped him on the shoulder. "It's good to see you, old man. What are you doing here?"

"Give me some of that nasty coffee, and I'll tell you."

He poured Greg a cup of coffee, then sat back down in his chair. "So. What are you up to?"

Taking a sip, Greg said, "I stopped by your place yesterday. I let myself in the back door. Remember I still have the key your dad gave me? I waited over an hour. When you didn't show, I had to leave. I should have left you a note but didn't have time."

The rest of his words faded into the background as Matthew thought about what Greg had said. *So Greg was the reason for the scare. No one had broken in. Sam's safe there, and we can go back home. Great!*

"Did you hear what I said?"

"Yeah, something about the governor. What?"

Greg sat up in his chair. "I said I'm working for the governor's office now. They have me on the payroll. I guess you could say for security reasons. Kind of a cushy job if you ask me, but I don't mind. I'm almost sixty.

I need something easy." He laughed.

"That's great. Look, I don't mean to rush you, but I'm on a case right now that won't wait. Why don't you come by for dinner one night soon? I'll cook."

"I never turn down a free meal." Greg stood. "Do you still cook like you used to? Of course you do," he answered his own question. "I wouldn't miss it for the world." As he started to walk away, Greg turned back and asked one more question. "Is there a little woman in your life yet?"

Matthew raised his brow, giving Greg a stern look. "You know how I feel on that subject."

"Sure I know. But I thought by now you would have figured it out. Let's see, how does that old saying go? Oh yes. It is better to have loved and lost, than never to have loved at all. Look at me. I'm living proof. Me and your dad. He might have been unhappy after your mom died, but trust me, he was always happier than me. Katherine was the best thing that ever happened to him, and he wouldn't have changed a minute of his life with her. Except maybe he would have made it last longer if he could have. But like Tad always said, look what they made." Greg's eyes rested on Matthew. "He had you and his memories to keep him company. I never had anything."

"Now don't go get all teary-eyed on me. I haven't changed my views, and I don't plan to." Matthew paused, his gaze looking past his old friend and out the window. "If I did, though, I know who I'd grab up in a minute."

"I see the sparkle in your eyes just thinking about her. You better do it before it's too late! You might not have another chance. Look at me. Still alone at fifty-eight. What a life. It stinks." Greg slapped Matthew's shoulder. "Well, I'll let you go. Call me. And make it soon."

Matthew walked out with Greg because he wanted to get back to Samantha as quickly as he could. It was great seeing his dad's old partner, and now Matthew's friend. Maybe he should take heed to what Greg had said. No. He had seen the way his dad missed his mom. He didn't ever want to go through that pain and suffering himself.

When he parked in the motel parking lot, he checked with Guidry. Everything seemed fine so he relieved him of duty. Matthew ran up the stairs taking two at a time. He couldn't seem to stop his feet from flying. Where had this extra energy come from?

Was this what it felt like to come home to

the same woman every night? To come home to Sam every night?

All excited, maybe even feeling a thread of hope for the future, thinking of the possibilities, he swung open the door.

Matthew stopped dead in his tracks. "What do you think you're doing?"

CHAPTER 27

Startled from the sudden loud voice at the door, Sam looked up and glared at the man who filled the space. She turned her head away with a quick snap. *Do I explain or not?*

The bathroom door slammed open at the same time and Marie jumped out with her gun pulled and ready to fire. "Dang it, sir." She lowered her weapon. "Are you trying to get yourself killed?"

"At the tone, the time will. . . ." Sam let the words she heard fade into the background as she made her decision. She would teach him a thing or two . . . or at least give him something to overreact about. "I can't talk now, Amanda. I have to go. But I'll call you back soon."

Annoyance consumed her. What did he think she was? An idiot? Maybe this would teach him a lesson. She knew she was in hiding in this secluded motel room for a reason. Of course she wouldn't call someone and give away her location . . . if for no other reason than to keep from putting her friend in jeopardy.

Slamming down the phone, she jumped to her feet and turned, jammed her hands on her hips, and faced Matthew. "How dare you talk to me like that! Who do you think you are?" Sam glared at Matthew in defiance.

"Detective, don't —" Marie started to call out but Sam interrupted her.

Sam held her hand up toward Marie and mouthed, "Don't." She hoped the woman could see what she was trying to say without having to say it. *Don't protect me. I know you know, but he should have had sense enough to know I wouldn't do such a stupid thing. Let me handle it my way.* That was what she wanted to say and hoped her eyes said it all. Marie shut her mouth and slipped her gun back in the holster. Shaking her head, the woman went back into the bathroom and closed the door behind her. Probably to handle the matter she went in to handle to begin with . . . before Matthew pitched a fit.

Without a word, he shut the door to the motel room. "I shouldn't have yelled, but you don't seem to understand how dangerous it is to let anyone know where you are.

Please, sit down."

"I will not," she snapped, still irked by his attitude.

Matthew closed the distance between them, holding her gaze like a magnet. His eyes held a glint of an indefinable emotion. Was it concern? Compassion? She wasn't sure, but one thing she was sure of, he was too close. So close, she had to sit just to give herself room to breathe.

"You do realize you're in protective custody for your safety? What if he had tapped your girlfriend's line? He could be on his way here right now." He quirked his brow. "That *was* your friend, Amanda, right?"

She practically bit a hole in her bottom lip, trying to keep quiet, not wanting to out and out lie.

"He could be on his way here right now! Lucky for us, we can get out of here. Get your things together. We'll finish this discussion in the car. Hurry up, Marie. We're going."

Matthew turned and left the room again. Sam assumed he was going downstairs to check them out of the motel, just as he assumed she would do as she was told. "Men!"

The bathroom door opened and Marie

stepped out. While drying her hands, she said, "He's just thinking of you, Sam. He's trying to protect you and at the same time catch a killer, in addition to the other cases he is working on. The man has a lot to think about. Just remember that when you try to understand him."

That took some of the steam out of Sam's sail, but not all of it. In a huff, she tossed her things in her little black bag. She wanted out of there as much as he did, so of course she did as she was told. And Marie's words did help her to understand him a bit more, but she wished he would have trusted her and known she had the smarts not to do something so stupid.

"Good girl," he said when he returned, then grabbed the few items he had unpacked and threw them in his bag. "I'll get these down to the car. You two double-check that we aren't leaving anything and come straight down," he commanded as he zipped his bag closed, grabbed hers, and headed out the door.

He was always giving orders. Sam wanted to scream. Instead, she stepped over to the door and slammed it behind him. "I wish your head had been in it!" she said in irritation at the closed door.

"Feel better?" Marie asked as a smile

spread across her face. "He always gives orders. He's used to that. He has men working for him all the time. Don't take it personally."

"Humph. I admit, that felt good." A small smile played at her lips also. "To have been such a sweet, wonderful man last night, he sure is a demanding ogre today."

"Just remember. He's doing his job."

Yes. He's doing his job, and I'm work to him. No more. No less. Running her fingers through her hair, she said, "Well, if we want out of here, we better start searching."

Finding nothing left behind, they ran down to the car. Matthew had the motor running, yet stood outside the car with the passenger door open, waiting while keeping a sharp eye out. Sam got in as Marie climbed in her car.

Sam said nothing to the detective, although she was curious where they were headed now as she climbed in and he closed the door behind her. Something changed his mind about having to stay hidden. But she wouldn't dare ask. He would have to volunteer the information.

Maybe they were going back to his house. That would be wonderful. She didn't know what changed his mind and his attitude, but she was very grateful. Another hour in that room, and she would have gone stark raving mad.

Minutes later and miles down the road, Matthew broke the silence. "For the record, my house wasn't broken into by the killer. It was an old friend of my father's. The one I told you about yesterday. Greg. He has a key and used it but forgot to leave a note."

Inside she smiled at that, excited to know his house was a safe hideaway again. She loved his place, warm and welcoming, but didn't dare let him know how happy it made her. She hoped as far as he was concerned, he believed she was still agitated. She planned to keep up the silent treatment.

Out of the corner of her eye, she saw Matthew glance her way, so she quickly averted her eyes.

"Do you want to know what we did today on the case? We made some headway."

Of course she wanted to know, but she couldn't tell him that and keep quiet at the same time. Finally, acting as if it didn't matter one way or the other, as they pulled to a stop at a red light she said, "If you want to tell me."

When he didn't respond, she turned her head to look at him. His gaze was locked on her. Obviously, her eyes betrayed her. He apparently saw the excitement there, because she saw his smug expression. Shrugging off his self-satisfied attitude, she thought, *Big deal. So he knows me better than I thought.*

"Okay. Okay. I want to know. Tell me," she said, giving in to his victory. "What did you find out? Are you close to catching him? What?"

"I knew you'd break. I'm a cop. I know these things."

"Ha, ha, funny," she said, sarcasm dripping from her voice. She hated that smirk on his face, but she had to know now. "Okay. Okay. So you win. What? Tell me." She punched him lightly in the arm.

His lips turned up in a half grin as pure delight penetrated his eyes and he wiggled his brows. "One of my informants tracked down some information, so now we know the killer works on a boat that's pulling out midnight Friday night. We ran a check and found two boats scheduled to leave at that time."

"How do you know your information is correct?"

He huffed. "We don't. But we have to use whatever we get and try to go from there. Anyway, we pulled in a few men from the crew that fit the description you gave and came close to the drawing the sketch artist made. We managed to question them. Unfortunately, none of those were him, but we still have a couple more to locate. When we do, we should have our man."

Matthew sounded very confident, which gave her an idea. She touched Matthew's shoulder lightly and said, "Why don't you bring me in and let me look through one of those hidden windows, or whatever, to see if I can spot him?"

"No!" he barked.

She jerked her hand back at his gruff reply. "Why not?" she asked, confused. "I thought you wanted to catch him?"

"I do." Matthew slowed the car down as he turned onto his street. Curving around the lake, he pulled into the driveway. "But it would be too dangerous for you. After we get him and arrest him, then we'll have you look at him. But not until then."

Sam sat back on the seat and looked out the side window. Sometimes she didn't understand him. It seemed to her that if she could point him out of the few left to interrogate, it would help. She closed her eyes as she tried to let Matthew's response sink into her thoughts and maybe make some sense.

None of it made sense. "Matthew, why won't you let me come in? Sure, it might be dangerous, but wouldn't it help you get the killer faster? The sooner the better. I'm in danger until you get him. Didn't you just say a minute ago you would do whatever it took? I'm willing to take that chance. Do my part."

In a very quiet voice Matthew said again, "No."

"But —"

"Samantha," he said her name in a whisper, interrupting her question. Matthew pulled the car around to the garage and put it in park. Turning in his seat, he faced Sam.

The solemn look on his face softened Sam's heart along with the way he called her name. Although she wanted to, she couldn't feel anger as she waited for his next words.

"I can't let you go down to the station and put your life in jeopardy. I. Me. Matthew Todd Jefferies . . . the man, not the cop."

He reached out and cupped her face. Wetting his lips, he added, "I have to do this without putting your life in more danger than it already is. Can you understand that?" His thumb caressed her cheek.

Sam's heart pounded like a big bass drum. She thought it would beat right out of her chest. At least now she knew he wasn't just using her to catch his man. If he had been, he would let her walk into the station and try to pick him out of a lineup.

"Do you understand?" he whispered as his fingers stroked the side of her face.

Leaning into his hand, she closed her eyes and let the pleasure devour her. Her heart raced as breathing became hard to do. "I'm not sure, but it sounds like you care what happens to me."

"I told you, you were a smart girl." Matthew reached his other arm out to her and drew her to him. Sam fell into his embrace. His lips found hers with no problem; like a magnet they drew together.

The warmth of his mouth covered hers. Her hands found refuge in the softness of his wavy hair.

Down deep she wanted to hear him say he wouldn't, couldn't put her life in danger because he loved her, the magic words that would make everything all right, the words her own heart had been working up to. Yes, she admitted to herself, she had fallen in love with this man.

The pressure of his hands on her back shot pleasure through her. He pulled her closer to him. One more inch was all that separated her from being totally in his lap.

The horn blasted, shattering the silence around them and scaring Samantha out of her mind. They both jumped.

Sam quickly pulled back to her side of the car. Her heart beat triple time. Heavy breathing was still coming, and she couldn't slow it down. Her eyes flashed on Matthew. What were they doing? Acting like schoolkids. At that same moment, Marie's car pulled in beside his.

It took Matthew almost as long as it did Sam to regain composure. "Let's get inside. We shouldn't be out here like this anyway."

Of course, always the cop thinking about correct procedure. You don't make out with a possible witness in your car. She wanted to laugh, but it wasn't funny. So much for the magic words she wanted to hear.

As they got out of the car, Matthew grabbed their bags and brought them in with him. She and Marie followed him inside. In the kitchen, she watched him place the bags on the counter. She knew what was next. He would tell her to go to her room. Rest, relax, she needed it; after which, he would add an apology, swearing it would never happen again. He had made a mistake.

She stood, head held high, feet apart, ready for Matthew's onslaught of words.

"Samantha." His tone was as soft as it had been in the car. Holding up his hand, as if to say wait a minute, he then turned his eyes on Marie. "Can you give us a minute here?"

Marie's eyes widened as she glanced back and forth. Sam was sure the woman didn't know what to do. It looked like part of her wanted to stay and defend what Sam had not done but been accused of, but part of her didn't want to disobey her immediate boss. She shrugged as she looked at Sam one more time and then said to the detective, "No problem, boss." And with that, she left the room.

Surprised at him asking Marie to leave them alone, Sam just stared at him. Maybe she wasn't ready for what he had to say. She trembled.

Matthew sighed. "I'm not doing the proper thing. I know you should go down to the station, point him out, make a positive ID, but I can't let you."

She held her breath, waiting. Still, the promise to keep his distance was coming . . . that was his way.

Instead, Matthew closed the space between them, wrapped his arms around her, and pulled her head to his chest, holding her lovingly in his arms. "I can't let you do it, because if something happened to you, I would never know what love was." He kissed the top of her head. "I think I'm falling in love with you. The thing is, I don't want to fall in love with you, but it seems I'm not the one in control. And now I can't take a chance of losing you. Can you understand?" His brow furrowed as he asked her that.

Sam pulled her head away from his chest but stayed wrapped in his arms. The magic words had been spoken. He was falling in love with her. She was at a loss for words herself. Swallowing hard, she moistened her own lips. "You sure know how to sweep a girl off her feet."

CHAPTER 28

His lips came down on hers and he kissed her soundly.

"Don't wake me if I'm dreaming," she whispered.

"Trust me, you're not dreaming. Unfortunately, the ugliness of the mess we are in is all around us. It will catch up to us soon, but in the meantime we will deal with it . . . together."

Sam gently caressed the side of Matthew's face. "I don't know what happened to you today, but it's wonderful. Don't change."

His lips came down on hers again, this time in a long, sensuous kiss. This man thought he was falling in love with her, and she knew she loved him. Could it get any better than this? Her hands wrapped around his neck, pulling him closer.

When they pulled slightly apart, he looked into her eyes as his hands moved slowly down her back in slow circular movements.

"Samantha Cain, you just don't know what you do to me."

Sam kissed his mouth and then buried her head in his chest as he continued to hold her close. She sighed. They stayed locked in an embrace for a long, long time.

Finally, Matthew hugged her one more time and kissed the top of her head. "As much as I'd love to stay like this forever, we need to put some space between us so I can get my mind back on work. As you can see, once I start thinking about you, I can't seem to stop."

"I haven't noticed, but I'll keep my eyes open." She winked. "I don't know about you, but I'm hungry."

He pecked her on the lips. "That's not a bad idea. You set the table, and I'll whip us up something after I toss our bags in our rooms. And I'll let Marie know it's safe to come back in here. I just didn't want to share my feeling for you for the first time in front of someone else."

This was a new side to Matthew, one she loved even more. He dropped all of his barriers. Would it last? She hoped so. She hoped they weren't rushing things, and she prayed they were thinking with their heads as well as their hearts.

He returned within seconds and started

pulling things out of the refrigerator and cupboard. "Marie is on the phone in the office. She'll join us shortly she said."

"What are you making us?" she asked.

"Ham and cheese omelets. Do you like omelets?"

Yielding to temptation, Sam walked up behind him and wrapped her arms around his waist. "He cooks. He cleans. I think I've found me the perfect *little woman.*" She chuckled. "Thank You, Lord." Leaning her face into his back, she placed a light kiss between his shoulder blades. He laughed as his masculine scent teased her nerve endings. She then released him so she could do her share. She pulled plates down from the cupboard and silverware from the drawer, then quickly set the table as he placed a plate of bacon in the microwave and pressed a couple of buttons, then pushed down a couple slices of bread in the toaster.

"I didn't know love could be so wonderful. Here I've been fighting it all my life. Was I crazy or what?" Matthew said as his blue eyes caressed her lovingly. When the bread popped up, he put two more in and slapped some butter on the toasted ones.

"No way. You were just waiting for me and don't you forget it. You can't just fall in love with anyone. Only that certain someone.

And I'll tell you now. I'm it. I hope you believe in God. I know He's been there for me these last few years. And I know He brought us together." As she rambled on and on. she realized he hadn't said he loved her. At least not, "I love you" specifically. He had said he thought he was falling in love, and then just now said love was wonderful. But that was pretty darn close, and enough for her at the moment. She blew him a kiss, then grabbed two glasses. "Milk or orange juice?"

"Juice. I've never really thought about it before. I know about God, because of my father. He made sure he continued to take me to church after Mom was killed. But eventually his job got in the way. I'd like to know more. Sometimes with the job, it's hard to believe there is a God."

"Don't worry. There is, and I will share Him, the Gospel, with you so you can have your own relationship with Him. You'll be even happier then." This told her Matthew needed to know and accept the Lord for salvation. This was evidently one of the reasons they were brought together, so she would make it a priority to share the Gospel with him. "One thing I'll say right now is, to have a good relationship as a couple, God has to be in the middle of it. For Marty's sake, as well as mine and yours, I will definitely tell you all about Him and salvation." As she poured them each a glass, she remembered just a short time ago they were fighting because he thought she had put their hiding place in jeopardy. And now she was witnessing to him. Sam needed to tell him the truth. "I have a confession to make."

He turned and looked at her. "Oh no. The look on your face tells me I'm not going to like this."

She shrugged. "Yes, you will. Earlier, when I was on the phone and you walked into the motel room, I was checking the time because I was worried about you. Marie suggested I call time."

"So she knew? Why didn't she tell me even though you wouldn't?"

"Because I asked her not to. She started to, but I shook my head no, and she understood what I was saying. I guess you could say it was a woman thing."

He smiled. "Good confession. I'm glad. I thought you were smart enough to know not to call your friend."

"You should have trusted your instincts about me. Because it didn't sound like it when you came in the room."

"I panicked." He pulled a chair out from the table. "Sit. Let's eat." Grabbing the pan off the stove, he stepped back to the table, cut the omelet in thirds, and scooped out part on her and Marie's plates, and then the rest on his and placed the pan back on the stovetop. "Marie," he called, "come and get it before it gets cold."

Sam sniffed the aroma. "Smells wonderful. There is one more thing. I would like to set straight with you about what really happened three years ago."

Pulling the bacon out of the microwave and placing the strips on a plate, he then put it on the table. "I've learned in these few short days that your husband told many lies. I don't have to know everything, but it would probably be for the best if you told me what went down on the last day." He grabbed the saucer with the stack of buttered toast and added it to the table.

Lifting her hand to her bangs, she brushed them aside. She had quit wearing a bandage when she showered at the inn, never replacing the old. "Do you see this?" she asked as she revealed her old scar.

He stood fast, staring. He frowned. "Martin did that?"

"Martin did that to me the night he shot himself. For some time he had been accusing me of infidelity and some other morbid things, but that night he'd lost all control.

When I came home, he was waiting for me. He was drunk. After shouting accusations at me, he grabbed me by the back of my neck and dragged me over to the mirror. Yelling —" Her voice cracked. She swallowed hard. She hadn't realized how painful it would be to tell the story, a story she had kept secret for so long.

Matthew touched his lips to her scar and whispered, "It's okay. You don't have to say another word."

She shook her head. "No. I have to finish. For my own sake, if not for yours." Sam continued the story. "Martin yelled at me to look at the tramp in the mirror, slamming my face against it over and over. The mirror shattered, but he kept slamming me against it. Finally, I blacked out. When I came to, he was gone. Blood was everywhere. I was weak, but I knew I had to get to the hospital. By the time I was stitched up and released, I drove myself home. Martin's mother was waiting for me. She told me Martin had called and told her he couldn't put me through what his father had put her through, and she rushed right over. The front door was unlocked, so she had let herself in. She saw the blood and broken mirror but didn't know what to think.

"Together we went out to the garage and

found him. He had told her earlier, he couldn't be like his dad. That was why he took his life that night. She swore me to secrecy, because neither Martin nor his mother wanted to tarnish the image everyone had of his father or his grand-father. I didn't like it, but I did it out of the love I once felt for Martin, the Martin I had known in the beginning. Plus Marty. He didn't need to think ill of his father. We had managed to keep it from him so far. One day, maybe, I'll tell him the truth."

"Oh, baby. I'm so sorry. The department treated you unfairly. Everyone assumed you had pushed Martin to his death, but in the end he did what he did out of the love he felt for you. In a sick, twisted way, he saved your life." Matthew pulled her up into his embrace and held her close.

They stayed that way for a few minutes, and then she kissed his cheek. "Enough pity. I'm just glad it's over, and you know the whole story. Let's never talk about it again."

"That's all right with me."

Slipping out of his embrace, she sat back down. "Let's eat. Soup's getting cold." She smiled.

"We had that —" Matthew cocked his head slightly, interrupting his own words with silence, and looked questioningly at the ceiling. "Was that yesterday? No the day before. Today it seems like we've been together forever. Doesn't it?"

"With many more to come." Sam sniffed the food in front of her again. "Maybe," she added. "Do I smell onions?"

He pulled a face. "You don't like onions?" He clicked his tongue behind his teeth three times. "That will never do. I put onions in practically everything I cook." He shrugged. "Oh well, I guess that means you get to do the cooking after all."

"Not on your life. I'll learn to love them." She took a big bite. As she started chewing she said, "Mmm. This is wonderful. Onions and all!"

Matthew smiled as he took his first bite. "It doesn't take much to make you happy, does it?"

"It takes one big cop, with dark wavy hair, steel-blue eyes, and a warm heart." Sam never believed she would fall in love again. "Do you know anyone who fits that description?"

Matthew smiled. "It better be me," he said, and they both laughed.

Marie walked in. "Am I too late? Smells good, and I'm starved. Glad to see you two made up. You don't know how much pressure you put on me when the two of you aren't getting along."

"I think we'll all do fine. Thanks for your understanding," Matthew said. "Help yourself to juice or milk. Your choice."

"What understanding? I just like everyone getting along," she said as she poured a glass of milk. "Keeps the stress level down and makes it easier for me to do my job." She smiled at Samantha. "You know what I mean?"

The three of them finished the meal with very little conversation. The food took their complete attention. Everyone seemed to have worked up a big appetite.

As he took his last bite, he glanced at his watch. "I've got some more work to do." He stood up and started cleaning up the dishes.

"I'll get that. Don't you worry. I do know my way around in the kitchen, I promise," Sam said, then added, "Just not much as a chef."

"I'll help her, unless you need me to do something, too, boss."

"Great. You help her. I have to go to the station for what I need to do. I hate to eat and run, but I have to. It's almost two." Matthew made his apologies as he stood to leave.

Sam followed him to the back door and walked outside with him. "Hey. Can I have just one kiss before you go, to prove to me I'm not dreaming." Sam met him halfway. One long, wonderful kiss and he was gone. Going back inside, she locked the door.

Walking on air, she helped clean the kitchen.

"I can see you two have come a long way," Marie said. "I've never seen the detective so happy. Glad y'all worked things out."

"Me, too. I didn't think I would ever find love again. But I was content, because I had my son and he means the world to me. When we finish here, I'm going to go for a workout. Want to join me?"

"Of course. That's what I'm here for. To stay by your side and keep you safe. Besides which, my passion, when not being a cop, is to work out. I want to stay in top shape. When you started talking about men and how they treat you in the workplace, I understood. Been there . . . done that, as they say."

"I figured as much. I'm going to go slip on those gym shorts and a T-shirt, and I'll meet you in the back room.

She made another stop in the bathroom. In the mirror, even with the bruises, her face seemed to glow. "I am in love," she told her reflection. After brushing her teeth, she continued to her original destination.

In the weight room, she adjusted the weights on the machine and did a few warm-up exercises. Marie was already running a steady pace on the treadmill. Sam started a slow workout. She did steady reps working out her arms and upper torso and then reps that worked the lower portion of her body. Half an hour of the weight machine was enough for her. She grabbed the jump rope that hung on the wall and started jumping. Fifteen minutes later, she moaned, "Enough." Returning the rope to its rightful place, she did cool-down exercises.

"Do you only do the treadmill?" Sam asked Marie. "I've never seen anyone run steady for almost an hour."

"It's endurance. I have to keep my endurance up. You never know when you'll have to be on a foot chase. I don't want to be the one to lose my perp because I lost my energy." Marie laughed as she continued to run steady.

When finished with the cool-down exercises, she dragged herself from the room. "I'm going to shower."

"I'll be right outside your room. No problem." Marie stopped the treadmill and followed Sam out of the room.

Sam strolled to the bathroom and stripped

for a shower. The water streamed over her body pounding, massaging all the right places. Sam let the water do its magic, then washed and rinsed from head to toe, keeping a washcloth over her stitches. After drying, she wrapped the towel around her and went to her room.

Opening the bedroom door to the hall, she saw Marie sitting outside just as she said she would be. "I'm going to lie down and take a nap . . . I think. I know I'm going to lie down anyway."

"That's probably a good idea. You get some rest. I'll be out here."

Closing the door again, she slipped on a pair of shorts and T-shirt and then lay across the bed, listening for Matthew's return. As she waited, her thoughts recalled his kisses. She closed her eyes, reveling in the afterglow. Before she knew it, she fell asleep, taking that much-needed nap so her body could continue to heal.

CHAPTER 29

"Where is the other one?" The cops finished interrogating the man they had found, which told Matthew what he already knew. "It must be him."

"I have to agree," Johnson said. "We couldn't find him, though. We searched everywhere."

"We've got the bar staked out. And the patrol car is keeping an eye out at the motels downtown near the river," Davis added.

Before Matthew could respond, his phone rang. "Jefferies," he said into the receiver.

"This is Officer Holmes, from the Cincinnati Police Department. We received an inquiry on a set of prints you are looking for an ID. We've got it. Eighteen years ago, we arrested a sixteen-year-old for the death of his mother. He was tried as an adult and convicted, sentenced ten years to life at a state penitentiary for the criminally insane."

"Is he still in prison? What's the story?"

"Six years ago he was released after serving his ten years. He'd also been pronounced cured at the time of his release. It was a long, sad story with a lot of years of sexual abuse. The doctors found out his mother had sexually abused him, and when the kid finally thought he was old enough or man enough to put a stop to her, he refused to play any more of her sex games. If we'd had the technology then that we have today, he probably would have gotten better help and truly recovered. But you apparently can connect him with a crime down in Louisiana."

"Yes. We have three dead women we believe we can connect him to."

"That's too bad. He was one sick kid, but it was hard to blame him after what the doctors had found."

"What do you mean?" Matthew questioned.

"In the beginning, his mother would leave him locked in a room when she left to go to work at night. Sometimes he'd slip out and wander the streets. As he grew older and she took notice of his body maturing, she found pleasures with him, and instead of locking him up before leaving, she would tie him up, leaving just enough slack for him to stand up and use the pot she left for him to relieve himself in. She told him it was for his own protection. And for years he believed it. But, like I said, he grew up. As he grew, he wised up. That's when he strangled her to death."

Matthew interrupted, "Those three women we believe he has killed are all middle-aged women. Maybe he thinks they are his mom, and he's killing her over and over. Did she work nights at a diner?" Matthew asked.

"As a matter of fact, yes."

"He sexually abused the first two after they died. He would have done it to the third one, but a witness stopped him. Our psychologist ascertained he was rebelling against something in his early life and determined it was probably a form of abuse by his mother. She was right. It's sad what he went through, but it doesn't give him the right to do what he's done. We have to catch him and lock him up. For good this time. What's his name?"

"Robert Thomas Howard."

"Thanks for the information. Please fax me a copy of the complete report along with the most current picture you have, if you don't mind." Matthew gave him the fax number, then hung up the phone.

"We've got him now. Check the lists. See

if there is a Robert Howard or a Thomas Howard. Or anything similar."

Johnson's face lit up. "Lieutenant. It's Bobby Howard. And that's the one we are looking for now."

Pounding the desk with his fist, Matthew shouted, "We got him. Now all we have to do is find him."

"Don't worry. We will."

Matthew wished he could stop worrying. Instead, he would only worry more. Samantha was the woman he loved. Everything Martin had said about her had been a lie. Now that he found her, he couldn't lose her. He wasn't his father. He couldn't make it through life without her. Of that he was certain. She was a breath of fresh air in his once very drab life.

He was robbed of ever knowing a mother's love. He didn't want to be robbed of ever knowing a wife's love. *Yes. When this is all over, I'm going to ask her to marry me. I'm not afraid anymore . . . of love, of her, or of a commitment.*

"Sir, did you say something?" Johnson asked.

A smile forced its way to Matthew's lips. He didn't think he had said anything aloud, but who knows? Buck Johnson must think Matthew was going over the edge. "You get the APB out?"

Johnson nodded.

"Then go home and get a good night's sleep, Johnson."

"Yes, sir."

After Johnson left, Matthew, overwhelmed with a feeling of elation and hope for the future, picked up the phone and called Greg. After inviting him for a spur-of-the-moment dinner, he said, "Yes. Tonight. I know it's last-minute. Can you make it or not? I have a surprise for you."

"How can I say no to that? Of course, I'll be there. Seven okay?"

They agreed on the time. Matthew made a few more calls to the right people, picked up the fax on the Howard case along with the picture, set proper wheels in motion, then called it a day. On the way home, he stopped and picked up a few ingredients to a special recipe he planned to cook that night. All the way home, he was very careful not to be followed. Nothing was going to ruin their future together.

"Samantha, I'm home," he called when he entered the kitchen. "Marie, where are you?" Neither answered him, and he heard no television or anything. *Déjà vu.* This time he wasn't going to panic and think the worst. They were probably in the back room again, working out.

Samantha missed her routine. He hoped she got back to it soon, only doing it from his house instead of hers. He hoped she and Marty both would feel at home in his house. *A complete family.* He couldn't hold back the grin that covered his face as he worked his way through the house. He was actually thinking about marriage. This was definitely new to Matthew.

As he stepped into the living room, Marie entered from the hallway. "She's in her room, boss. I didn't want to holler out loud and wake her. But she's fine . . . taking a nap. Since you're here now, I'm going to go shower, if that's all right with you. We worked out after you left, and I'm really in need of soap, if you know what I mean."

He laughed. "By all means. Go take your shower. We're having company tonight for dinner. I think you'll enjoy him. A retired cop."

"Great," she said as she headed to her room.

He made his way to Sam's bedroom and knocked lightly. When she didn't answer, he opened the door and peeked inside. He smiled. "Asleep again." She had found peace in his home with all the turmoil that was going on around her. He was so glad.

The last rays from the sun filtered through the blinds and shone directly on her sleeping torso.

Matthew leaned over the bed, dropping tiny kisses on her face as he whispered, "Samantha, wake up. I'm home." He kissed her again and again.

Her lips puckered toward the kisses until her eyes popped open. "What a way to wake up. You have my permission to do this anytime."

Running his fingers through her long brown hair, he nuzzled in the softness. "Woman, you drive me crazy. How can you sleep when the sun is still shinning?"

"Mmm, that feels good." She turned her head, giving him easier access to her neck. "All I can say is, I never used to take naps in the late afternoon. But sleeping while the sun is shining is not a problem. Remember, I work nights."

He nibbled at her earlobe. "Wake up now. I have a surprise for you. Someone's coming over for dinner."

Pulling out of his embrace, she sat up quickly. "And you want me to whip something up? You must be out of your ever-loving mind. I'm going back to sleep. I wasn't joking when I said I didn't cook very well."

Matthew started laughing. Not a small laugh, but a huge, robust laugh. "You're wonderful."

"Even if that's so, I still won't cook your dinner. Sorry," she pouted as she placed her hands on her hips.

"Come here," he said in a low growl. Pulling her to her feet and close to him, he lowered his head as his lips claimed hers. After one long hard kiss, he eased away. "Mmm, nice. *I'm* doing the cooking. Do you remember asking me what happened to make me change earlier and admit my feelings for you?"

"I remember everything about today. Why?"

"Because you're going to meet the reason tonight."

She looked suspiciously at him. "A person changed your mind about how you feel about me?"

"No, silly. My mind didn't have to be changed about how I feel for you. I think I've loved you since the first time I laid eyes on you. Well, second time actually. It just took me awhile to understand it and believe in it. Anyway, my father's old partner and best friend made me realize how I didn't want to chance losing you without ever loving you. He made me open my eyes and my heart."

Sam murmured as she snuggled close, "Thank you, Daddy Jefferies' friend." Raising her face, she pressed her lips to his.

CHAPTER 30

Later, in the kitchen, Matthew took items out of the grocery bag, pulled some things from the refrigerator, grabbed a couple of pots and pans, and got busy doing what he did well. Sam and Marie busied themselves setting the table.

"When we finish here, I'll help you with the cooking. I don't mind helping," she added, remembering the hard time she had given him when he first mentioned the meal. Changing the subject as quickly as she brought it up, she said, "I can't wait for you to get to know Marty better. He hasn't had a man, other than his grandpa, around him in a long time. You will be a very good influence on my son's life."

"You might end up with another cop in the family if you're not careful," Marie said jokingly. "Of course, you can't ask for a better teacher than Detective Matthew Jefferies."

He stopped dicing onions. His eyes sent a warm, loving look in Sam's direction. "I know she's joking with you, but seriously, I can't wait to get to know him better. You've raised a wonderful son. He's a smart boy."

"Thank you. What's the matter? You look a little . . . I don't know, worried maybe?"

He sighed. "I think I'd better remind you what you're letting yourself and Marty in for. It's only fair. Who knows? You might decide it would be best not to get involved with me, with my life."

"My father was a policeman and I turned out fine," Marie said. "In fact, my dad knew your dad. And I have two brothers on the force. My baby brother works for the FBI. I don't think that's too bad coming from a cop's family. So don't put it down, sir."

"Don't get me wrong. I'm not. I love what I do, and I love that my father before me did it, too. I'm proud to be the son of a policeman. But I also know the danger the family can be placed in, and I wanted Samantha to think it over before it was too late."

It was already too late. He was in her heart, and she couldn't just rip him out. A tiny knot caught in her throat. Sounded like he was having second thoughts though, and that frightened her a little.

"Don't look like that. It's you I'm thinking of right now. I know I love you and want
to be with you and Marty, but it won't be
as easy as it sounds. Cops lead horrible
lives. We're practically on call twenty-four
hours a day. Sure, we have set times to go
into work and times to head home, but the
case doesn't always allow us to stay on
schedule. It means phone calls in the middle
of the night and me rushing out at odd
hours, not able to explain a thing to you."

Sam moved closer to him as she watched
his blue eyes soften. "I'm sure I'd get used
to it . . . if you're sure you are not having
second thoughts about me."

"Unfortunately, the job is dangerous. He's
right there," Marie said.

"Not only dangerous for me, but for you
and Marty as well. Your lives could be put
in danger. Those nuts out there, you never
know what they plan to do next. They
wouldn't mind using you to make me play
it their way . . . that's what they did with
my mom. That's why I've always avoided
getting close to anyone."

Sam reached up and gently touched the
side of his face. "So what exactly changed
your mind? I know Greg, your dad's
partner, but what did he say that changed
your mind so completely?"

Matthew stopped stirring the pot for a minute and focused his full attention on Sam. Bending slightly, he kissed the tip of her nose, then brushed it slightly with his. "Greg let me know that even though my father suffered a lonely life, in the end, he always had his memories of Mom to keep him warm. Greg said the only thing that has kept him warm at night was a blanket and maybe a bottle of whiskey. Not much comfort in that."

Sam wrapped her arms around his waist and whispered, "Greg sounds like a smart man. I can't wait to meet him."

"We best all stop talking, or I'll never get the meal cooked. And to respond to your earlier offer, thanks, but no thanks. You two would probably help me most if you'd leave the kitchen. Not that I don't want you around. You either, Marie. I'm kind of getting used to having two women underfoot. But I think more clearly when Samantha is not around to distract me."

"We'll go in the other room, but when you get it going, I'll come in and sit with you while it cooks if you'd like."

"Deal. Or I'll come join you two in the living room."

Flipping channels from one to the other, she realized she was as bad as Matthew.

"Anything special you'd like to watch?"

"Not really. I don't usually watch much television."

Finally, Sam stopped on a movie. A great detective show. Her kind of film. They watched the movie in silence. After getting halfway through the flick, she heard her name being called from the other room. She liked the feeling of being loved and feeling at peace with the world. Even though danger awaited her out there in the dark of night, she knew she was safe with Matthew. "Thank You, Lord, for bringing him into my life," she whispered as she let out a sigh of contentment.

By the time the dinner was almost finished cooking, Matthew had joined them in the living room. He got Marie to sit in his chair and he sat by Sam. The doorbell rang a short time later. Matthew rose and answered the door. Sam stood slightly behind him, and Marie stayed seated.

"And this must be that special woman that makes your eyes dance with delight," Greg said as he walked into the house.

Sam felt her cheeks go warm as she thought about making Matthew's eyes do anything. His eyes made her do everything. Sam reached her hand out to shake Greg's as they were introduced. "It's a pleasure —"

"You don't get off that easy," the older gentleman said as he swooped her up in a big bear hug. "I'm family."

The three laughed as they walked back into the living room. Marie rose from her seat. "I'm not," she said as she stuck out her hand. "I'm Marie Boudreaux. It's a pleasure to meet you. I've heard some stories about you and Jefferies . . . ugh, the older Jefferies I mean, from my dad. Mark Boudreaux. Captain Mark Boudreaux."

Greg laughed some more. "So he's Captain now. I can only imagine the stories you've heard."

"Marie is here on special assignment helping me keep Samantha safe. It's a long story and we've got all night. Let's go in the kitchen and sit at the table so we can really talk."

"Something smells wonderful. Matthew, my boy, did you cook this, or did you?" he asked Samantha.

Sam had to laugh to herself but didn't bother to share the joke with Greg. He must know Matthew loves to cook. Matthew was a gift sent from God. She never was much good with the stove. She could nuke with the best of them, reheating leftovers or heating carryout from a good restaurant, but that was pretty much her limit. The meals she prepared were very simple but healthy.

The four sat down and enjoyed a wonderful meal of salad, french bread and shrimp fettuccine. The thick, creamy sauce was seasoned with onions, celery, bell pepper, and garlic. The food was delicious and the conversation, light. Greg told old war stories of the police force from when he and Tad patrolled together. And Marie chimed in with a few of her own: some about her, some about her dad. Matthew spoke up occasionally himself. Sam sat back and enjoyed hearing the stories and watching everyone laughing as they enjoyed talking about their jobs.

"My compliments to the chef," Greg said as he lowered his fork and eased away from the table.

"Here, here. That was good, boss. Best I've ever had."

Matthew took his praises graciously, and they all retired to the living room. Sam and Matthew sat together on the sofa as Greg made himself comfortable on the recliner and Marie took the overstuffed chair.

"I'm glad my boy found him a woman like his mother. He never got to know her, but I did. Trust me, you have a lot of her qualities," he said as he glanced at Sam. "One of them being," he darted his brows up and down as he paused in his statement, "you don't cook, do you?"

She laughed.

Matthew considered her with a curious expression. "I've never tasted anything she's made, come to think of it," Matthew admitted as his gaze darted toward Samantha. "She admits to not being the best in the kitchen . . . but can't cook?" Still not sure, he added, "I can tell you the last few times I saw her at her house, she was about to eat something. She must cook a little. Her son, Marty, looks healthy. So my guess is she can cook a little. Jump in there, Samantha. Tell the man you can cook . . . right?"

Marie and Greg both were laughing.

Sam smiled and raised both of her hands in the air. Shrugging, she said, "I'll never tell." For now, that would remain her little secret.

They talked most of the night. Greg shared secrets from the past . . . some of Matthew's well-kept secrets. Now Marie would know, too. How long before the whole force would know?

After a couple stories were told and Matthew's worried eyes darted to Marie, she said, "Don't worry, boss. Your childhood stories will remain a mystery at work. My lips are sealed." She pinched her fingers together, then slid them across her lips, as if zipping her mouth shut.

Some of the stories were priceless. Sam would treasure them forever; others, more humorous escapades, made the night an enjoyable experience. She loved Greg immediately.

Sam watched Matthew as he reminisced with his old family friend. His eyes sparkled whenever it was a story including his father or mother or both. Matthew listened excitedly whenever Greg told a story about Matthew's parents, Tad and Katherine. She could tell he never got tired of hearing about his mother. Matthew missed out on a lot there.

She smiled to herself as she thought about her mother and how she would eat Matthew alive. Diane did not have a son and would love being able to treat him as one. Her mom had never trusted Martin, and her worries had turned out to be true. How do mommas know these things? Sam couldn't wait to share Matthew with both of her parents and Marty.

Later that night, after they said their goodbyes and Greg left, Matthew put his pager on the counter and his cell phone in the charger. Marie said good night and went off to her room. As he double-checked the locks on the doors and windows, Sam headed for the spare bedroom. Pulling out the T-shirt she slept in, she sensed Matthew's presence at the doorway. Looking up and finding him watching her, she smiled. "Good night," she whispered.

"Good night."

His eyes were waiting, wanting. She eased herself over to the door as he opened his arms to welcome her in them.

"Samantha, I don't tell people I love them, but I told you, and I meant it. I love you. You are the best thing that has ever happened to me. When all this is through, and your life gets back to normal, I want to be a part of it. Of yours and Marty's life. I hope you realize this."

Sam's heart leapt out of her chest. "Yes," she squealed. That was pretty close to a proposal. She knew it hadn't gotten to that, but. . . . "Thank you. I want it, too."

"Sweet dreams," he whispered as he bent and kissed her lightly on the lips, then turned and went down the hallway toward his room.

She watched his back until he disappeared behind the door. "Good night, sweetheart," she said softly as a smile spread across her lips. In all her days, Samantha could not ever remember being happier.

The next morning, Sam awoke to the ringing of the phone. Glancing at the clock, she saw it was early. Slipping on her robe, she ran to the kitchen. By the smell of the coffee, Matthew had been up for a while.

"Jefferies," Matthew said in the phone as she entered the kitchen.

Sam couldn't hear what was being said, but she saw his reaction. Marie, too, walked in while he was on the phone. His body stiffened as he listened. Something was wrong. Was there another murder?

"Who was it?" he asked. Silence as he listened. "Where? Was he told anything?"

More silence. Sam wanted to know what was going on, but she had to wait, then he said, "I'm on my way."

"What happened?"

"Oh baby. I don't know how to tell you this." He hung up the phone and moved around the counter closing the space between them.

"What happened, sir?" Marie asked.

Sam's heart stopped beating as she held her breath, waiting for what he couldn't tell her. The killer found Marty? Was he okay? Were her parents okay? "So tell me. What?

He's killed another woman? Please, tell me. You don't know the thoughts that are running through my mind." As bad as that would be, another woman being killed, it would be worse to her if it was her son. She couldn't lose her son. Her stomach twisted.

Matthew reached out to take her hands. "It's Amanda."

Sam gasped as her knees started to buckle. Matthew grabbed hold of her and held her upright. "Amanda? Is she all right?"

"She's alive but in bad shape. This guy has gone off the deep end. I'm heading over to her place now. Marie, you stay here . . . no. On second thought, Sam, he has no idea where you are. Right now, I'm going to bring Marie with me so she can maybe help with Amanda. Being a woman, she might be able to get a few more details from Amanda than what she might tell me."

"I have to go with you! I need to be there for her, too."

"No." Matthew shook his head. "You can't. Don't you see that's what the killer wants? He's trying to flush you out, and he knows she's your best friend. He figures you'd rush to her side to help her. That's got to be what his plan is, and we can't fall into it. We'll go to Amanda and make sure she gets all the help and protection she needs. But you can't. You have to stay here. Promise me," he begged. "Promise!" he said again sternly when she didn't answer right away.

"Okay, okay. I promise. But hurry. Get to her. Help her, then let me know she'll be okay. I'll be waiting for your call." Her hands shook like crazy. What was she going to do while she waited? The slow passing of time was going to kill her.

Sam followed them to the back door and watched as they each jumped into their own car and started backing out of the driveway. Quickly, she locked the door and ran to the living room. She peered through the picture window as taillights disappeared and they raced to Amanda's aid.

Seconds later, Sam dropped to her knees by the couch. "Oh, dear God," she prayed, "let her be okay. Please don't let her die because of me. She just found happiness in her life. Please don't take it away from her." She prayed and cried until there were no tears left to shed.

Chapter 31

Matthew arrived with sirens blasting and lights flashing. Marie pulled in right behind him. Police cars were everywhere. Amanda's apartment was a mess with furniture upside down, drapes pulled off the wall, the phone ripped out of the socket, smashed to pieces, lamps turned over, and shattered remnants of figurines everywhere.

"What a mess!" Glancing at Officer Johnson, Matthew asked, "Where's the victim? Is she okay? Do we have any witnesses?" He knew who had done this, felt it in his gut, but had to ask. The more evidence they had when the killer was caught, the deeper they could bury him.

"The victim is on her way to the hospital. Been beat pretty bad, but they talked like she would be okay. We have the boyfriend, Charles Chambers," he said pointing toward the man who was being kept in the middle of the breezeway. "He wants to get to the hospital, so you might want to talk to him first. And the neighbor across the breezeway, Maria Gabriella. She called 911."

"I think I better let him breathe a little first. Give him a couple minutes to calm down some." Matthew nodded in thanks. "Marie, find out which hospital and get on over there. See what, if anything, you can get from Amanda. Johnson, grab another uniform and you two go door-to-door to see if anybody heard or saw anything suspicious last night or in the past few days. We need to canvass the area. We have his picture, a few years old, I admit. But use it along with the sketch and see if anyone saw him. We'll get enough to put him away for life . . . when we get him."

"I'll get right on it. Don't worry, sir, we'll get him."

"And I'll get back with you as soon as I know anything from the hospital," Marie said as she left.

"Thanks," he said to her and then to Johnson, he added, "I know we will. I'll go talk to Chambers and Ms. Gabriella." Matthew walked toward the two, flashing his badge toward Charles. "I'll be with you in one minute, sir, if you'll wait over there." Matthew pointed to the other end of the breezeway.

"Please hurry, though. I need to get to the hospital," Charles said.

"I understand, sir. They said she was going to be fine, so try to relax so you'll be able to answer my questions. You'll be more help that way." Matthew turned his attention to the neighbor. "Ma'am, what exactly did you hear, and did you see anything?"

The older woman fiddled with the lapels of her robe. "This morning, I heard a lot of commotion through the wall, and then when I was putting on a pot of coffee for Joe, my husband, I heard the neighbor scream. And when I say scream, she screamed. That was around five thirty this morning. I immediately called 911. After what happened to Samantha's place, I didn't know what else to do. Joe was in the shower, or he could have gone to see if he could help her. But me, what could I do? Nothing. So I stayed inside till the police got here."

The older man standing near Amanda's door trying to sneak a peek must be Joe. Matthew found it hard to believe the woman wasn't curious enough to look out a window or something after calling for help. "And you didn't see a thing? Didn't look outside at all?"

She looked down at her feet.

That proved it to Matthew. She was not telling him the whole truth. "Mrs. Gabriella, in order to catch the bad guy, we need to know everything. Did you see anything? I need your help, ma'am. All you can give me. You never know what's important."

"Okay." The older woman looked nervous. "I admit it, but I was watching for the police. I wasn't being a busybody like everyone thinks I am. While I was watching for them, I saw a dark-haired man go running away from our building and jump in a little black car. He sped off in the same direction the police came from."

"Had you seen him before? Do you know the kind of car he drove off in?"

When she shook her head no, Matthew said, "I'll have an officer take you down to headquarters so we can get a written statement from you." He glanced at her attire. "As soon as you're ready," he added.

Matthew left her, gave instructions to Officer Myer, who was standing guard outside Amanda's door while the Crime Scene Division worked inside. Next Matthew walked over to talk to Charles Chambers. "Mr. Chambers, let's take a walk. You look like you could use a little fresh air."

The boyfriend's eyes were red, as if he had been crying. Feeling sorry for the guy, Matthew knew how he would feel if it had been Samantha. "My officer said Amanda is going to be all right. Really. She's lucky you got here when you did."

Charlie was shaking his head. "Don't you see? It's all my fault. She wanted me to stay over last night, but I was mad. It's so stupid now! I was mad because she wouldn't consent for us to live together for a year and then get married. I wanted us to get married and told her so, just not right now. First I wanted to get my degree. That's a year away. I went back to finish school for her . . . so I could do great things, give her the world."

Matthew let the boyfriend talk out his grief. He needed to get past it so they could get on with the investigation.

"I was so determined that she wouldn't support me in any way, 'cause all you ever hear about is how men use women to get their law degrees, then run off with their secretary later. I didn't want to ever be one of those statistics. If I hadn't pushed so hard or been so pig-headed, we would have been together at her place or mine, and this wouldn't have happened to her."

Matthew stopped them at a cement bench out in the courtyard. "Have a seat, Mr. Chambers."

Charlie sat down, dropped his elbows on his knees, and rested his face in his hands. The man looked drained; his eyes threatened to tear again.

"Mr. Chambers, listen to me. I'll tell you like I told Samantha, Amanda is going to be all right. Because of you, we got help to her in time. That nut didn't kill her. In fact, I don't think he planned to kill her. I think attacking Amanda was meant to be more of a warning to Samantha, another way to scare her and pull her out of hiding. It scared her, and she wanted to be here. But I wouldn't let her come."

Charles was a friend of Samantha's, so Matthew knew he could confide in him, which in turn hopefully helped in calming him down some so he could be of some use to the investigation.

Using the backs of his hands, Charlie rubbed his eyes. "Sorry. Call me Charlie. From what Amanda told me, I think we might all be good friends in the future." He then extended a hand toward Matthew.

Matthew shook it, then started his questioning. Charlie gave a detailed report of the guy. The description fit Robert Thomas Howard all right. The attacker practically ran Charlie over in the doorway as he fled from the scene.

"Instead of running after him, I went in to check on Amanda. I just knew that guy had raped her or even . . . killed her." His forehead furrowed as he drew his brows together in a frown. "Thank God he hadn't. Not yet anyway. But he had slapped her around and had been choking her when I unlocked the door and started walking in. The noise of the key turning in the lock or jingling in my hand must have stopped him. I think he wanted to kill her."

Matthew wrote as Charlie spoke. Sounded like Matthew had been wrong in his earlier assessment of the situation. He had thought this was more of the same, like when he had broken into Samantha's apartment and tore it up, putting fear into her and trying to scare her out into the open. But it wasn't. It sounded like the guy had flipped right off the deep end.

From all accounts, once a serial killer changed his pattern, it started the wheels in motion, and he went completely out of control. All along, Matthew had known Samantha was being stalked because of the killer's fear of his crime being witnessed, but maybe that was just the beginning of his change. Now the man was going to be more determined than ever to get to Samantha.

Noting everything Charlie told him, Matthew said, "We need you to drop by the station later today so we can get a written statement. I know right now you want to get to the hospital and see for yourself Amanda is all right." And Matthew wanted to get back to Samantha as quickly as possible.

"Thanks, I sure do." Charlie shook his hand.

"Do me a favor. Tell Amanda as soon as it's safe, Samantha will get in touch with her, but right now her life is in extreme danger, as you both know. Watch your back, and drive safe."

"Will do and we understand. I'll see you later," Charlie said and left for the hospital.

Matthew walked back over to the apartment. The Crime Scene Division was finishing up collecting physical evidence, and they were about to leave. Another policeman stood watch at the door. Myer had left to take Maria Gabriella to the station.

"Sir, this call is for you." The uniformed officer handed the walkie-talkie to Matthew.

"Come in," Matthew said, speaking into the black apparatus in his hand.

"We have two possible witnesses over here. Do you want to talk to them before you leave?" came the voice across the walkie-talkie.

"Be right there." He handed the black object back to the policeman. "I'll check back in over here, before I leave."

One more thing he needed to do before interviewing those two witnesses. Call Samantha. He went to pull out his cell phone.

"Dang it!" He didn't have it. He'd left his phone at home. Matthew retraced his steps to Mrs. Gabriella's and asked to use her phone. Amanda's phone was out of commission.

He heard Samantha pick up the phone. She sounded like she was breathing hard.

"Working out your worry?" he asked.

"I hoped it was you. I almost didn't answer the phone, but I decided to take the chance. How is she?"

"Amanda will be fine. I told Charlie to tell her you'd call her as soon as it was safe for you. He understood and promised he would. But listen. This man has gone over the edge. Whatever you do, don't leave the house. Stay there. He has no idea where you are. Do you understand me?"

He heard a big sigh. "I understand."

"I don't know when I'll be home, but I'll get there as soon as I can." He wanted to stress one more time not to go anywhere, but hopefully what happened to her best friend would frighten her enough to keep Samantha inside. She had a strong determination, always trying to prove she could handle any situation.

For now he had to put Samantha on the back burner of his mind. She was safe at his house. He had too much to do to be distracted by his thoughts of her and not much time to do it in. He headed for the two witnesses.

CHAPTER 32

His phone call about Amanda had caught her by surprise. She had spent the morning working out trying to keep from worrying. After she'd done all she could, she started cleaning his home from room to room. There was that nervous energy at work again. Her friend would be fine. That was the important thing.

A smile touched her lips. Her friend would be fine and Matthew took time to call her and give her the update. With all that was going on, he thought of her needs and worries and made that phone call.

After they hung up, Sam peeked into his office thinking about cleaning in there. "The only room I haven't touched," she said out loud. Stepping in, she glanced around, and then decided not to touch a thing. He probably had everything right where he wanted it.

She couldn't help herself as she glanced

at one of the bulletin boards, and then stepped closer to it. The pictures covering it were of the three bodies. They were not a bloody mess like you would see in the movies. This was real life, she reminded herself. Each woman's face was puffy, with eyes bulging and bruises around the face and neck. They were sickening. Sam had to turn and leave. She couldn't think about them right now. All she could see was Amanda's face, thinking Amanda could have been one of those victims.

Thank You, Lord, for protecting her and for not allowing the man to hurt my best friend. It's me he wants, Lord, but I pray You help them catch him before he can harm me or anyone else. Please let this nightmare end.

Shivering, not from cold, but from the eerie feeling of being in the room with those pictures of dead women, she left. She wasn't afraid. She knew the Lord would look out for her. She only prayed she would hear His direction.

Walking back in the kitchen, she decided to make a fresh pot of coffee. As she reached to grab the Mr. Coffee pot to fill it with water, her hand froze midair. Her eyes noticed Matthew's cell plugged in to the charger. He had left his phone. And laying next to it was his pager.

"Great." *How could he forget so much today?* She half smiled to herself, remembering what he had said to her only yesterday. *You make me forget everything.*

"That could be a bad thing. It must be bad, because now you've gone off and left something I know you need. I hope you didn't forget your gun." As that thought crossed her mind, a dash of alarm gripped her heart. No. He couldn't have left that, too. *He'll be okay. He knows what he is doing.*

She had to quit worrying. Things would be all right. *Trust in the Lord. You've asked, you've prayed. Quit worrying. Start believing and receiving,* she told herself.

Sam filled the pot with water as she had planned at first, poured it into the well, and then pulled out the section to hold the grounds. Placing a filter inside, she scooped up two large dippers full of Community Dark Roast, then added another half scoop. "There. That ought to be perfect." Putting it in place, she turned on the coffeemaker and sat back to wait.

CHAPTER 33

Matthew made his way to one of the witnesses waiting for him.

The elderly gentleman said, "I saw a man sneaking around that apartment." With arthritis-stricken fingers, the old man pointed toward Samantha's apartment. "That was several days ago but weren't none of my business. With young folks today, you never know what they're up to."

Matthew shook his head as he wrote down the old man's statement, which included a description that fit Howard.

Next he turned to an older, full-figured woman who had been out walking her dog. They had kept them about fifteen feet from one another. "What did you see?" Matthew asked as he walked up to her.

"I saw a young man, dark hair, average height, run out of that building and jump in a black car, and then he took off." She turned to a Labrador retriever and said,

"Sit." Turning back to Matthew, she added, "The next thing I know the police are swarming the place."

The same thing Mrs. Gabriella had said. "How young? A teenager? A young man in his twenties? What?"

She squinted her eyes as she appeared to think. "I'd say in his early or mid-thirties. Nowadays, you never can tell. I'm almost ninety-one. Bet you didn't know that, did you, young man?"

He smiled, shaking his head, then thanked her. Walking her toward the older gentleman he said, "I need you both to drop by headquarters to give a written statement and look at a few mug shots. If you need a ride, we'll have an officer escort you to the station." They both agreed, so Matthew made the arrangements with the policeman standing nearby, then returned to Amanda's apartment.

With every witness, every fiber, he was building a case. There was no way Matthew would let this guy slip through his fingers . . . or the courts for that matter.

CHAPTER 34

The coffee smelled heavenly as it filled the pot. The black murky water was just what she needed. Pulling down a cup, she started pouring coffee into it.

His cell phone started ringing. *Should I? It could be important.* After several more rings, she flipped open the phone. "Jefferies' residence, may I help you?"

"Matthew Jefferies," the caller said.

"I'm sorry, but he isn't in right now, could I take a message?" Sam tried to be helpful.

"Look lady! This is a matter of life or death. He told me I could reach him anytime at this number, if he wasn't at his desk at the station. Now let me talk to him."

Sam chewed on her bottom lip. What should she do? *A matter of life or death,* he had said. *Whose?* Should she take a message, try to reach Matthew and get him to call the man back, or what? "I'm sorry, sir. He truly isn't here right now, but if you care to leave a message, I'll see that he gets it."

"Jefferies told me — aw, never mind! Take a message, but make sure he gets it right away. Jefferies told me to call if I hear anything. Tell Jefferies I got the man's name and where he's staying. I'll be waiting for him outside the Arts and Science Center downtown near the Kidd. I'll be sitting down near the river, on the levee, trying to stay out of sight. Don't want to take no chance of being caught. I'll wait half an hour. If he ain't there by then, I'm out of there, and he'll be sorry. Tell him to bring some money if he still wants this information. You got that?"

Sam was writing as fast as she could. "Yes. I do. You've got some information he wants. You'll be waiting for him, right? He's got half an hour." She glanced at her watch noting the time.

"Yeah, you got it." The line went dead.

Sam's hands were shaking. She punched in Amanda's phone number to get him the message immediately. It rang and rang. No answer. That was strange. Maybe they'd left. Sam tried calling him at the station. "He probably isn't back yet," she mumbled to herself.

His number rang a few times, then someone else picked up. "Homicide,

Guidry" came the voice on the phone.

"Oh, Officer Guidry, this is Samantha Cain. Could I speak to Detective Jefferies, please?"

"I'm sorry, ma'am, but he's not here. He's working a case right now. I'll try to get word to Detective Jefferies, if it's important."

Sam breathed a sigh of relief. "Yes, it's very important. It's urgent. Tell him it's a matter of life or death."

"Is something going on there? 'Cause if you think someone is breaking in, I'll send a unit right away."

Thankful, Sam said, "That won't be necessary. It's not here. It's not me. I'm fine, but he has to meet someone —" she glanced at her watch — "in twenty-five minutes. Can you get a message to him right away and have him call me?"

"No problem. I'll get word to him."

Sam waited for what seemed like eternity, but in reality it was only a few minutes. When he didn't call her back right away, she doubted Matthew could get there in time. "I wish Marie was here. She would know what to do, but no. I'm glad she is there for Amanda. Maybe I should go and stall the man. That would help." Looking up the number for a taxi service, she ordered one right away. Sam was close; it shouldn't take long.

As she waited, she thought, *Boats, river, levee.* Could it be connected to her case? She doubted it, but it was important to another case, so she would do what she could to help him. And she would do it with the utmost care.

In the corner room, where her things were still sitting, she rummaged through her black bag for the .38. Matthew insisted she keep it with her at all times. That was as close as she had come to having the gun with her.

Sam switched from shorts to a pair of jeans, stuffed some cash in one pocket, and then, after double-checking the safety on the gun, slid it in the other pocket.

Grabbing the pad she had written the note on, she tore off the top piece of paper and shoved it in the pocket with the cash. Then she swiftly scribbled another note for Matthew and stuck it under a magnet on the refrigerator where she knew he would see it when he got home, in case the police didn't talk to him first.

A yellow cab was there in less than ten minutes. "Arts and Science Center please, and hurry."

She didn't mean to sound so desperate, but the driver turned around and gave her a strange look before saying, "Look, lady, I drive the speed limit. If that ain't good enough, get out and call for another one. I don't play those cloak-and-dagger games."

"Sure. I didn't mean speed. Sorry." Sam sat wringing her hands. She tried to rehearse in her mind what she would tell this guy. How would she know him? She never met the guy and didn't think to ask his name, and then she thought, he would be the one trying to stay hidden. Sam knew she wasn't trained to talk to an informant, but how hard could it be?

Glancing at her watch, she saw the time for Matthew to get there had almost run out. She was doing it for him and that was all that mattered. Like he had said before, you do what you have to do.

Back to the man she was looking for, Sam realized if he was trying to stay hidden, there was a good chance she wouldn't even see the man, but she had to try. For Matthew's sake. And, of course, he was not going to show himself, since he was expecting a man, not a woman.

When the taxi stopped, she paid the driver the price he asked. Slipping out of the yellow car, she stood frozen in place as she looked up and down the sidewalk. It looked deserted. "Shouldn't be hard to determine who he is," she whispered. "He should be the only one here."

Carefully, she moved toward the steps leading to the levee.

CHAPTER 35

"Sir, this call is for you." The uniformed officer caught up with Matthew and handed him the walkie-talkie. "It's headquarters."

Matthew was about to leave. Everything was wrapped up at the scene. Only thing left was to go back to the station and complete his report.

"Come in," Matthew said into the black box.

"You had a call from Miss Cain," said Officer Guidry. "She said it's urgent you call her right away. We beeped you and called your cell phone, sir, but when we got no response I radioed you at the scene."

"Is she all right?"

"She said she was fine, but it was very important that she give you a message right away."

"Got it. I'll give her a call right away." Matthew handed the walkie-talkie to the uniformed policeman. "Loan me your cell.

I'll get it back to you as quick as possible."

No questions asked, he gave Matthew his phone.

"Thanks." Quickly, Matthew called. No answer. He ran and jumped in his car. Starting his engine, he strapped himself in and pulled out in a hurry. He turned on his siren and flashing lights. They cleared a path for him as he raced toward home.

He punched in his home phone again. Still, there was no answer. The phone rang and rang. "Come on Sam. Pick up. It's me. Take the chance."

No answer.

In no time, he was there. He rushed inside. It was empty, but he found the note hanging by the magnet. Scanning it quickly, he crumbled it in his hand and muttered, "She didn't. How could she be so foolish?"

Racing out the door and back into his car, he fled toward the river. *Samantha is gone. She is trying to help me.* What she didn't know was that the snitch who called was following up on the killer who was after her.

"Dear God, please keep her safe. Help me get there in time." This was new to Matthew, but Samantha believed in Him. *It's her God. She loves Him. He must love her.*

The closer he got to his destination, the more he questioned what was about to happen. Had the killer slipped some false information to Matthew's snitch to turn the tables? Was it a setup?

He let dispatch know where he was going, just in case. Taking corners practically on two wheels, he sped to make the meeting in time. Hopefully, the information was for real and it would be enough to help catch the killer and put him away for life and not some sick plot by Robert Thomas Howard, aka Bobby.

Less than a block away, he cut off the siren, remembering it could be a setup. If so, Jake wouldn't be aware of it, but gut instinct told Matthew it was probably more than a meeting with his snitch. He had to get there in time to save Samantha.

Matthew's adrenaline heightened as he anticipated what was about to go down if his instincts were correct.

CHAPTER 36

The steps to cross the highway were steeper than she recalled. At the top she crossed over to the other side, and then took time to catch her breath. Sam looked out over the levee in search of the man. Buildings had been added around the downtown area along the river since the last time she had been there with Marty to watch the fireworks display. The July after Martin's death. She had tried to get his mind off of his father. Now, because of the legalization of gambling a few years ago, they had cleaned up downtown and added shops and hotels.

With careful strides, Sam raced down the steps and headed toward the concrete structure of seats along the levee. A massive cement area had been added along the levee, as well as benches for lovebirds to cuddle on. Flower beds planted here and there added to the view. She wished she was there to enjoy it.

Searching to the right, she saw the USS *Kidd* docked down at the end of a long pier. Glancing around, she noticed one man walking away from her, going back over to the highway area. Could that be him? Probably not. He was supposed to be hiding. He had a sleeping bag tucked under his arm. The homeless slept anywhere they could find to feel safe, as long as officials didn't run them off, and the number had increased after Hurricane Katrina.

Docked on the edge of the water further down, she could see the two floating casinos, but because of the distance, she could barely hear the music and noisy people.

Swallowing hard and taking a deep breath, she murmured, "Here goes." She walked along the concrete path in the direction of the pier to the *Kidd*. Her gaze traveled first one direction, then back the other way, searching the levee for a man . . . hiding. She didn't see a soul.

This was an excellent view of the muddy Mississippi River. The current was rough, even though there was no wind and no bad weather approaching. It was said, if something went in the river, there were doubts it would ever come out again, or if it did, it would be miles downstream. Due to the undertow, there had been many bodies never found of people who jumped over the side of the bridge, committing suicide.

That thought sent shivers down Sam's spine. She shook slightly, feeling as if a ghost had walked over her grave.

Since the man was hiding, she decided she needed to take a closer look around the pillars holding up the pier. This would be a perfect hiding place. When she started her descent, she didn't go down the wide cement stairs that had been built like bleachers for people to sit on to enjoy the fireworks display on the fourth of July. Instead, she went down the concrete slope. It was easier. This way she could move down toward the water and not have to watch her footing.

As she neared the bottom of the cement, she noticed a person sitting, huddled over, almost next to the water under the walkway to the ship. His body leaned slightly against the large cement structure bracing the pier.

"Maybe that was what he called being hidden," she said under her breath as she started toward the man.

When the cement ended, which was two-thirds of the way down the levee, the ground became hard-packed dirt mixed with loose gravel. The level of the river was down. No grass grew on this section of the levee at all.

She walked down the decline toward the man, toward the water's edge. Moving very cautiously, she eased closer and closer to the hunched-over body.

The closer she got, the more she didn't like it. He hadn't moved a muscle. He should have noticed her approaching by now. He should have turned and looked in her direction. Maybe it wasn't the one she was looking for after all. She hoped not, now that she was less than ten feet away. He still sat with his head bent over. Maybe he was drunk and had passed out in a drunken stupor. Yes. That was why he hadn't noticed her approach.

Step by step, Sam moved closer. When she was almost up to him, she slipped on some gravel that rolled beneath her feet. She started to fall but caught herself. Straightening up, she took the last five steps, placing her right next to the man.

Sam squatted by his side. "Mister," she said as she touched his shoulder lightly. He still didn't move. If he was asleep, he was one heavy sleeper, if drunk . . . dead drunk.

A slight breeze stirred off the river. At that moment, Sam got a whiff of whiskey. She was right. "The man's drunk," she mumbled aloud.

Looking closer, she saw marks on his

neck, red marks along with some bruises. Suddenly, she remembered where she had seen those types of markings before, on the victim's bodies in the pictures hanging on Matthew's bulletin board in his office.

Was he dead, too? Panic rose within and pin needles pricked her body. She had to get out of there. Every nerve stood on end.

A wire wrapped around her throat before she could turn. A horrifying scream broke the silence around her. Sam's scream shattered the stillness as her hands reached up and caught hold of the wire starting to close tightly around her neck.

The man is dead, not drunk. And I'm next!

Those thoughts flashed through her mind as she screamed and fought for her life.

CHAPTER 37

Matthew whipped up to the curb in front of the Arts and Science Center. As he was coming to a stop, he called in for backup.

He leaped out of his car and slammed the door shut. As he turned toward the levee, he heard a scream. He would know Samantha's voice anywhere.

"Samantha!" he screamed as his mind shouted, *Hold on, baby! I'm on my way.*

His heart pounded as he rushed around the building.

Another scream sounded, but the distance seemed further. He was not going to lose her — or the killer.

There was no time to waste.

CHAPTER 38

Sam pulled with all her strength till the wire cut into her fingers. The warmth of the blood oozed around the wire and trickled down her hands. "He's not going to get me," she swore under her breath. She had too much to live for: Marty, Matthew. God had just blessed her with a future for her and her son; she wasn't going to lose that without a fight.

Be not afraid. You can do all things through Christ. Strength started to flow through her veins as those words came to mind.

She couldn't knee him in the groin; he was behind her. She had to do something, anything. Quickly and with all her strength, she lifted her right foot up and pushed backward into his knee. She hit it so hard, she heard a pop.

"Aaahhhh," he cried out.

On target. The wire dropped from around her neck, giving Sam the opportunity to run as fast as she could. She didn't know how badly she had damaged him, but she wasn't going to hang around and find out. Sam took off up the levee, across the loose gravel, and away from the water's edge, toward the cement incline. It was much slower running uphill.

For a second, she stopped and looked around for help. No one. She had to hide. The floating casinos were too far, and she knew the streets were deserted. Hiding on the *Kidd* was her only chance. It was closer. She had to make it to the ship and hide until Matthew found her. Hopefully, he would get the message and be there soon.

Quickly, she ducked under the linked chain that stretched across the beginning of the pier, and then ran toward the USS *Kidd.* Just ahead, a locked gate stretched across the walkway. The gate's bars looked like a jail, only the bars extended out one foot on both sides of the railing.

The gate was too high to climb over, and the slits were too narrow to slip through. Without wasting any time, Sam threw one leg over the side railing and eased along the edge of the pier. Step by step, she slipped her feet in the openings between the bars, working around that extra distance. She made it from one side, back down the other side, and then reached the rail. Holding on tight, she crossed her right leg over the railing onto the other side of the locked gate and pulled the other leg behind her. She made it, one movement at a time.

Once on the other side, Sam ran as fast as she could. As she ran the last few feet on the pier and crossed over onto the ship, she paused for only a second to see how far behind she had left him. He was limping after her. At least she had slowed him down, and she had a lead.

This scum wasn't going to catch her. She could pull the gun out and shoot him, if she thought she could hit him, but Sam didn't trust herself under these real circumstances. Better to keep the distance. Hide — that was what she needed to do. She doubted she could shoot a person. It was one thing to shoot at a target. It was another to shoot at a real human being. She couldn't do it. Matthew would get there and save her. She needed only to hide out and wait.

In the distance, near the building, she saw a moving shadow but didn't have time to stop and be sure. *Let that be Matthew. Please, Lord, let that be him.*

Hurrying around the deck, she ducked through a portal and ran down a flight of stairs, moving as quickly as possible and scanning for any feasible hiding place.

Running down a short narrow hallway and taking every turn, she saw plenty of doors to run through. She even opened a few, hoping it would throw the killer off or at least slow him down some more.

Unfortunately, it didn't seem to. Before she knew it, she heard his feet dragging down the hallway in her direction. She hadn't lost him at all. Sam ducked into one of the small rooms and glanced around. She had to hide.

There it was. A great place for her to crawl into and hope he didn't find her.

She crossed the room. Along the back wall was a storage area for lifejackets. Sam lifted one of the seats, crawled into the big box-looking thing, squatted down in the bottom, and curled up into a fetal position, then let the lid close over her. The gun handle poked in her stomach while the barrel pushed into her leg.

Her heart pounded in her chest, the beating so loud she was afraid he might hear it. Sam tried to slow down her breathing so she could ease the hammering of her heart. Just when she had it almost under control, she heard a bang. The metal door clanked against the wall as he threw it open and stepped into the room. Listening very closely, she managed to hear his feet. The first step slapped as it hit the metal flooring and the second one dragged behind it.

He wasn't even trying to be quiet. The man wanted Sam to hear him, she decided. This was part of his plan to scare her to death. She swallowed hard. It was working. *Be not afraid,* she reminded herself.

"I've got you now," he called to her.

I'm okay, she told herself. *Stay calm.* Sam's body shook all over. She couldn't fall apart. She had to be strong. She had to be tough. Sam didn't want to be another statistic for this sicko. She was not alone. The Lord was with her, and Matthew was on the way.

She wiped the sweat off her hands by rubbing them against her jeans. Her hands slid across the hard object in her pocket.

The gun! She had no choice now. She had to get ready, maybe even use it. Trying to straighten herself a bit so she could slide the gun out of her pocket, she eased her hand in the pouch, touched the cold steel, then cautiously, trying not to make any noise, pulled the gun out of her jeans.

Her hands were still shaking and now they held a gun. She had told Matthew about the danger of guns when the user didn't know what they were doing. Now she was afraid she fit that description perfectly.

Think! she yelled at herself in her mind. Matthew had gone over this with her to be sure. *Remember.*

Feeling with her hands, because she was in total darkness, her fingers found the safety. Clicking it off, she took hold of the gun with her right hand in firing position, and held it steady with her left. Aiming it straight up, she sat waiting and ready.

The killer's feet were still moving around in the room. "I know you're in here, and I'll find you."

She could hear him opening cupboards and knocking things around as he called to her, warning her. Next she heard him lifting the seats one at a time, and then letting them slam shut. Sam's heart clamored as it banged up against her ribcage. *Oh God, oh God, help me, please,* her thoughts cried out. She could hear the whacks and crashes getting closer and closer.

Finally, she heard him next to her as he grabbed the handle on the lid above her. Sam sat waiting . . . but ready.

"Are you in here?"

A flood of light filled the box as the seat was lifted open. Sam didn't breathe. She waited. Her eyes adjusted. He still had to look down in to see her. She knew this and counted on it. The box was deep.

Her hands shook more and more with each passing second. His shadow covered her first, and then she saw his head. As he bent over to look in, she fired the gun twice in quick succession. Sam saw him fall backward.

She scrambled up and out of the box, holding the gun tightly in her right hand. She looked over at him, afraid to run around him. There he was, laid out on the floor.

A small puddle of blood stained the floor next to his face. A moment of relief washed over her, and she started to ease around him and head toward the door.

As she made her way past the body on the floor, the killer caught her by the ankle. "Oh, no you don't!" he hollered.

His hands wrapped around her foot as she tried to pull away. He pulled her foot right out from under her.

Sam landed with a thud on the floor. She lost her air but not the gun. Her hand held on tight. Her bottom hurt, but she didn't have time to think about it. She had to shoot again. Sam turned the gun on him. As she started to pull the trigger, he knocked her arm up into the air. The bullet rang out, but missed the target.

The killer knocked Sam flat on her back

and covered her body with his, holding her arm out, keeping the gun out of his face. A stale odor of sweat invaded her senses as they struggled. His cold eyes, which she remembered all too clearly, stared down at her. The dark stubble on his tanned face didn't hide the etched lines of pain and anger shadowed beneath the facial hair.

Sam's hand was still wrapped around the gun tightly as she gagged from the smell of his body odor. *Oh Matthew, where are you? Please Lord, let him get here in time,* she cried out in her mind.

She wasn't going to give the gun up, or her life for that matter, without a fight. Sam pulled her arm in and pointed the gun toward his chest. Just when she thought it was right to pull the trigger, he twisted it back toward her.

Sam never thought in a million years she would be doing this. She should have waited for Matthew, or been more prepared. She should have practiced shooting more, worked out more, and built up her strength. *My strength comes from the Lord,* she reminded herself as she twisted the gun one more time in his direction.

Her heart cried out to Matthew again, but still, he wasn't there. Her finger squeezed the trigger. The sound reverberated in the metal room.

Chapter 39

Matthew followed the sounds and knew he was close. As he worked his way down another flight of steps and eased around the corner, he caught a glimpse of a man entering a room at the far end. Sprinting down the tiny hallway toward the shadow he had seen, he heard shots ring out. Matthew reached the room, stepped through the door, and simultaneously fired his weapon. The man was on top of Samantha. Both Matthew's and Samantha's shots rang out at the same time. Everything seemed to freeze. The killer still sat astride Samantha, but Matthew knew he had hit him. In another instant, Matthew saw the killer snatch the gun out of Sam's hand, and he turned it on Matthew as he turned his whole body around and off of Samantha in one quick motion.

Matthew fired off two more shots at the perpetrator, straight to the chest. When the bullets hit, the killer, Robert "Bobby" Thomas Howard, dropped the gun and fell backward across Samantha.

Immediately, Matthew pulled the perp off of her, turned him over, and laid him on the floor. Squatting down, he twisted the killer's hands behind him and slapped the cuffs on him. Samantha lay perfectly still. At a glance, she looked to be fine. "Samantha," he called as he rose to his feet.

No answer.

Matthew sank down close to her. Blood was on her blouse. "Samantha, talk to me. You're okay." He wasn't sure, but she had to be. The blood soaked a large area. She had been hit, but Matthew wasn't sure where. Thank God it wasn't the heart, too low for that.

"Samantha, Samantha, hang on! I'm here! We're going to get help! Hang on!" he said to her, hoping she was listening to him. Punching buttons on the borrowed cell, he called the station. Backup had already been sent. Now on his words two ambulances were being dispatched.

Matthew turned to Sam. Careful not to move her since he didn't know the extent of her injuries, he leaned down near her face and whispered, "Hold on, baby. Help is on the way. You're going to be okay. Hang in there. Stay alive. Don't you dare die on me now." He kissed her lips. "Stay with me, baby."

When the first cop appeared through the door, Matthew barked orders at him, "When the ambulance arrives, get them up here ASAP!"

Another policeman on the scene inspected the killer. "He's alive, but barely. He's losing a lot of blood."

"There is one coming for him, too. Don't let him out of your sight. Not for one minute. Go with them to the hospital and stay with him."

She still hadn't said a word. Could it be shock? Her eyes had opened, but she just lay there. He didn't know what was going on, but he knew she was alive. "Hold on. Help is on the way."

A short time later, the ambulance attendants carried Sam up top, and Matthew followed her all the way to the emergency vehicle.

"Take good care of her," he told the men and watched in despair as they drove away, siren screaming and lights flashing.

Keep her alive, Lord. Give us a chance.

CHAPTER 40

At the station, Matthew talked to the chief, giving him all the details, then rushed through the necessary paperwork on Robert Thomas Howard. Anything that wasn't mandatory would have to wait. He needed to be with Samantha.

Howard was in critical condition, still under tight security at the hospital. By the time Matthew's report was completed, he had received the details of Howard's mother's death, which gave him a better understanding of the man's warped mind. Not that it excused anything he had done, by any means.

Matthew turned in his completed report, gave a statement to the press, then left for the hospital. When he arrived, he found Samantha was in surgery. The bullet had done some internal damage that the doctors were attempting to repair.

"She's in good hands. Have faith," the

nurse told Matthew as he stood next to the desk. "You can wait in the waiting room. Drink some coffee and relax. As soon as she comes out of surgery, we'll let you know."

The first thing Matthew did was get word to Charlie and Amanda, then asked if they would contact Samantha's parents. After that, time dragged by.

Matthew poured a cup of strong, nasty coffee that hospitals were famous for having. It might not taste good, but he knew he needed something to keep him going. Right now he wanted to fall completely apart worrying about what could be happening to Samantha.

Marie walked into the waiting room and went straight to the detective. "How is she, sir?"

"She could die during surgery, and it would be all my fault." If he had caught the killer earlier, she never would have become involved in Howard's sick story. Matthew also realized the only reason a gun had been around for her to get shot was because he insisted Samantha relearn how to use the gun and keep it with her for her own protection.

She had tried to tell him it would be more dangerous in the hands of someone who didn't know what they were doing. She was right. A one-time practice at the firing range wasn't enough to make her proficient with a gun. Sure, under normal circumstances, the practice would have helped. But hers were nothing near normal. It was all his fault.

Had she not had the gun, she might be fine right now. He had heard her scream and when he heard that, she had been just on the other side of the levee. Somehow, she managed to get away from the killer long enough to run to the USS *Kidd*. On the *Kidd*, she managed to stay out of his clutches, probably by hiding, up until right before Matthew caught up to them. He had seen the killer climbing around the locked gate and fled after him, knowing in his gut, the killer was chasing Samantha.

Without the gun, she would have only been fighting with Howard when Matthew arrived. He was that close behind the killer. Matthew could have overtaken him, and Samantha would be safe at this very moment. It was all his fault.

"Sir, if I had stayed with her, maybe she wouldn't be there fighting for her life. So it's just as much my fault as it is yours."

He knew Marie Boudreaux was just trying to make him feel better, but it wasn't working. He wouldn't be better until Samantha was perfectly fine again.

"Her friend, Amanda, is fine, sir. She had to get a lot of stitches and she is going to hurt like the dickens, but everything he did to her will heal. That will make Sam happy when she learns this. In fact, they are coming here when she gets released from the emergency room. Which should be soon."

He heard her speaking but really didn't hear what she was saying. His mind stayed on Samantha. Marie went and poured him a hot cup of coffee when she poured herself one, and then came back and sat in silence but waited with him. Time crept by.

Amanda and Charlie finally arrived. Her bruises were ugly, and her stitches were many, but she was all in one piece. No broken bones, and he hadn't raped her. She would heal.

Samantha would be glad to hear it.

Quickly Matthew gave them the news on Samantha, then told them that the killer was in the hospital fighting for his life but under lock and key.

The doctor came out to the waiting room. "The damage has been repaired and Samantha is in recovery. Everything went well."

Shortly after, Samantha's parents arrived and were introduced to Matthew and Marie. Amanda gave them an update on Samantha's condition.

"Where's Marty?" Matthew asked.

"We left him with our neighbor. We didn't think he should see her right now. When she's better . . ." Sam's mother tried to smile, but Matthew could tell she would rather cry.

"I'm sorry your daughter is going through this. It's all my fault. I should have gotten to her sooner. I should have —"

Diane grabbed Matthew's hand and held it tightly. "Son, don't blame yourself. She'll be okay. She's in God's hands." Reaching into her purse, she pulled out a small Bible and shared some scripture with him. "So you see. We only need to trust Him. He's in charge, and He'll see her through."

"But what if she doesn't make it?"

"She'll be with Him in heaven. Either way, she wins, and we'll get through. But, I believe, He'll bring her through this. He's given me peace."

"I hope you're right."

They all sat in silence, waiting. It could take a couple of hours for the drugs to wear off. When they did, she would be fine. Matthew had to keep reminding himself of that. Marie left to go back to the station. Matthew promised to call as soon as they knew something.

Matthew swallowed a big swig of cold coffee from his fourth cup, then tossed it into the trash can. Time passed slowly, but finally a nurse came into the room. "She's waking up."

"How is she?" Matthew asked as he rushed to the nurse's side.

"She's weak at the moment, but her vitals are stable. She should continue to strengthen."

"When can I see her?" Sam's mom touched the nurse's arm. "When can we see her?" she added as her gaze moved to her husband.

"We can let you in for a minute or two and only a couple of you at a time." Her gaze moved to each one of them as she spoke.

Running his hands through his hair, Matthew said, "Thank you." He wanted to go. He needed to go. But Matthew knew he wasn't blood. Her parents only knew him as the cop who had saved their daughter. Matthew looked at Amanda. He knew he was pleading with his eyes and hoped she got the message.

"Let's let Matthew go back there first," Amanda said as she slipped her arm through Diane's and held her gently. "Remember what I told you? I believe he would be the best medicine for Sam right now."

The mother hesitated, but her husband laid his hands gently on his wife's shoulders and whispered, "Come on, honey. Amanda said she loves the guy. Let's give her what she needs right now, not what we need."

Diane nodded in agreement. Everyone returned to their seats and waited it out.

"Tell her we're here and give her our love," Diane said.

"Mine and Charlie's, too," Amanda called out.

Matthew nodded as he rushed out of the room.

Would she be all right? The doctor said he repaired all the damage. What if he missed something? Would she ever forgive Matthew for not getting there sooner? Could he forgive himself if Samantha didn't make a complete recovery? Could they get past this and make a life together for themselves? For the three of them?

He loved her, and if he couldn't have her, his life would be meaningless.

Passing through the double doors into recovery, Matthew followed the nurse into Samantha's section. Quietly, he entered her room.

His heart dropped to his stomach as his gaze fell on Samantha, her face so pale, her body so limp, just lying there. Her eyes were closed, and machines were hooked up to her. Matthew's eyes scanned the monitors. Looking at the needle in her arm, he winced. His gaze traveled up her arm to her face. The loss of blood left her weak and pale, the paleness emphasizing the bruises to her face.

Stepping to the side of the bed, he said, "Hi, sweetheart." He bent down and kissed her cheek. "Welcome back to the land of the living. I'm so glad you're going to be all right."

She opened her eyes and looked at him but didn't say a word.

"Amanda and Charlie are here. They called your parents, and they are here, too. Marie was even here for a little while. I promised her I'd let her know how you are doing. You kind of grew on her. You have a way with people." He touched the back of her hand gently. "Everyone is waiting to see you, but I pushed to get to see you first. Hope that's okay." Gently, he brushed a few strands of her hair to the side of her face.

"Marty. Where is Marty?"

"He's with one of your parents' neighbors. Your mom said they would bring him up later. When you're in your own room."

Her fingers jerked as she asked very softly,

"Is it over? Did you get him?"

"Yes. I wish I'd been there sooner to protect you, sweetheart. But I promise, I won't let anything happen to you again." Looking down at her, he whispered, "I love you."

Her eyes fluttered closed. When he saw her even breathing, Matthew realized she had fallen back to sleep. Since the doctor had said that was what she needed, he slipped quietly out of the room. Besides, he needed to give her parents a few minutes with her, too.

"She looked great, but she's fallen back asleep again," Matthew said.

Her mom had to see Samantha for herself. Matthew understood that. She promised not to wake her.

When her parents came back to the waiting room, Matthew said, "You ought to go get Marty and bring him back. She asked for him. He would be the best medicine for her. By the time you get back, she should be in a room."

"That's a great idea. We'll stay here with the detective," Amanda agreed.

"Matthew, please. Call me Matthew."

Her parents left to go get Marty.

While they sat in the waiting room, Amanda and Charlie talked over old times they had shared with Sam. Matthew listened and enjoyed hearing the stories of Samantha as a child and some of the escapades she and Amanda had been involved in. Some of the stories even included Charlie and Martin. Amanda then went on to mention the hard times Sam had these past few years taking care of herself and Marty, but her son made everything worth it.

Matthew took a lot of it in but mostly stayed focused on his desire for her to be totally well and his need to be near her.

About the time the nurse came out to let them know what room Samantha was being transferred to, Marty and his grandparents came walking in.

As a group they went to the fourth floor and headed to the room. When they got there, Samantha was already sitting up. Everyone walked in and gathered around the bed, giving Marty the closest spot to his mom.

"Momma! Oh, I'm so glad you're okay. Don't ever do this to me again. Granny and Papaw told me you are going to be all right, but I was scared." Tears were running down his face as he held his momma's hand, squeezing it tightly.

"Oh, baby. Momma didn't mean to scare you. You kept me strong through this whole ordeal. Thank you for being my big man for me." She smiled at her son as a tear trickled down her cheek.

Matthew felt such joy. He was going to be a part of that family. A proud feeling swept over him. *What a lucky guy I am. Thank You, Lord. Samantha was right. She said to trust You.*

"Guys, do you mind stepping out in the hall. I need to talk to Matthew for a minute."

He smiled and thought good thoughts till everyone cleared the room. Samantha turned her eyes on him. The smile from her face was gone. What was she going to say? Why the look? Everything was over. Only the best could possibly happen now. What was she thinking? Matthew wasn't sure he wanted to know, but he braced himself.

Chapter 41

How would she tell him? What words could she possibly use that would make him understand? As she was about to speak, Matthew bent over the bed and placed a warm, loving kiss on her mouth.

Her heart raced as the warmth of his lips pressed against hers. Love swelled inside her as her heart drummed out of control. Joy mixed with fear raced within her. Could she do this to Marty? Could she do this to herself?

She attempted to raise her head off of the pillow so she could sit up. A pain shot through her side and stomach, and she groaned.

"Aren't you supposed to stay still?"

She nodded. "Probably."

"Please do what they say. I'm so glad you're going to make it. You sure had me worried." Matthew kept his face close to hers. His eyes peered into hers.

She had to tell him. Again before she could form the words, he leaned over and brushed his lips gently against her cheek. "I was so scared. My life would be nothing without you."

She swallowed hard. "I don't know if I can go through this again."

"What do you mean? I thought you understood it was over. We got him. You don't have to worry anymore."

Sam didn't know what to say, but she had to continue. "What about your next suspect? What if the fears you've had all your life come to pass and they go after me to get to you? Or even worse, they go after Marty. Use him against you. I don't think I can take that chance with my son."

He breathed a sigh and then smiled.

She watched the changes on his face. Why wasn't he afraid? A thought flashed through her mind. *Everything happened for a reason. At least I'm alive. My son won't lose another parent.* Where did that come from? She couldn't stop the thoughts, but she still knew what she had to do. Yes, everything happened for a reason. This happened to make her see clearly, she couldn't put Marty through it.

"I understand what you're saying, but you are wrong. I was wrong then. In fact, today

I blamed myself for what happened to you. If you had died, I would never have forgiven myself. I insisted you use the gun." Matthew caught her hand again and held it tightly. "Marty could have lost his mom . . . but he didn't. You were right. No one should handle a gun if they don't know exactly what they're doing. If I had listened to you, or at least let you listen to yourself, you wouldn't have been shot.

"Unfortunately, I wasn't thinking like a cop. Shoot, I wasn't thinking period. I just wanted you to be safe. Thank God, you're all right now." He squeezed her hand tighter. "I prayed. I knew God loved you, so He would listen to me, even though I don't know Him . . . yet."

Yet? This might be the good that will come out of what has happened, but I can't take a chance and marry a policeman for my son's sake. Matthew will have to understand. I love him, but I love Marty, too. And I have to put him first.

"Samantha Cain. Are you listening to me? I love you, and I will never let you go. It's you and me and Marty together forever. I want you to marry me. Will you marry me?" he asked, his voice strong and clear.

She looked into his eyes and watched as the love poured out of them. Against her will, tears started to form in her own eyes. *What do I do, Lord? I love him, too. Sure I want to marry him, but I can't. It wouldn't be fair to Marty. It wouldn't be fair to Matthew.*

"Samantha!" Matthew's voice started to rise. "Why aren't you talking to me?" He dropped her hand. "You hold me to blame for what you're going through, right? That's it." He paused, and then added, "You're right to do so. I can't blame you, because I know I did this to you. But it won't happen again. I'll keep you safe. You and Marty both."

"You can't promise that. Well, you can promise it, but you don't control things. You can only try."

Dragging his fingers through his hair, he groaned, "You are right. I don't control it. Your God does. And He allowed us to meet again and fall in love. Don't you think He had a purpose in that? Don't you think He could have stopped that if we weren't meant to fall in love? He's your God. I only know what you've told me and what my dad tried to tell me as a young man. And let's not forget your mom."

She couldn't take her eyes off of Matthew. He was the same but different. Sam was worrying about the future instead of living for the day. *What does the Word say? Worry about nothing, pray about everything.*

"We could have a beautiful life together, no matter what the outcome." He went on. "We were meant to be together. I've waited my whole life for you. I love you. Please, don't make me go on without you. I couldn't do it."

A look of horror crossed his face when she did not respond to his open admission of such an overpowering of love. He shouted, "You do still love me, don't you?"

"Yes," she whispered as she closed her eyes and lifted up a silent prayer. *Help me, Lord. Show me the answer.*

Calmness filled the room as a smile spread across his face.

"That's all I needed to know." Snatching her hand again, he leaned down to her face. "Say yes to marrying me," he whispered before his lips covered hers.

Sam savored his kiss of love. She wanted it to go on forever. Life would be grand if it didn't matter that their lives would be in danger, but Sam lived in the real world. Things do happen, even to good people. She couldn't put her son in jeopardy like that. She had to say no.

When Matthew ended the kiss, he caught her bottom lip with his teeth and eased away, slowly releasing his hold as he moved back. Her tongue touched her lip, spreading the warmth he had radiated within her.

"Samantha, I'll let you know now, I won't take no for an answer."

Her gaze rested on his loving face. From it she drew courage she never knew she had. God put them together for a reason. A moment ago, she knew it was to save Matthew's eternal life. But could it be more? He loved her and she loved him. What more could she ask for? He made her believe they could face anything together.

"Your parents shared a word from the Bible earlier in the waiting room. It talked about trusting God and fearing not. That is what being a Christian is all about. Trusting God. Knowing He is in control. You need not fear. He sees the big picture. Your mom said you'd be okay because you are in the Lord's hands. I even asked, but what if she dies? And do you know what your mom said? She said then you would be right next to Him in heaven. How could you lose? How could Marty lose? How could I lose? It's a win-win situation." Matthew stood up straight and grinned from ear to ear. "How can you argue with God?"

With a peace in her heart, she fixed her stare on his beautiful blue eyes and said, "Yes. I'll marry you."

Looking up, he said, "Thank You, God." Catching her face in his hands, he leaned down and kissed her hard on the mouth. After the kiss, he pulled back slightly, his voice almost in a whisper, and said, "Girl, you scared me. For a minute there, I thought you were going to say no."

"I almost did," Sam confessed. "In fact, I meant to."

As he dropped his hands from her face, she automatically reached out for them, catching them in her grasp. He squeezed gently, then rested her hands back down by her side.

A joy deeper than she ever thought possible overwhelmed her and she shouted joyfully, "There is no arguing with God's Word. Thank you for reminding me."

"We'll both thank your mom, too."

Her eyes held Matthew's gaze as her shaking hands covered her mouth. Water rimmed her eyes. Tears of joy rushed down her cheeks. She whispered, "Bring the family in. Let's share the news."

"It will be my pleasure." He rushed to the door and swung it open. Marie had joined the family out in the hall. Everyone was waiting, and their eyes all rested on Matthew as he opened the door.

"Come in . . . everyone. We have some

great news to share with you all." He rushed back to her side as they were filling the room.

"I love you," he whispered, for her ears only.

She laughed. "I love you more than anything in the world," she said a little louder than intended.

"More than me?" Marty cried out. Samantha winked at her son and said, "As much as you. Everyone, Matthew asked me to marry him." She looked back at Matthew. "For the record, Matthew, I could never tell you no."

"Truly?"

"Never . . . about anything."

"That's my girl," he whispered as his lips pressed against hers.

And all the people in the room cheered, including Marty.

ABOUT THE AUTHOR

Deborah Lynne, beloved inspirational romance, mystery, and romance-suspense writer, has penned eight novels: *After You're Gone, Crime in the Big Easy,* The Samantha Cain Mysteries (*Be Not Afraid, Testimony of Innocence, The Truth Revealed*), *Grace: A Gift of Love, All in God's Time,* and *Passion from the Heart.*

She is an active member of ACFW, RWA, and HEARTLA. She enjoys sharing her stories with her readers as well as the knowledge she gains as she grows as a novelist with other writers who share the same dream — of becoming a published author. She and her family enjoy their relaxed life in Louisiana.

http://www.author-deborahlynne.com
www.oaktara.com

The employees of Thorndike Press hope you have enjoyed this Large Print book. All our Thorndike, Wheeler, and Kennebec Large Print titles are designed for easy reading, and all our books are made to last. Other Thorndike Press Large Print books are available at your library, through selected bookstores, or directly from us.

For information about titles, please call:
  (800) 223-1244

or visit our Web site at:
  http://gale.cengage.com/thorndike

To share your comments, please write:
  Publisher
  Thorndike Press
  10 Water St., Suite 310
  Waterville, ME 04901